THE CYBORG'S CRUSADE

BOOK 1

Benoit Lanteigne

80 Mapleton Rd, Unit 11-80
Moncton, New-Brunswick, Canada
E1C 7W8

Benoit Lanteigne

80 Mapleton Rd, Unit 11-80
Moncton, New-Brunswick, Canada
E1C 7W8

https://thecyborgscrusade.com

Book Layout © 2016 BookDesignTemplates.com
Edited by Eliza Dee, Clio Editing
Book Cover Design by 100 Covers

The Cyborg's Crusade / Benoit Lanteigne. -- 1st ed.
ISBN 978-1-7387526-9-0

CONTENTS

Once you've finished reading, please consider leaving a review, or at least rating the book. This helps a lot and would be a great show of support.

Do you want a free short story that serves as a prequel to The Cyborg's Crusade? Then, join the cyborg's fan club on my website,

https://thecyborgscrusade.com/fanclub.html

Day of the Deus Ex Machina

Chapter 1

Damn it. Why the hell did I come here? I should never have listened to him... What was I thinking?

—Thoughts of James Hunter, Hocmar 28, 2134, on the Nirnivian calendar

The second that James saw the deformed statue, he deemed it painful to look at. The sculpture depicted a man, but not one of normal proportions. The arms were far too long, paired with short legs, and the right eye appeared thrice the size of the left—nothing compared to the elongated spike forming the nose, or the mouth contorted in a grimace. Now that he sat leaning against the grotesque shape, the figurative ache turned literal as the sharp stone dug into his back.

Even with the intense heat, James shivered. The recent revelations chilled his blood, and no matter how hard it tried, the sun couldn't warm him again. He rubbed his chin, pondering all he had learned. His hand brushed against his stubble, and he scowled at the itching sensation. Usually he shaved every day, a habit his unplanned trip had broken. Then again, next to his companion, a bit of extra hair was nothing...

The freak still stood a few feet behind, laughing to his heart's content. What a horrendous chortle. How James yearned to shut him up via his fist. "Gwa ha ah aha ha! Ha ha aha! Ha ha! Come on, why do you take things so seriously? You still don't get it, do you? Gwha ha ha ha ha! You should laugh more; it'll do ya good! Gwha ha ha ha ha! Wha ha ha ha! Gwa ha ha!"

With considerable effort, James ignored the taunt and focused on his current predicament instead. A cruel decision lay before him, and it required thought. As he considered his situation, a gust of wind blew dust into his mouth. James coughed before shielding himself with his hand. Though now gone, the gale had shattered his concentration. He sighed, about to resume his musing, but then his stomach churned, causing him to gag and cover his lips. How long since he had taken his medicine? Panicked, he reached for the brown pouch lying beside him. A search inside it produced a syringe offered earlier by the one they used to call Doctor Death.

James gritted his teeth while he contemplated the needle. Between an injection and a fatal sickness, the latter choice appealed to him quite a lot. He rested the syringe against his arm like the cyborg had demonstrated. Fear paralyzed him, except for a slight trembling. At that moment, the despicable voice said, "Gwa ha ha ha! Radiation kinda sucks, huh?"

James took a deep breath and relaxed. A touch of pressure and the needle pierced his vein. Pain assailed him, so he countered by imagining the sweet melody his good friend often played on the violin. He pushed on the plunger, and the brownish liquid left the plastic tube for his bloodstream. The task done, James exhaled while he peeked at the sky. A small white bird flew around the scene. How did a living being survive here?

After chirping a few random notes, the avian landed on a rock a couple of feet away from James and waited, studying the human intruder. Gauging him. Blue eyes... did his imagination trick him? Could birds even have blue eyes? He'd never paid attention to such details before. In any event, the feathered observer troubled him. Maybe he should scare him away. Perhaps he could throw something. Biting his lip, he grabbed a pebble, only to drop it with a groan. Despite his anguish, pity stalled his hand, and he endured the staring bird. In the end, the animal showed mercy and took flight, leaving him alone with his torments.

How did it come to this? I mean, it's crazy... I'm just a regular guy. I have no business here. I wish... I wish I could erase the last few years, forget everything that happened. My life used to be so simple. Back then, I hated it; I found it boring. Let me tell you: boring's good. Boring's great! I should've been thankful...

—Thoughts of James Hunter, Hocmar 28, 2134, on the Nirnivian calendar

Chapter 2

October 16, 2007

Just another day; another day like so many before, or so I thought. As it turns out, it was the most important day of my life. The day everything changed. The day of the deus ex machina.

—Thoughts of James Hunter, Hocmar 28, 2134, on the Nirnivian calendar

At least it didn't rain. Humid air weighed on their shoulders, but so far they remained dry. Between steps, James sneaked a peek toward the gray clouds. They grew more ominous by the minute, so he halted for an instant and studied them. As he brushed a bead of sweat off his forehead, his fingers grazed his black hair. He pondered whether they'd reach their destination before their luck ran out. He hoped so, since he'd suggested the stroll. Nadia had wanted him to borrow his dad's car, but he'd insisted he needed some fresh air.

The second his girlfriend entered his mind, James glanced sideways toward the woman next to him. Her shoulder-length blond hair bounced with every step. The poor soul shivered and rubbed her own arms in hopes that the motion might warm her up. Her cold body matched the frigid reaction she'd offered when he'd suggested they walk in this weather. Not helping matters, he'd begged her to attend the matinee showing. Despite the harsh temperature, however, the furrows on Nadia's brow subsided and her crimson cheeks returned to their normal color. In short, any sign of grumpiness vanished from her delicate features now that the date had started.

Perhaps sensing his gaze, Nadia smiled and said, "You're not thinking of canceling on me again, are you?"

James scratched behind his ear. "Uh, what? Oh, of course not!"

"Good! You did it twice already, and I'm working next weekend."

"Sorry, it's been a rough couple of weeks." The moment he uttered the words, James tapped the pocket where he kept his wallet. His own touch surprised him.

"Don't worry"—Nadia paused for a sigh—"I'll pay for your ticket... and the snacks."

"No, I have money. I'll—"

"We've been together for over a year now. I recognize the signs." She patted his shoulder. "Frank screwed you again?"

"Kind of. He swears he'll pay me tomorrow. He always does, it just takes a while. Really, it's fine, Nadia. Patrick lent me a few bucks."

"Keep it. Frank thinks 'day' and 'week' are synonyms." She shook her head. "I don't understand why you're still working for that asshole."

"I know it's a sucky job, Nadia, I know." James couldn't conceal the annoyance in his voice. "It's not like I have any options. What the hell do you want me to do?"

Until then, their footsteps had echoed on the sidewalk in unison, but at that moment, the duet morphed into a solo. Nadia stopped and glared at him with crossed arms. Blushing, James spun around and faced her, though his stare met the ground instead of her deep blue eyes.

"Oh, James... I can't believe you said that."

"Please, let's not go there. Not today. Let's not ruin our date again."

Nadia bent her neck and rubbed her brow. "I'm sorry. I don't want to fight over this. James, I don't care if you work for Frank or not, but you do. You hate that job, and I can't stand watching you give up on yourself, because I love you!"

"I, uh..." James shrugged. "Look, it's not like I didn't try. I want to do better. I really do, but I keep failing. I tried to study, I tried to be somebody, but I guess I'm not all that smart."

"Then try again. You're worth the shot, and I'll be there to cheer you on no matter what."

"Nah, I'm too old for that stuff."

His girlfriend giggled. "You're twenty-seven, not exactly over the hill."

"Yeah, but it feels like seventy-two. I'm sorry, Nadia." He approached her and grabbed her wrists. "I'm not special; I'm not a unique snowflake. What can I say? I'm a total loser, I know—"

"You're the only one who thinks so. And, James, you're special to me." She hugged him, and James wrapped his arms around Nadia's waist. Her head rested right under his chin and, as a reflex, he kissed the top of her hair.

Special to her... she said that right before it happened. A sweet thought, but she meant it less and less every day. She began wondering why she wasted her time with me. Realizing she could do better. Seeing me as a loser. I can't blame her. She was right: I was a loser. Still am. I'd even say I'm a sort of ultimate loser—an all-time loser.

—Thoughts of James Hunter, Hocmar 28, 2134, on the Nirnivian calendar

At that instant, a spark flashed in his peripheral vision. Curious, he focused his attention toward the trees along the road. The wind explained the leaves' motion and yet... was somebody there? He had the distinct impression someone was watching them, but why would anybody spy on him of all people? Growing ever more suspicious, he pushed Nadia away, breaking the embrace.

"What's wrong, James?"

"Nothing, I just want to check something out." He took a few steps toward the trees in order to prove himself wrong.

"Where are you going? The movie's starting soon."

He peeked over his shoulder before fixating on the dubious bush again. "I know, I know, baby. I'll be right back."

That feeling of being watched—I'd had it before. Everybody does from time to time. There didn't seem to be anybody around, but to be sure, I got a bit closer... and poof! A flash of light... Deus Ex Machina...

—Thoughts of James Hunter, Hocmar 28, 2134, on the Nirnivian calendar

Chapter 3

Mashar 17, 2133, on the Nirnivian calendar

The world whirled around James. Soon, all distinct shapes vanished, superseded by a haze of colors. Shades of green, red and blue filled his vision. An agonizing pain flared across his body, and James screamed. His stomach floated up to his throat, while his intestines... he preferred not to think about them. Then, at last, the forms returned, though muddled. The sensation lasted only a few seconds, but it brought James to his knees as he gagged and vomited on the pavement. Once done, he wiped his mouth and coughed. Revolted screams erupted around him.

James almost mumbled an apology for the mess, but then he realized: who was yelling? He and Nadia stood alone and yet... wait, those dark figures surrounding him on the ground... shadows? And over there, feet and legs... where had these people come from?

Perplexed, James tried getting up, but he wobbled and fell. His new position gave him a view of the trees he had scrutinized before the incident, except they had morphed into a yellow brick building. James's heart raced and his body tensed. Trying to relax, he took a few deep breaths through his nose and scowled. That stench, a mix of decayed food, feces, and puke, permeated the air. Of course, his own actions explained the last odor, but still, Moncton never smelled so bad. No wonder, with all the garbage littering the street. However, the road he'd strolled along had been so clean just moments ago.

As he pondered the change in scenery, James's vision cleared. He took it as a good sign and attempted to stand up again. Though he swayed, he remained on his feet. Perhaps because of his movement, the confused chatter around him intensified. Bronze-skinned people glanced at each other and recoiled, a few pointing at him. James scanned the crowd in search of Nadia. Unable to locate his lover, he found his attention drawn to a stranger in the distance instead. The man held a leash, but without a dog at the end. A pink glob of goo replaced the expected canine. The horror waved its many tentacles, sometimes caressing passersby. James gasped. Covered in perspiration and shaking, he averted his gaze and spotted a young boy with a miniature leg sticking out of his belly through a hole in his shirt.

Propelled by a burst of adrenaline, James dashed in the opposite direction. A mere three steps and he almost crashed into a woman with a single gigantic eye and a flesh-colored lobster claw for a left arm. James's mouth gaped. In a panic, he shielded his eyes as he collapsed on his knees once more and whimpered. Tears streamed down his cheeks. What kind of nightmare was this? He must've fallen asleep; the movie had ended up being boring, so he'd dozed off in his seat. No worries, though. Soon, he'd receive an elbow in his ribs from Nadia, who'd scold him for his rude behavior. After such an ordeal, he'd enjoy his girlfriend's ire. Seconds passed, but the anticipated blow didn't come.

I was in a different place, like nowhere I'd ever seen before. I guess it's obvious, but I was terrified. If I had known more about this new world—if I had known what would happen there—I would've been even more scared.

—Thoughts of James Hunter, Hocmar 28, 2134, on the Nirnivian calendar

"Hey, you, the visitor!"

Loud footsteps accompanied the gibberish-filled shout. Swallowing hard, James risked a peek toward the source. A man and a woman wearing black uniforms approached. Something glimmered on the upper left of their vests. The closer they got, the clearer the shape became, and James discerned some kind of badge he'd never seen before, though he found himself reminded of police officers. If only they hadn't aimed their guns at him, he might've been relieved by the presence of law enforcement. Under the circumstances, however, he patted his abdomen while shuddering.

"Me?"

"Yes, you. Please stay calm and put your hands up where I can see them." James obeyed without hesitation. "Sorry, visitors can be unpredictable, so we have to be careful."

"Uh, visitors?"

Before the cop could answer, the kid with the belly leg James had spotted earlier said, "Sir, what's going on?"

The officer glared at the child. "Shut up, you filthy mutant! I'm busy, get out of here." Then he sighed and returned his focus to James. "Visitor is our name for beings from another universe. They've been popping up once in a while, and you appeared out of nowhere, so I think you're one of them. Good thing we can understand each other. That's rare with visitors. Can you tell me your name?"

"My name's James Hunter." He gulped. "I don't mean any—"

"I'm sure you don't, and I know you must be confused and afraid, but could you please tell me what you call your species? We're trying to keep records of visitors."

James resisted a nervous laugh and shook his head. "Is this a joke? I'm a normal human from Earth, are you saying you ar—"

Before he could finish his sentence, the people started yelling at each other. Most ran away, glaring at James. Even the cops grew a touch paler. The duo stopped moving as if unsure how to proceed. Breathless, James looked around. Only disdain answered his gaze. He rubbed his brow, puzzled by this turn of events, when a groan echoed from his right side. James spun around: a bare-chested brute towered above him. Before he had a chance to duck, the club the goon brandished collided with James's skull with a resounding bang that was followed by a sharp pain. Blood dripped into his eyes as he tumbled onto his back. In a hazy chaos, the officers ordered the assailant to drop his weapon, and then there was darkness.

***

Sitting at her desk, Rose reached for a large book. She consulted this volume so often she opened it at the correct page in a single try. Then she located the passage she sought. As she'd assumed, she remembered the quote right. She studied these texts so much she could recall every word without effort. Still, she preferred double-checking. Her mother had taught her that erring on the side of caution usually proved to be a good idea, and she had taken that lesson to heart.

With a sigh, Rose closed the book and grabbed her pen. Before she wrote anything, a beeping sound interrupted her. The interphone. A second later, a female voice echoed through the speaker. "Rose, it's Kristina."

Rose frowned. Her personal assistant had been sent on an errand and she hadn't expected her to return so soon. Then again, Kristina had shown her efficiency on several occasions. That she'd finished her task early shouldn't be that surprising.

Rose opened the door and the blond woman stepped inside. She smiled. "Hey, Kristina, I'm always impressed by how quick you are."

"No, I'm not done." She pointed at the phone. "You shut off the ringer again, so your dad asked me to deliver a message to you."

A tingle of anticipation ran down Rose's spine. "Oh?"

"Another visitor appeared out of nowhere."

"I see." For decades, strange creatures had been appearing at random in Nirnivia. While not a frequent occurrence, it happened roughly once a month. They shared little in common with each other. Some were humanoid and possessed intelligence, while many seemed to be animals. In most cases, the poor souls died, Nirnivia's atmosphere being unsuitable for their physical needs. When they survived, their circumstances baffled and terrified them. That fear often manifested in violence. Scientists had studied the phenomenon and reached the conclusion that reality comprised multiple parallel universes. By pure bad luck, the visitor had stumbled upon what they called a multiverse crack and slipped into a different world. While the coming of a visitor was a tragic event, Rose wondered why her father had sent Kristina to inform her of this since she couldn't help with the situation.

"It's a human. A male. And the people reacted how you'd expect."

Rose gasped. A human had appeared long ago, and his arrival had scarred their country. She suspected the average Nirnivian citizen wouldn't welcome another one. Especially since people were beyond stressed. A recent war with a rival nation called Ostark had ravaged Nirnivia. Though a truce had been in effect for years, the two countries had never reached a final agreement and so tension remained high. Fear that the hostilities might restart simmered in silence. And those villains BBR worsened matters. A terrorist organization, BBR believed the ceasefire to be a mistake and aimed to end it. So far they'd failed, but they kept throwing fuel on the fire. So, in short, humans were disliked to begin with, and Rose feared that the craziness everyone had endured would only feed the flames of hatred.

"Oh no... is he all right?"

Kristina nodded. "Someone gave him a bump on the head, but he's fine. The cops put him in jail for his own protection."

"What?" While gritting her teeth, Rose clenched her fists. "That's unacceptable! He's not a criminal. He doesn't deserve to be thrown in prison."

A shrug came from the assistant. "It's temporary. At least he's safe there."

"No, I won't stand for it. Come, let's go talk to Dad."

***

No hangover James had ever suffered had caused a headache this intense. A tad more pressure and his brain might explode. He figured he must've indulged in a night of binge drinking with his friend Patrick, not that he remembered the party. How much had they consumed, anyway? Judging by the nightmare he had woken from, a lot. Mumbling a curse, he patted the top of his skull, then frowned as his touch detected a bump covered in dried blood.

James lay motionless for a while before noticing that his mattress had doubled in firmness. No way had he slept in his own bed. Seized by curiosity, he opened his eyes. A gray fog greeted his effort, though it soon swirled into clarity, revealing black bars casting their shadows on him. James gasped and shuddered. They'd thrown him in prison. Panicked, he felt his respiration accelerate.

I had never been in jail before. I'd done some bad things, like everyone, but nothing worth locking me up over.

—Thoughts of James Hunter, Hocmar 28, 2134, on the Nirnivian calendar

Twiddling his fingers, he attempted to calm himself. He'd probably instigated a minor disturbance, so they'd put him in here for his own safety. No doubt he'd be released without a fuss. A guard stood near the locked door. James gathered his courage and cleared his throat.

"Um... I'm sorry, sir..."

"Shut up, you human scum."

James's eyes grew wide. Human scum... such a reply only made sense if...

He gulped. Beads of sweat formed on his brow. The events he'd deemed a bad dream were real.

I realized I probably wasn't even on Earth anymore. Somehow, I'd appeared in a hostile new world. Someone being suddenly teleported to another world—it's a huge cliché in scifi and fantasy stories. I always hated it, too. It's such a cheap

plot device to give characters a reason to explain every little detail about their own universe. The kind of lame trick I'd have to use if I was a writer, because I'd suck at it. Not only was I stuck in this uber cliché, I was stuck in a cramped cell devoid of any comfort. Not a good day overall.

—Thoughts of James Hunter, Hocmar 28, 2134, on the Nirnivian calendar

Trapped in a cell, with the only person available not interested in a chat—given those facts, few choices presented themselves. With a grunt, James sat up and studied his surroundings. Other than the small bed, a discolored toilet stood as the single piece of furniture. James bit his lip. Thanks to his shy bladder, he dreaded the thought of using it. Much like the toilet's porcelain, stains marked the floor, suggesting pitiable living conditions; not that he'd expect otherwise in a place like this.

James stayed immobile on his mattress and pondered his situation. He'd spent a few minutes in this new world and ended up knocked out and confined. Of course, he understood a stranger appearing out of nowhere might surprise people, but the crowd had only freaked out for real once he'd mentioned he was a human. They knew the word—why? More importantly, what did that mean for him? When he considered the mob's reaction, he doubted they'd ever set him free. Was that his future—to remain here until death? James cringed at the idea. And it might not even be the worst. What about torture or execution? Unable to contain his nervousness, he jumped to his feet and paced around.

An hour or so passed and nothing changed. James's stomach growled, but no food came. At first, he endured in silence, but soon the rumbles increased. As he wondered whether his captor would ever feed him, he glanced at the guard. He might answer if asked, but their previous exchange had lacked courtesy. Once he overcame a moment of hesitation, James waved the notion away.

A few minutes later, footsteps echoed in the hallway. Curious, James turned his head. Two men walked toward his cell. Much like the police officers he'd encountered earlier, they wore uniforms, though of a dark blue shade rather than black, and the golden buttons on their shirts contrasted with the silver ones the cops had sported. On their heads rested berets matching the uniforms' color. Whoever they might be, the guard at the door straightened up on sight and saluted. James gritted his teeth.

Once the strangers were close enough, James glimpsed small badges the shape of a shield near their right shoulders. They featured a winged sword with the letters NISDA engraved underneath. The same emblem decorated their hats. Like most people James had met so far, they could've passed for human beings. The instant they reached the door, the one on the left gestured toward James and mumbled something inaudible to the guard, who nodded. The visitors then stared at the prisoner. Without even thinking, James recoiled.

One of the mysterious strangers smirked. "Hey, human boy, you're coming on a trip." The man brandished a bandana. "We can't let you see where we're going, so I'll have to cover your eyes. Don't try any funny business."

A second later, he jammed the key in the proper hole, turned the handle and swung the door open. The two men entered. "Damn, I can't believe we have a human on our hands," one of them said. "Maybe we should shoot him and pretend he resisted?"

James stopped breathing and glanced backward. Of course, only the wall waited for him. He began trembling.

Resistance seemed futile. Both potential assailants dwarfed his five-foot-ten frame and bulged with muscles. Besides, the guns holstered on their belts rendered any slight chance of a successful physical attack nil.

"Don't even joke about that!" the other replied, elbowing his colleague in the ribs. "The Melkar ordered us not to harm him. You don't want to cross her, do you?"

"No, no, of course not."

James let out a relieved sigh and mumbled his thanks to God. Whoever she was, he owed this Melkar a debt. Still, he couldn't help but worry. The woman who wished to meet him inspired dread in these two big guys—what did she intend for him? What if she saved him, only to deliver an even worse fate?

Chapter 4

The bandana covering James's eyes accomplished its task to perfection. Not a single ray of light pierced the material, plunging his world into total blackness. His escort guided him by pulling his arm. They showed a lack of restraint, and soon his muscles were sore—not that he dared complain.

James could only guess where they went. After a short walk, a fresh breeze tickled his skin and ruffled his hair. He stood outside, no doubt, but it didn't last long. A clunk echoed and someone pushed him. James tensed up, dreading the coming impact, but he landed on a cushioned surface. A moment later, an engine roared, followed by a sensation of movement. They had thrown him in a vehicle.

How long the drive took, James couldn't tell, but the guards remained quiet for the whole trip, leaving the motor as the sole sound. Deprived of his senses, his imagination concocted various scenarios. What would he find once they arrived? Perhaps the Melkar the men had mentioned earlier? What fate should he expect? Freedom? Captivity? Torture? Slavery? His mind contemplated each option, going from bad to worse, and long before they reached their destination, perspiration drenched his clothes.

Though for a while, it felt like the journey might last forever, the car eventually stopped. The door popped open, and once again the strangers yanked James away. He mulled asking a few questions, but he swallowed them back before they reached his lips. They walked for at least ten minutes, then fingers caressed the back of his head and removed the scarf.

A bright light assailed James, so he cringed and covered his eyes with his hand. In a matter of seconds, however, his pupils adapted. Curious, he scanned the area and noted the metallic hallway surrounding him. On the wall to his left, he recognized the same shield emblem his companions sported on their uniforms, except on a much larger scale. Again, the letters NISDA appeared below. More interesting than the environment, a group of mostly bronze-skinned people waited before them.

The first person James focused on turned out to be a hunched old man with his hands joined behind his back. He wore the same deep blue attire as James's escort, though decorated with several medals, and a cap rested on his head. A benevolent smile appeared on his wrinkled pale face. He watched the approaching trio with his eyelids almost closed, yet James sensed an intense alertness emanating from him.

A few feet to the senior's left, a blond man glared at James. Like his elder, he sported a far lighter complexion than his cohorts. He flashed an amused smirk the instant their gazes met and subtly flexed his arm, which proved thrice the size of James's. Beside these two, many others filled the scene with dark blue. James ignored them all, for he spotted the sole person who deviated from the trend: a woman in a white dress, nothing special... if you missed the wings sticking out from her back.

She was so beautiful. Not a top model, but good looking. Long red hair, deep blue eyes. And tall—almost as tall as me. I guess her freckles were up for debate, but I liked them. Still, her beauty was more than that. She had this grace to her. The way she moved; the way she looked at me. It was like an aura of some kind elevated her physical appearance beyond that of any woman I've ever met. I can't explain; there's no good word. I had never been particularly religious, but when I saw those wings, I immediately knew what it meant.

—Thoughts of James Hunter, Hocmar 28, 2134, on the Nirnivian calendar

The woman opened her mouth to speak, but before she had the chance, James said, "Are you... are you an angel?"

Despite his interruption, she beamed. Such warmth; James's legs weakened. Perhaps flattered by the comparison, her cheeks reddened a little. "No, I'm not. I am only a simple winged woman." James furrowed his brow a bit as he considered her statement. "My name is Rose Ricdeau, and I owe you an apology, Mr.—um, Mr. Hunter, isn't it?" After a brief hesitation, he nodded. "This is a time of war for my country, and people are frightened as a result. They often overreact. The police officers who found you didn't know what to do, so they imprisoned you. I wasn't happy when I learned about it, but I can understand their actions. I hope you will forgive us for this unfortunate mistake. I swear we mean you no harm, and I assure you that we do not condone jailing innocents. You are currently restrained. I wish to free you, but you must remain calm and follow us. If you run away or cause trouble, I doubt I'll be able to protect you. Do you understand?"

Her appearance had nothing on her voice. So soft... almost musical. It's a bad old joke, but I could've listened to her read the phone book out loud for hours. I was scared—terrified even, but just hearing her voice helped. It's crazy, but it was like her voice was so enchanting, anything she said sounded rational and wise. Even if she'd suggested dancing on the highway naked, I might've accepted. For freedom, I didn't even hesitate.

—Thoughts of James Hunter, Hocmar 28, 2134, on the Nirnivian calendar

James exhaled. "Y-yes. I'll do whatever you ask. I, uh, I promise."

Right on cue, Rose stepped toward him. The blond brute jumped forward and jammed his arm across her chest. She glanced at him and touched his bicep. "It's all right, Brucie, he's not dangerous." She concentrated on James once more. "You won't hurt me now, will you?"

"N-no!"

The one called Brucie grunted. "Ain't no way I... let those guys do their job, won't ya?"

Both of James's guards acquiesced, and one said, "He's right, Your H—" Rose fired a quick stare at him. The man gulped. "Um, I can do it!" In a nervous motion, he fished the key from his pocket. Thanks to his fumbling fingers, he dropped it. "Ah, crud!"

Rose peeked at the glimmering object on the floor and evaded her apparent bodyguard. Refusing to be foiled, Brucie blocked her once more. Silent up until now, the old man chuckled. "It's fine, son, let her."

The bodybuilder scowled and groaned, but he nevertheless obeyed. By the time she reached the key, one of the soldiers accompanying James had already picked it up. Still smiling, Rose presented her palm, and he gave it to her as requested. Now that she stood so close, James discerned the braid running along her face on the left. Properly equipped, she removed his shackles. The bonds irritated the skin on his wrists, so, being liberated, he massaged them.

Rose winked at Brucie. "You see? I'm alive and well. No need to be so worried."

"Just doing my job, ya know!"

"And very well, I might add." Rose looked at James again. "We have some business to conduct elsewhere. Please follow us." Nodding, James trailed the group along a corridor. Several of the men fell back until they fenced him in, rendering escape impossible, or at least implausible. "You're probably confused, Mr. Hunter. You deserve an explanation about what's going on. Rest assured, it will come, but I am afraid now is not a good time."

James only gave her half his attention, reserving the rest for the setting. In particular, several black domes ornamented the ceiling. He believed them to be cameras. The sheer number seemed excessive.

"I'll be honest: your arrival is... problematic for us at the moment. Some even proposed we leave you in jail for a while, but that felt cruel to me, and I don't do cruel."

They came to a steel door equipped with a slot instead of a knob. One of the men slid a plastic card in, and the barrier swung open. The movement James predicted, of course, but the door's thickness made him gulp. Over two inches of solid metal. What might even break through such a reinforced barrier? Beads of sweat materialized on his brow. The utter strength implied a great desire for safety. Could this be a military facility? If so, why bring him here? As he pondered those questions, a wrinkled hand patted his shoulder.

"Now, now, my boy. I know you're scared, but this is a high-security complex. You can't escape."

James turned his head and gawked at the elder. Yes, the thought of fleeing had entered his mind for a fraction of a second, but he had rejected the notion before the old man spoke. At the most, his legs might've twitched. How did the senior know? Fearing for his life, James swallowed hard. Thank God the old man then let out a pleasant laugh, reducing the tension.

"Oh, don't worry, nobody blames you for wanting to run. Just don't do it."

"Yeah, if ya run, I'll kick your ass." The bodyguard sneered with a trace of menace.

Rose glared at him. "Shut up, Brucie!"

"Ah, come on, Rose, ya know I'm kidding!" He bent toward James and whispered in his ear. "Psst, human dude, I ain't kidding."

The assumed Melkar glowered at the bodybuilder, both hands resting on her hips. "You're not funny, Brucie! Forgive him, Mr. Hunter. He has a strange sense of humor, but he's mostly harmless."

"It's okay!" James faked an enthusiastic grin. "I like jokes! Ha ha!"

Brucie snickered at the reply, but a sidelong glance from Rose stopped the hilarity. From there, a mere minute passed before they reached another door. Again, a key card proved to be the solution. Rose gestured toward the revealed chamber.

"All right, Mr. Hunter, you must stay in this room for now. I'm sorry for the inconvenience. There's some food in the mini fridge—water too. Feel free to sleep in the bed if you're tired. There are also some books should you fancy reading. Most are historical in nature, so not very entertaining, but you might find the information useful. There's even a small bathroom, though no TV for now. We'll leave two guards at your door, so if you need anything, ask them. Stay inside. The guards won't let you out anyway. We do not wish to hurt you, but we will if you don't cooperate.

Please understand, we're not trying to imprison you. We are trying to protect you. Your confinement is temporary, I promise. I'll come back and explain, hopefully soon, at worst tomorrow."

James blushed. "I... I understand."

A sad smile formed on Rose's visage. "No, you don't, but you will soon. I swear. Try to relax, Mr. Hunter, though I know it's difficult given the circumstances."

"Thank you for the room."

The winged woman lowered her neck at the standard courtesy. "Please don't thank me. After what happened, I don't deserve it. We must leave now. Please go inside."

James acquiesced in silence and stepped into the room. The gigantic door closed behind him. Now alone, the tension that had accumulated in his body released in a flash. His muscles weakened until he almost collapsed. Exhausted, he stumbled toward the bed, sat and took a few deep breaths. Still drained, he tumbled backward, the mattress bouncing under the impact. He lay down, scrutinizing the decorative swirls on the ceiling.

Whether James dozed off or not, he couldn't tell. In any case, his vitality returned. Soon, images of Nadia, his parents, and his good friend Patrick popped into his brain. He missed them so much. What if he never saw them again? What if...

His stomach growled and interrupted his reverie. After a sigh, he sat up and studied his surroundings.

Beside the bed, he discovered a small table. An alarm clock rested on top and displayed 4:33. Even assuming the digits meant the same as on Earth, the information provided zero help, so he disregarded it. Rather, he rubbed the table's wooden surface. It ended up far less than smooth. In fact, his touch detected countless scratches, and the motion left his fingertips covered in dust. Perhaps room service had lacked time for preparation due to his sudden arrival. James shrugged. Poor housekeeping or not, his hunger persisted.

Bored with the useless piece of furniture, James spun around and walked to the fridge tucked in a corner. As he advanced toward the appliance, part of the refrigerator's white color morphed into gray and grew distorted as if reflected in a carnival mirror. James blinked twice and scowled. He inspected the cold box for a while, but the effect vanished. Figuring his sleepiness played tricks on his mind, he dismissed the illusion. He pulled on the fridge's handle and explored the contents, exposing three items: a pitcher containing a clear liquid he hoped to be water, a package of meat and what might be sliced cheese. A loaf of bread short of a sandwich, but maybe these people understood it belonged at room temperature. That in mind, James approached the cupboard standing nearby and, yes, he found what appeared to be a loaf on the shelves, along with various crackers and snacks.

James licked his lips in anticipation—and a bit of apprehension, given he had no clue what he was about to eat. He reached for the bread, only to stop. On the bottom shelf, a basket filled with large blue fruits begged for his attention. A small memo leaned on the hamper. Intrigued, he picked it up and read: "I washed the druikinaka, so no pesticides for you! —Rose." James figured these might be safer than random meat, so he snatched an azure sphere and sank his teeth into the delicate yellow flesh within. Juice slid on his tongue, and a potent sweetness tickled his taste buds, like he'd ingested a fistful of gummy candies. Not that he disliked the flavor—on the contrary—but out of astonishment, he dropped his fruit.

I remembered the dust on the table, so I preferred not risking the five-second rule. Anyway, there were plenty more, so I figured I'd just take another. Before I had the chance, someone grabbed me from behind. It was so weird. Arms crushed me, but I couldn't see them. I struggled, but they held strong. Then the invisible guy shoved a rag or something over my nose. It stank—a lot. I'd never smelled anything quite like it before, but somehow it seemed familiar. Yeah, that doesn't make any goddamn sense, but it was like what I imagined chloroform might smell like, and maybe I wasn't too far off, since I lost consciousness.

—Thoughts of James Hunter, Hocmar 28, 2134, on the Nirnivian calendar

Chapter 5

The scent of rotten food and decomposing trash assailed James's nose. That ended up being his first sensation following a bout of dreamless sleep. In the span of a day, he'd suffered more loss of consciousness than ever before in his life. No way such an ordeal was beneficial for his health. Like in prison, a headache tortured him. Unlike with his previous blackout, however, he dismissed the idea of recent events being a nightmare.

Resigned, James opened his eyes. As expected, the world blurred around him and then stabilized. He lay in the dirt, leaning against a house and among garbage cans. He moved his arms and pushed himself up in an attempt to return to his feet. He almost coughed and groaned but bit his tongue once he spotted a pair of legs wrapped in beige pants. The sight paralyzed him for a few seconds, and the trembling began. He recalled the attack in the room. This had to be the perpetrator.

James lifted his neck and got a clear view of the assailant. At the last moment, he fixated on the ground again, inhaled, and made another try. A bare-chested man stood a few meters before him. Thank God his back faced James. A tattoo adorned his right scapula. It formed a gray triangle containing the acronym BBR in crimson ink. Far worse, several knives and a pistol hung from his belt. A cold sweat drenched James's brow. With effort, he raised his gaze and focused on the stranger instead of his weapons.

An unknown device rested on the brute's ear, and he muttered incomprehensible words into it. James deduced the machine to be a transmitter. His attention settled squarely on the fingers holding the gizmo, or precisely the fingertips. Those nails looked incredibly sharp. With his other hand, the man twirled a dagger in mesmerizing yet hazardous patterns. Somehow, he managed not to injure himself.

Swallowing hard, James slowly got to his knees, his perspiration exacerbated as he prayed that his deliberate progress muzzled any sound he produced. Once up, he peeked at a nearby alley and considered springing for it. Though tempted, he paused and risked a final glimpse at the goon. James's mouth gaped as he suppressed a yell. The freak's arm changed color. Initially, it adopted a shade of green, followed by red and cyan. If that wasn't impressive enough, the knife also copied a chameleon. Then, for its ultimate trick, the stranger's skin blended with its environment, rendering it invisible. Well, almost; in quick motions, slight distortions perturbed the camouflage.

Without a thought, James ran as quietly as possible and entered the closest available path. Unaware of whether his abductor engaged in pursuit, he switched streets often in the hopes that the erratic trail might lose him, should it be necessary. The farther he got, the faster his speed grew. He crossed a few people as he raced. Most gawped at him in surprise, and one woman even asked if he was okay. James denied her a reply and maintained his sprint. Not that he paid attention, but as he proceeded, the buildings became less and less dilapidated, and the junk littering the soil diminished until it vanished. The population also increased. About ten minutes later, he arrived in an open area. A mob of perhaps a hundred was spread over the place, walking around or talking to each other.

Since he dreaded a repeat of his arrival, James stopped at the outskirts. He glanced at the crowd while he huffed for air and fidgeted. So far, they ignored him and continued their usual business. Still, should he stay here or retreat? While he reflected on the question, a vendor riding a bike rolled up beside him and waved a sandwich.

"Hey, sir, best horchoir in the city; half price for you!" James swung his head sideways and the merchant shrugged. "Come on, pal, it's like two b—"

Frustrated, James turned around. He noticed a large monitor mounted on top of an edifice. The screen depicted a brunette sitting at a desk, a generic azure backdrop stretching behind her. A boring visual in James's opinion, no matter if decorated with a golden logo composed of the capital letters M and N.

Adjusting her spectacles, the lady stared straight at the camera and said, "As if we needed an extra visitor, a human was discovered this morning near Junction Avenue. Unlike last time, the cops incarcerated the subject immediately, and he is now in NISDA's custody. It's unclear what the military intend for the human, but everyone here at MegaNews agrees a swift execution would be the safest co—"

Execution, huh? I cringed. These guys hated my guts, but why? Fear of death filled my mind for a while, but then it hit me: "unlike last time." My stomach churned. More humans had appeared out of nowhere like me. How many? How long ago? I couldn't tell, but obviously we weren't welcome.

—Thoughts of James Hunter, Hocmar 28, 2134, on the Nirnivian calendar

Before he finished contemplating the implications of his sudden realization, the reporter's discourse cut off, superseded by static. The white noise's pitch augmented until it was so shrill that James grimaced and covered his ears. Next, the image froze. Patches of ashen grains concealed the journalist, only to vanish and resurge until the haze masked the whole picture.

James gawked at the useless TV as he scratched his skull. What had happened? In any case, no one else reacted. They kept going as if nothing were wrong. Then the monitor turned black. James recoiled in shock. A few flickers and a man emerged from the darkness. Yes, a simple man, except... more machine than flesh. His torso and arms were fashioned of shiny metal. The framing hid his legs, but James assumed robotic appendages replaced them too. Of his original body, solely the bald head remained. Burns ravaged his face into an unrecognizable mess. On the left, a single blue eye peered toward the horde; on the right, an electronic contraption substituted for the other. Enclosed in silvery steel, faint blue lights arranged in a smiley glowed from an orifice, providing sight where it had been lost. Though of poor quality, the crude visage shaped by the LEDs presented the only smile the mutilated soul could offer. He lacked a mouth. A speaker sewn to his jaw supplied his voice.

Oh God. Just remembering it, I... he was so freaking ugly. No doubt he'd had an accident; maybe he'd survived a fire or something, so I pitied him, really. But... I couldn't bear to look at him, yet I couldn't stop either. It was so... gross. Sorry, I feel like a piece of crap just thinking that, but yeah. And no one gave a damn. A cyborg took control of the TV, and that wasn't worth a gasp. Well, I guess it was, 'cause I gasped, but whatever.

—Thoughts of James Hunter, Hocmar 28, 2134, on the Nirnivian calendar

"People of Nirnivia," the mechanical man said, "you know who I am, and I realize you despise me, but please listen to my message. Your leaders—in particular, Ms. Rose Ricdeau—are lying to you. They are using your beliefs for their own selfish goals. Ms. Ricdeau is not the Melkar. She is a mere mutant who uses her unique deformity, namely her wings, to pretend she is special. She is dangerous—"

That godforsaken voice. So monotonous. No trace of emotions. I'd rather have a rat jammed in my ear canal. Speech synthesis from hell, I tell you.

—Thoughts of James Hunter, Hocmar 28, 2134, on the Nirnivian calendar

James missed the rest of the monologue, for a loud whimper distracted him. He spun toward the source: a shivering boy pale as snow. The child stepped backward while he glared at James and directed the foot protruding from his abdomen at him. "It's... it's the human! I was there! I recognize him!"

James held his breath for a second or three. Withdrawing a bit, he scanned the crowd. The revelation stunned most of them. Quite a few retreated. In the distance, however, four thugs dressed in rags gazed at each other and nodded. Not taking any chances, James resumed his sprint after a yelp. Fingers seized his shoulder and his elbow. Somehow, he wiggled free and plunged into an alley.

"He escaped from NISDA! Get him! Don't let him get away!"

As he rushed, James's heart pounded. Though he didn't dare check on his pursuers, the enraged shouts confirmed they trailed him. In fact, the roars' volume doubled. The pack gained ground every instant. Soon, a tossed rock landed in front of him. James hopped over the boulder, avoiding tripping.

A deluge of projectiles flew through the air. Subpar aiming be praised, the sticks, stones, and even pens failed to touch James. He exhaled as he appreciated his luck when his instinct warned he should duck. He obeyed. A brick soared an inch above his skull and smashed into a window. Shards of glass scattered; a clang echoed, accompanied by swearing. With a sigh, James skimmed the damage. Exploiting his reduced pace, a ball struck him on his bottom. While solid, the curved surface cracked upon contact, and sludge smeared his pants, ruining them. James's lips contorted at the gooeyness. Perhaps an egg had smacked him, or a putrid fruit. Whatever it might have been, a shot of adrenaline gushed within his veins. Properly motivated, James reached an unprecedented speed. He thus fled the gang, but to little gain, for he bolted into a dead end.

As he clenched his fists, James mumbled a curse at the wall blocking the road. He rubbed his chin, wondering what he should do. With no choice but to backtrack, even if that implied reuniting with the chasers he had foiled only moments ago, he turned, about to retrace his steps, but a feminine voice cleared her throat. Startled, James studied the scene. Ridden by a woman clad in a leather jacket and jeans, a motorcycle advanced from the shadows. A red scarf obscured her mouth, leaving her short brown hair and hazel eyes as the two recognizable traits. The disguise added menace to her persona, and the sword strapped to her back and the gun holstered on her belt accentuated the effect. She pulled down the bandana, exposing dual parallel scars on her left cheek.

"You human, kid? Get on. Take you outta here."

James scowled. "How do I know I can trust you?"

The rider chuckled. "Can't. Don't know what boss wants with you. Heh, might be unpleasant. Maybe deadly. Maybe not too bad. Stay here, you're screwed. Come with me, might live. Won't force you." She pointed behind him. "Choose fast, almost here."

What to do, what to do. That woman hardly seemed trustworthy. At the same time, it was obvious the mob would tear me apart. Their furious screams got closer, so I figured what the hell. I was likely to die either way, so I delayed the inevitable and jumped on the motorcycle. Like I said before: I'm not that smart.

—Thoughts of James Hunter, Hocmar 28, 2134, on the Nirnivian calendar

***

The moment James's bottom touched the seat, the woman departed. She performed a U-turn and took the same path he had come down earlier. Now rolling in a straight line, she accelerated. The engine released a furious roar, and the resulting force propelled James backward. Thank God he clutched the driver by instinct, burying his face in her hair. A flicker among the strands drew James's attention. Frowning, he focused on the area and discovered a metal crown embedded in the lady's skull. Confused, he wondered what the contraption might be. Not for long, however, for they reached the very mob he'd fled mere minutes ago.

Without hesitation, the woman plunged toward the horde. James averted his eyes, dreading the impact. None occurred. People jumped left and right, shrieking. Those paralyzed by fear, the rider weaved around.

She didn't hit any of them. I swear, it was a miracle.

—Thoughts of James Hunter, Hocmar 28, 2134, on the Nirnivian calendar

Though initially shocked by the vehicle storming at them, the crowd soon recuperated. They glanced at each other and brandished their fists at the offenders. A few gave chase, but on foot they stood little chance of overtaking the pair. One of the chasers yelled, "Hey, it's that Wrathchild traitor bitch helping the human asshole."

Not concentrating on the road, Wrathchild offered her companion a side glance. "Don't listen. Had veterinarians do test." She smirked. "Ain't no female dog."

Despite their superior speed, she opted for caution and swerved into a small street. James exhaled as he hoped the retreat cut the hunt short. Then a soaring bottle grazed his ear. It shattered on the asphalt with a chink. A rock followed, and next a banana-shaped fruit of all things. The projectiles missed their mark, yet James's muscles tensed up. He mumbled to himself in an attempt to calm his nerves. His worries proved futile. They outpaced the flock, who vanished in the distance in a second. Before he could relax, a rumbling sound arose from behind.

James gulped. He deduced the implications. Terrified, his brain ordered him not to look, but the temptation ended up too strong. Out of breath, he took a glimpse. A bare-chested thug covered in tattoos had mounted his own bike and raced after them. A lone hand steered; the other wielded a club. The message seemed obvious: he'd prefer to risk an accident than not to pummel them.

Glaring at his prey, the goon shouted, "I'm gonna kill you, bitch!"

Wrathchild groaned. "Amateurs... gotta hate 'em." With that, she braked.

"What the hell are you doing?"

No response. Because they'd virtually stopped, the brute caught up in a flash. He chuckled and lifted his bat. Sweat soaked James's clothes as he squirmed and whispered a prayer.

Their aggressor's head tumbled off his neck. Blood splattered on James's shirt; a drop or two soiled his brow. He whimpered as he gawked at the woman's extended crimson-stained blade. When had she unsheathed her sword?

"Jesus Christ!"

"Who? What?"

"Forget it!"

Dear God... I... I couldn't believe it. She murdered him. I saw someone die. Sure, he threatened us, so it kinda was legitimate, but still... I felt sick. If I hadn't lost my lunch already, I probably would have at that point. At least seeing a guy being slaughtered like an animal discouraged the mob. They ran away. I guess they realized I wasn't worth it.

—Thoughts of James Hunter, Hocmar 28, 2134, on the Nirnivian calendar

Freed from the tails, Wrathchild slowed down. She changed course and almost crashed into a teenager dressed in rags. The youth froze in place as his lips contorted in terror. A sharp tug on the handlebar dodged a collision, but they intercepted the ball he bounced on a house's wall. The sphere bumped their muffler and ricocheted.

"Okay," Wrathchild said once they'd passed the adolescent, "must leave city." She negotiated a curve when James spotted a white car coming in the opposite direction. The instant the automobile popped in their vision, the revolving lights on the roof illuminated. Shades of red and blue glowed on their skin as a siren blared. "Ah, crap!" Without delay, she veered into an adjacent lane. Determined, the cops followed, and a blast thundered. James's eyes watered. They'd shot at them!

Wrathchild switched routes often, but her erratic behavior failed to fool the police. The nimble bike possessed greater cornering ability, and the frequent twists held the car at bay, yet not enough to escape. As they progressed, she zigzagged in an effort to thwart the cops' aim. Nonetheless, James glimpsed sparks around the front wheel's rim. A bullet had struck it, or so he assumed. He sobbed, and then a blade materialized next to his face. As James wheezed, his pupils traced the edge until they met Wrathchild's fingers.

At first, I thought she went insane, but I heard a clink and... it's crazy, but... I mean, I'm not certain, but... I think she blocked a bullet.

—Thoughts of James Hunter, Hocmar 28, 2134, on the Nirnivian calendar

Now under heavy fire, the motorcycle kept going. James's grip on Wrathchild strengthened as he wept. What a mess, and yet he figured he'd no doubt survived the worst. Fate intended otherwise. A new police car appeared before them, obstructing the path. A pistol emerged out of the opened window. Tears skimmed along James's cheek while he squealed. Consumed by madness, his driver charged at the vehicle.

"Please, stop! We're done for, just stop. Please!"

"No."

"But they'll kill us!"

"Over dead body."

James moaned. "Yeah, exactly!"

The woman disregarded the objection, instead glancing at a wooden board lying on the ground and a trash can. She turned slightly toward James and winked. "Be right back."

She jumped off. To this day, I still wonder if I imagined what happened. I mean, it was impossible. At the speed we were going, she would've died. I was so stunned that the fact that the bike was driverless and would lose balance didn't cross my mind. She ran down the street and grabbed a garbage can. The cops shot at her. Luckily, I was considered far less dangerous, and they ignored me. She laid the garbage can down in the center of the alley and set the plank on top, creating a ramp, if you can call it that. Then she jumped back on the motorcycle. None of the bullets touched her. She did it all in a few seconds. She moved faster than her vehicle.

—Thoughts of James Hunter, Hocmar 28, 2134, on the Nirnivian calendar

Back in command, Wrathchild aligned the bike with her improvised slope. She pressed a button on her controls. A bang echoed and the motorcycle dashed forward. Again, James screamed in horror as they hopped. Through the car window, the officer's mouth gaped. Mesmerized by the stunt, he neglected to pull his trigger.

James's yells doubled as they approached the white roof beneath them. Convinced they wouldn't make it, he closed his eyes. At the last minute, he peeked: their tires grazed the metal, but they cleared the obstacle. The landing shook them. James tightened his grasp on Wrathchild, avoiding a lethal fall.

He gasped. "Please, I changed my mind. I want to be torn apart by the mob."

"Too late. No time. Cops can't stop me. NISDA might. Gotta get outta here before show up."

Though James discerned the words, their significance eluded him, given that he pondered whether a twenty-seven-year-old man without any cardiac condition could suffer from a heart attack. Based on the irregular pounding in his chest, he expected the answer to be yes. The question soon faded, however, for they arrived at a bridge hovering above not a river but rather another road.

Wrathchild smiled. "Gotta be unpredictable."

She flipped a switch. Panels on either side of the bike slid back to reveal two cannons. Wrathchild chose her target and fired a mini-missile at the railing. It detonated on contact, revealing a gap after the smoke dispersed. Against logic, she headed toward it as James swallowed hard.

"No, no, no, no! You gotta be shitting me!"

Wrathchild snickered. "Nope!"

Indeed, she wasn't. The nearer the hole, the paler James became. They reached it and dove. Properly motivated, his vocal cords attained an unprecedented high note. A fierce wind suffocated him as the asphalt and traffic below grew bigger and bigger.

Don't ask me how, but she did it. She freaking landed between two cars. I don't know what happened next. Maybe I passed out, or I repressed the memory. Too bad I couldn't just forget the whole thing.

—Thoughts of James Hunter, Hocmar 28, 2134, on the Nirnivian calendar

***

Still clutching the driver, James exhaled and inhaled in a rhythmic fashion. His stomach churned. The taste of blood lingered in his mouth, though he lacked memories of an injury. While Wrathchild slowed to a leisurely pace, the trip ended up rockier than earlier. A look down provided an explanation: they'd traded the asphalt road for a dirt trail. What happened? The last he recalled, they'd raced through the city, but now a sea of vegetation replaced the buildings and streetlamps. Confused, he almost rubbed his brow when a croak echoed.

The sound startled James. Had he not held on so tight, he might've fallen. Instead, he lifted his neck and realized spectators observed them in the form of black birds resting in the trees' branches. One changed his perch as he studied the intruders; another flew away, perhaps scared by their engine's rumbling. James lowered his gaze and glimpsed a flower. A purple insect gathered nectar among the delicate petals, or at least that was what he assumed.

What a change. I dared hope maybe, just maybe, I'd be okay. Why do I have to be so stupid?

—Thoughts of James Hunter, Hocmar 28, 2134, on the Nirnivian calendar

"Can relax grip," the woman said. "Out of danger."

James opened his jaw, but before he answered, he spotted an animal on the path. The distance proved too great to discern its exact shape, but the long ears reminded him of a rabbit. A smile appeared on his face. He used to own a pet bunny. The poor thing had died in a mere few months, but he remained fond of those balls of fur. The creature tilted its head, examining the approaching vehicle. Once it deemed the potential threat close enough, it hopped toward the woods, leaving James with a final peek at a caramel patch amidst the white hair. Freed of distraction, he remembered Wrathchild's comment and loosened his embrace.

"Right... sorry."

"Is fine." She paused for a second. "Speaking of apology: sorry rough ride. Had no choice."

"Rough ride?" Pictures popped into James's mind. The crowd pursuing them; bullets striking the bike; a sword nearly jabbed into his skull; jumping off a bridge. Without a doubt the deadliest experiences he'd lived through, and she brushed it aside like she discussed a breakfast marred by burnt toast. "Jesus! Rough ride! Are you kidding me?" Adrenaline surged through his veins. His heart pounded. "You almost killed us! What the hell was that? It was just impossible! You broke the laws of physics! How did you do that?"

Wrathchild shrugged. "Was easy. Don't give shit about physics."

"That's not how it works! Hell! That was like a crazy-ass action scene from a summer blockbuster movie directed by some director who's high on drugs!"

Wrathchild chuckled at his remark and hit the brakes, raising a cloud of dust. The particles irritated James's lungs. He erupted in a cough.

"Crap! Guy wanted longer chase. Gotta go back."

"AAAAAAAAAAH!"

"Kidding!"

I'm not a big fan of the B word—I swear I'm not, but if you ask me, I think her veterinarian should redo those tests.

—Thoughts of James Hunter, Hocmar 28, 2134, on the Nirnivian calendar

Chapter 6

In a valley fenced in by trees, the crimson man leaned against his military van. His weight was so heavy that the door bent under the pressure. A cloud of insects surrounded him. Every couple seconds, one landed on his limbs and attempted sucking the blood essential for its subsistence. The beast ignored them. Why bother chasing the winged menace? His rock-hard skin crushed their stingers. At least, Stalker assumed that was the reason for his boss's nonchalance. How he wished he possessed such an ability at the moment, but alas.

Though his mind tried tricking him, Stalker forced himself immobile. The desire for bug swatting he squashed, as well as the impulse to fidget. He simply needed a little extra time. His mission had ended in failure and thus required a proper excuse. Maybe the human had died before he arrived, murdered by his hosts? What if the news of a visitor proved a mere false rumor?

Enthralled by his pondering, Stalker almost tapped his chin with his finger. He aborted the motion at the last instant. Despite his effort, his superior glared toward him. Did a slight muscle tremor betray him? Strangely, the red monster examined the ground where Stalker stood as he scratched the edge of the single twisted horn protruding from his forehead. Footsteps in the mud; goddamn footsteps in the mud. Stalker cursed his stupidity for falling into an obvious trap. Should he admit defeat and reveal his presence? He rejected the idea and instead prayed the boss shrugged off the prints when a female voice said, "Danger! Stalker is scared. Terrified."

Prey to a sudden adrenaline burst, Stalker glowered at the truck's cracked-open window, or rather the blond woman sitting in the backseat. *Allison, you three-eyed fool,* he thought as he entertained the idea of shoving her own ponytail around her throat and choking her. With a grunt, he swallowed his rage. The straitjacket binding the poor soul and the electronic crown she wore reminded him of her condition. Furious or not, his illusion shattered.

The scarlet brute crossed his arms. "Give up, Stalker. Ain't got no human there. Stop the camo games and fess up, will ya?"

After a sigh, Stalker reverted to his original color scheme. Now visible, he rubbed behind his neck, embarrassed. "Sorry, boss." He slanted forward and twitched. "I messed up. I got him out, but he woke up so fast! It's my fault: I should've tied him, I..." His cheeks blushed. "I forgot my rope."

A harrumph interrupted Stalker's apology. He fixated on the laptop resting on the soil beside his leader's leg. On its screen, a bandaged visage appeared, denying a peek at the rotten flesh below, except for a few missed spots. Concealing the rare strands of hair remaining, a fedora sat on the walking cadaver's skull.

"Don't blame him." The words sounded hoarse, as if uttered by decayed vocal cords. "It's not his fault." His bloodshot white orbs serving as eyes enlarged. "gorthaca can knock out a guy for hours. The effect must be less potent on humans. Stalker couldn't—"

The crimson beast spun and grimaced at the computer. "Shut up, Plague! I ain't need no science lesson from ya today!" He groaned, faced Stalker again, and advanced. "It's okay, Stalker, you infiltrated Valardir. They got insane security, 'specially fo' Nirnivia." Once close enough, he wrapped his arm around his subordinate's shoulder. Though Stalker interpreted the gesture as friendly, it nearly crumbled his bones. "I'm impressed." He smirked and poked Stalker's sternum. Stalker shivered. "Just don't fo'get your rope no more. If you do, I'll put it to good use myself, if ya catch my drift."

Done with his speech, the abomination recoiled. Stalker took a deep breath or two and wiped his brow. While he recuperated, a motor echoed in the distance, and he gritted his teeth. "Crap. Is that NISDA?"

Waving the comment away, the leader rummaged through his yellow vest's pocket and fished out a minuscule pair of binoculars. He studied the road and grinned. "Hmm... Wrathchild's here. She's not alone. Looks like she caught our boy! Ain't that nice?"

***

Relaxed pace or not, James's nausea worsened the more they rolled. The moment Wrathchild stopped moving, he brought his palm to his mouth. His guts burned and grumbled. Despite assuming he'd emptied his stomach's contents earlier, he hopped off the bike on all fours and retched. Mere air came out, however.

The driver's familiar feminine voice said, "Hey, Diabo! Here's human you want."

Diabo? What an improbable name...

Footsteps interrupted James's pondering. Filled with curiosity, he returned to his knees and spun as he wiped saliva from his lower lip. During the motion, he glimpsed the chameleon he'd encountered in that guest room. He frowned at the sight, but not for long. A large leg landed next to him. After a gulp, James raised his gaze and witnessed a crimson muscle mass.

"Ain't he a charmer," the cross-armed creature mumbled while James fell on his bottom.

He looked at me with those disgusting yellow eyes. I... I didn't know what to do. He reminded me of a demon all right, and my "good Samaritan" had called him Diabo—the Portuguese word for devil. My friend Patrick is a quarter Portuguese, and his grandma... whatever. Was he actually the lord of darkness my priest had warned me about as a kid? I had a hard time believing that, but I could tell he wasn't friendly either way. I thought I was scared before, but it was nothing compared to the feeling I got staring at him and his motley crew.

—Thoughts of James Hunter, Hocmar 28, 2134, on the Nirnivian calendar

"A human..." The red beast pinched James's chin between his thumb and pinky. An intense pressure crushed his face, enough for pain. He whimpered and jerked his neck in an attempt to escape but remained stuck in place. Two fingers immobilized him. "Ain't gonna lie, I wasn't sure I believed it." Then the abomination forced James's jaw open by squeezing and pulling down. He peeked inside the oral cavity and grunted. "Get him in the truck, won't ya, boys? Maybe we can cut him up later. I wanna see what he's made of." The monster let him go and walked away, revealing a BBR tattoo on the back of his hand, much like the one the chameleon sported on his shoulder blade. Freed, James crawled in the opposite direction as he wept.

"Don't mean question order—" Wrathchild bit her lip. "Really necessary? Sounds extreme."

Oh God... Vivisection seemed bad already. I feared it'd be a dissection by the end. Yeah, I know the word vivisection. Thank you, Doctor Death. Anyway... she kind of screwed me, but I guess I should be grateful to Wrathchild for trying to save my ass. It didn't help, though. Diabo ignored her objections. Goons approached me. I swallowed hard. I figured I was dead meat, but someone grabbed me from behind. I screamed, terrified. I got even louder when I started floating.

—Thoughts of James Hunter, Hocmar 28, 2134, on the Nirnivian calendar

***

Halfway to his van, Diabo's thugs screamed. Surprised, he scowled. He then peeked over his shoulder. A woman clad in a white gown stood next to the prisoner. She wrapped her arms around the human and stared straight at Diabo, or so he assumed. On second thought, he realized she gazed past him and at his vehicle's window, or rather Allison—not that he cared. Roaring, he spun and dashed toward the offender. A futile gesture. She flapped her wings and departed with his prize. In a desperate attempt, Diabo reached for her leg but missed it by an inch.

"Ro... Rose?" Wrathchild trembled as she pointed to the sky. "Outside? What's going on? Who is he? Why came herself?"

"Shit if I know," a shrugging Stalker said.

Diabo ignored their dialogue and glared at the fleeing duo in silence. A bit of pondering, and he smirked while he rummaged through his vest's pocket. He fished out a small remote control. "Ain't gonna go far, lemme tell ya." The instant he touched the device, Allison tensed up, her three eyes wide open as she wailed. Diabo's index finger hovered above a button when Wrathchild jumped in front of him.

"Don't! Not Allison—"

Furious, Diabo growled and closed his fist. The poor woman cringed and shielded her face with her hands. He punched, but she rolled away. The brute mulled striking again, but he reconsidered and focused on the remote. A voice from his laptop interrupted him.

"No, Diabo, she's right!" He glowered toward the zombie on the screen and gritted his teeth. Plague had no reaction, though his colleagues recoiled. "If you do that, they'll crash. She'll break her neck. You know what Daniel Ricdeau will do to us if you kill her, right?"

Diabo contemplated the alluring button for a minute while twisting his lips and then sighed. "Fine, whatever. Let's get the freak outta here 'fore NISDA shows up."

Chapter 7

Flying... every human dreams of it. I remember looking at birds as a child, wishing I was one. A cliché, but still lovely, isn't it? Yeah, we have planes. That's just not the same. I was the closest a human had been to soaring through the air like a bird, but I was too baffled to enjoy it at first. The angel came and saved me! Why? I didn't know who she was, really. I didn't know if I could trust her. Yet she helped me, a perfect stranger. I guess it's normal given the circumstances, but I was so happy to see her again.

—Thoughts of James Hunter, Hocmar 28, 2134, on the Nirnivian calendar

From above, the terrain offered a magnificent view. A green field stretched beyond James's vision, decorated with wildflowers and bushes as well as the occasional tree. In a few spots, various animals fed on the grass or scurried along. To the left, a river flowed and beyond it stood a forest. Facing him, the city loomed. The buildings grew larger the closer they approached. Once his shock abated, James relished in the scenery. The speed ended up exhilarating, the flapping of Rose's wings oddly soothing. Both combined formed the most pleasurable sensation. He hoped this moment proved eternal, but Rose's mood suggested otherwise.

"Mr. Hunter, what do you think you're doing?" she asked. "I understand you're scared, but you need us if you want to live! I told you before. I'm not supposed to be here. They'll lecture me for hours because of you! Listen—"

"Wait—"

"I'm the only one. The only one who can protect you! In your current situation, running away is suicide. If you crave death, Mr. Hunter, you'd be better off hurting me so I'd drop you. It would be far less painful than whatever BBR has in store for you!"

"No, please don't drop me, I—"

"I never said I would!" Rose sighed. "How did you do it? How did you escape? That was Valardir, Nirnivia's highest-security military complex!" She paused for a second. "Answer me, it's important!"

"I... I didn't!" James whimpered. "That chameleon guy kidnapped me! I swear!"

"Kidnapped!" Concern replaced the anger in Rose's tone. "Oh, Mr. Hunter, I'm sorry. I should've figured it out. Kidnapped... I don't know what a chameleon is, but it must've been Stalker. Damn it! Valardir is filled with traps and security systems, yet he scooped you away. Dad has work to do. Please forgive me, Mr. Hunter."

"Don't worry about it, Ms."—James scowled as he searched his memory for her last name—"Ricdeau. I'm so grateful you saved me, I couldn't believe it."

"Ha ha, I'm surprised too. I shouldn't have, but I did. Lucky you." She hesitated. "Please, Mr. Hunter, call me Rose when we're alone. I get plenty of courtesies as it is."

Due to their flight, a sharp wind blew on James. He'd hardly noticed thanks to his excitement, but now the cold breeze took its toll. Trembling, he rubbed his arms for warmth. "Sure thing, Rose. You can call me James."

She giggled. "Oh, no offense, but that's such a boring name. My own name is boring enough. I'll call you Hunter. It's a lot cooler. Try to relax a bit, Hunter. Your heart rate seems fast to me. It's okay, you're safe. BBR won't attack while I'm with you. Diabo can be terrifying, but there's far worse." She gulped. "If he knows I'm here…"

"Um, who exactly?"

"Ignore me, I'm rambling. He's in a whole different country, so he can't harm us. Besides, we'll be in Valardir soon."

As we flew, I realized it was the first time I had been alone with Rose. She was much more casual, her wording less formal than the overly polite speech she had given me earlier. She wasn't quite as angelic this way, but friendlier. I felt a connection to her despite having just met her. While we glided in the sky, my thoughts drifted. I came to think about how my situation was like a bad trope out of a sci-fi TV show or something. Complicating matters, the setting was another world filled with freaks who wanted me dead. Back then, I had no idea how close to the truth I actually was…

—Thoughts of James Hunter, Hocmar 28, 2134, on the Nirnivian calendar

***

A squeal spread across the room as the marker's tip rubbed against the porcelain surface. Some might consider the sound irritating, but he had grown accustomed to this particular annoyance over time. The one Nirnivians called Doctor Death scrawled a variable or two in his uncompleted equation. Once done, he paused and pondered his work. Confused, he tapped his right index finger on the area around the speaker that had replaced his mouth.

Despite how hard he toiled, the solution eluded him. He shook his head and peeked at the three other whiteboards covered with cyan writing. Releasing the sigh his mouth could no longer produce through his nose, he then gazed upon the computer standing on the main desk. While unimpressive in appearance, the machine connected to a vast network, offering an unprecedented amount of calculations per second. All that processing power, and yet for organizing his thoughts, the good old-fashioned method proved most effective.

He started pacing. Five minutes later, he stopped and snapped his fingers. A brilliant idea came in a flash. Ecstatic, he returned to his whiteboard and lifted his pen. Light glimmered on his metallic arm. He had sketched a lone stroke when a beep interrupted the motion. He stared toward the table sitting beside his canvas, or more precisely, the tablet-shaped minicomp resting on top. A text message, received at the least opportune moment. He swallowed his frustration and picked up the device. After a few pokes, he saw the sender's name. Any remaining trace of anger morphed into curiosity. He read the note as fast as possible. The LED face decorating his electronic eye changed. For an instant, the simple smile became a surprised circle, followed by a grin. A human had shown up in Nirnivia. Not only that, but Rose insisted he stay in Valardir.

"My, my," he said to himself, "it seems my deus ex machina has finally arrived..."

The Voice of God

Chapter 1

Mashar 17, 2133, on the Nirnivian calendar

The white cloth covered the lower half of the prisoner's face, though his eyes remained visible. He lay on a table, restrained without hope of escape. A shiver beset Janice Ricdeau as she observed her colleague pouring water over the rag. The captive stiffened and gasped. His pupils contracted in fear while they searched around for something that might allow respite. Janice looked away, grasping her own fingers to seek comfort. Sure, the one they tortured had committed heinous crimes, but such a crude treatment brought her no joy. Being a soldier, she spilled blood on occasion, but this... this seemed excessively cowardly and cruel. Give her a fair fight and she'd excel without hesitation, but brutalizing a downed foe left a sickening sensation in her stomach.

The assault lasted about a minute before Janice signaled her coworker. He stopped as instructed. Their victim coughed and took numerous deep breaths. Janice's lips twisted while her nose wrinkled. The technique appeared benign enough to the uninitiated, but she knew better. It simulated drowning and proved convincing. She waited a moment until the goon recuperated, then she leaned forward, faking a smile.

"Don't be stupid. Just tell us where Diabo's hiding and we'll leave you alone."

The detainee glared at her. "Screw you!"

Janice let out an unexpected chuckle. "Careful what you wish for. I'd eat you alive." The brief hilarity vanished. After a sigh, she shook her head. Why did they insist she conduct so many freaking interrogations? She assumed her superiors believed that her feminine touch might charm these fallen gentlemen, but the tactic lacked results.

Frustrated, she almost gestured for her companion to resume his task yet resisted the urge when she remembered how waterboarding felt. Her training had dictated she undergo the torment in case of capture. She had endured a mere ten minutes, a trifle compared to what their prisoners went through. The instant morphed into an eternity as an illusory death crawled closer. Since then, she had refused to perform the procedure; others fulfilled that duty while she asked the questions.

"Throw me a bone. Give me Stalker, Plague or Wrathchild instead." She beamed. "I'm being too generous. I'll pay for it, I swear!"

Unfortunately, the fool stayed silent as he kept staring. Janice groaned and glanced at her teammate. "Hit him again!" Though she gave the order, she averted her gaze. Once the punishment was administered, she decided on a new course of action. Perhaps if she exploited males' alleged greatest weakness...

"Come on"—Janice straightened—"tell me what I need and you'll get a special gift, how about that?"

No reaction despite her optimism, but her friend turned toward her with his right hand resting on his hip. He offered his most devious smirk. "Why do you only give special gifts to terrorists? Me and the guys like surprises too!"

Janice forced a snicker. "Oh, Bob, didn't you take Psychology 101? Women with daddy issues have a soft spot for bad boys."

"Daddy issues?" He slapped his brow. "Ah, Janice, that's so cliché."

"Don't worry, I have plenty of mother issues too, buddy."

***

Another tedious workday dealt with. Janice leaned against the building serving as their outpost. Located near what they labeled the neutral zone, the decrepit structure provided the lone sign of civilization. Her pal, Bob, sat on the ground and doodled with a twig. Once he completed a picture, he erased it by spreading the sand via his palm and started a different masterpiece including a house, a tree, and a dog. Janice's gaze alternated between his sketches and the setting sun. The immense fireball descended in the horizon, rendering the sky a pinkish hue.

Even at this hour, the heat oppressed them. Such was the price of living so far north. To think that past the neutral zone, the country named Ostark experienced even warmer temperatures. The mere notion triggered a shiver. At least their shift had officially ended; they were off duty and thus Janice traded the inadequate uniform for her favorite black T-shirt and a pair of denim shorts. Though less glamorous than her previous attire, the current one suited the environment better. The beer in her hand also aided.

"About that special gift," Bob said while he drew, "you weren't gonna do it, right?"

"Of course. I'm a woman of my word!" Bob darted an incredulous glance. "Oh, you're jealous, Bob?" She giggled. "Fine, I'll sneak in cupcakes for you tomorrow."

"Man, if that guy took you up on it, he'd be freaking disappointed."

"Hey, I clearly meant I'd bring him a treat for his sweet tooth. If he somehow imagined something else, he'd only have his sick and twisted mind to blame." Janice laughed and waggled an accusing index finger. "Same goes for you, buddy. You should be ashamed."

"Oh, I am, I am. Gotta give it to him, he was a tough nut to crack, huh? The bastard kept his mouth shut pretty damn tight."

"They all do. I can't remember the last time a BBR goon talked. I don't know why we bother."

"It's just for show." Now erect, her companion crossed his arms. "The bigwigs don't care about BBR. The truth is, they're doing us a favor."

Flashing half a smile, Janice raised a dubious eyebrow. "So, you're pledging your undying love for terrorism? Careful, I might tell on you." She stuck out her tongue in a playful manner.

"Come on! You understand what I mean. You're a grown girl."

The explanation remained unfinished. Janice poked her colleague's sternum and admired her muscular limb. The benefit and burden of training. Many claimed that her powerful body diminished her femininity, but she chose to ignore the critics. Besides, her strength proved valuable in her profession. "Grown woman!"

Bob sighed and nodded along. "Yes, you're a grown woman. My apologies, ma'am. My point is, BBR's right. This peace is a joke. The Nirnivian government pretends they're going after BBR so Doctor Death won't attack us while we have our pants down, but they don't really want to stop them. Whatever hurts Ostark helps us."

Before replying, Janice brought her bottle to her lips and sampled a sip from her beer. She closed her eyes and savored the bitter flavor with a satisfied grunt. "Maybe."

"Maybe? Are you kidding? They won't let us enter the neutral zone. Everyone knows that's where BBR's hiding."

"Great idea! We set a toe in there without Ostark's permission and we break our treaty." Janice forced a snicker. "That'd piss off the Doctor a whole lot more than anything Diabo can do." As she uttered her sentence, she noted a large cinder block resting nearby. Bored, she approached and jumped on top.

Bob slapped his forehead and mumbled a curse. "Are you dense or are you shitting me? You've got to be shitting me, please."

Disregarding the tirade, Janice positioned her feet over the brick's side. Forward she bent, and the concrete slab tilted on its edge while maintaining balance. Enthralled by his tale, Bob failed to notice his friend's prowess.

"They send troops into the neutral zone all the—" Janice lifted her left leg. The motion finally caught Bob's attention. "You sure you wanna do that when you're drinking?"

She acquiesced. "Yeah, it's too easy sober."

"Makes sense... I guess. Like I was saying, they send troops into the neutral zone all the time, and Ostark does the same. No one's broadcasting it, but it's not that hard to see if you look—" He then waved his own argument away. "Oh, and forget it, I've got better. If they want those bastards in jail, why do they only allow waterboarding? Give us Ostarkiran pain sticks and watch the assholes squirm."

"The Council made every form of torture except waterboarding illegal. And don't get attached. Thanks to my sister, Her Holiness, we'll lose that soon." In her mind, she added, "and good riddance." She realized Bob didn't share her aversion to waterboarding and decided she preferred avoiding a lecture. The discussion annoyed her enough as it was. She wished to relax, not debate.

"You are shitting me! Illegal? NISDA doesn't worry about pencil pushers and their laws."

It appeared he wouldn't drop the issue without encouragement. From her perch, Janice groaned and glared at him. "Listen, Bob, don't take this the wrong way, but you're asking the wrong girl—"

He smirked at her faux pas. "Woman!"

"That's only cute when I do it!" Janice wiped a pearl of sweat off her brow; her fingers caressed her luxurious dark hair. Next, she tasted her beverage. "I obey orders, I don't question them. I don't know about any secret torture. You want answers? Ask my father. He's in charge, not me."

"Ah, right, the old dog of the mili—"

A booming voice yelling Janice's name interrupted Bob. Surprised, Janice lost her equilibrium. The cinder block tumbled, and she risked a nasty fall. She leaped and landed back on the brick once it steadied, switching her leg and earning an impressed whistle from Bob. "Nice!"

"Yeah, I got a talent." Janice hopped down and faced the source of her distraction. Due to the gesture, her sunglasses slid along her nose. She adjusted the specs and spotted a tall soldier running toward them: Gerard.

"Janice, you have an urgent communication! It's the Commander!"

She placed her beer on the ground, opened her mouth wide and put her hands on her cheeks, feigning enthusiasm.

"Oh my, Daddy dearest is calling me. My oh my, what an honor for a simple sweetie." Bob adopted a confused scowl. "Long story."

That said, Janice seized her brew and gulped the remaining contents. The deed done, she flung the empty bottle, which shattered the moment it struck the soil. She then peeked at the shards and resolved to pick them up later; first, her superior waited. She reached for the radio Gerard offered her. The exchange ended in a few minutes at most. Though of a mysterious nature, a new mission required her presence. Whether she liked it or not, it seemed she'd be heading home.

Chapter 2

No doubt, the flight demanded a tremendous effort from Rose, yet despite the fact that they reached the city, she stayed airborne. They glided above the buildings. In the street, passersby strolled along until one of them pointed toward the hovering duo. More gazes joined his every second. Cars stopped in the road as their drivers fixated on the sky. A light scowl appeared on James's brow, and he wondered if perhaps the crowd explained why his rescuer avoided the soil.

While they progressed, the mob grew larger and followed. Soon, James spotted a security fence in the distance. Rose lowered her altitude, a move that puzzled him. The horde's screams assailed his ears but remained indistinct. Among the chaos, he noted barbed wire decorating the barrier's edge. He guessed the contraption posed little challenge for a determined infiltrator, though he supposed it served as a warning rather than genuine protection. At any rate, they cleared the sharp obstacle and Rose landed.

The moment she touched the pavement, Rose unloaded her cargo. A few deep breaths and James studied the structure standing before him. Low to the ground and presenting a silver wall devoid of features except for a NISDA logo, the edifice seemed quite small for what he assumed to be the complex he had visited earlier. Then again, a downward staircase led to a door, giving credence to the idea that most of the space rested below the surface.

Yells and shouts interrupted James's pondering. He peeked backward. The swarm pushed against the fence blocking their path. He swallowed hard. People hated his guts, he knew that already, but to such an extent? Perplexed, he almost asked Rose why Nirnivians despised his presence, but when he noticed his friend's condition, he forgot the question. Bending over, Rose huffed and puffed as perspiration covered her skin and drenched her dress. James gasped. Though she carried him without any complaint, obviously his weight exceeded her strength. Somehow, they had made it, but by her appearance, logic dictated they should've plummeted a long time ago.

Overwhelmed by gratitude, James blushed and began thanking her, but she seized his hand.

"Come."

Undeterred by her fatigue, Rose ran forward, pulling James. A couple of soldiers rushed at them, but she ignored their pleas and darted for the stairs with such speed that her companion almost tumbled. She swung the door open and shoved James inside. Before the thick metal slab shut, he took a final glimpse at the horde. He expected furious growls and fist shaking, but instead, he witnessed smiles and awe-filled eyes. Confused, he contemplated the possibility that they had assembled not for him but for his savior.

***

When James and Rose entered the building, they arrived before a wooden desk. Two headset-wearing soldiers in familiar uniforms operated the station while they hammered on computers. Behind them was a thick metal door. As James deduced, it likely led deeper into the military complex. The receptionists spotted him and Rose. Shocked, they jumped to their feet, pulling out their headsets' cords in the process. One of them extended his arm toward the winged woman.

"Oh my God! Your H—"

"Yes, it's me and I'm fine," Rose said, interrupting her wheezing. "I need a favor." She hobbled toward the counter. "I'm well aware of Valardir's procedures, but we're in a hurry. Could you, um, let us through without a fuss? Just this once."

The men exchanged glances. "Gosh, we want to, but we can't—"

Before he finished, Rose stumbled. Thankfully, she gripped the desk, thus preventing a fall. Panicked, the soldiers grasped her nonetheless, though the moment they realized she had avoided the danger by herself, they removed their hands as if they touched burning coal.

"I'm all right, I swear." She took in a breath before continuing. "Tired, but all right. Please, I'll make sure you won't get in trouble."

"We can't." The officer bit his lip. "The Koporal ordered us not to let you through until he spoke with you, and you know how the Koporal is."

Rose let out an exasperated sigh. "Oh yes, I've had my share of disagreements with Ron Tigh, believe me. I'll handle h—" By some miracle, she maintained her balance, but her leg wavered.

"Look, Your H—" He peeked at James. "Ms. Ricdeau, you're obviously exhausted. Why don't you sit down and relax until the Koporal shows up? I'll call him right away. It won't take long."

"But... okay, you win. I could use a breather." She peered over her shoulder and beamed. "Come and sit with me, Hunter. We'll have a chat while we wait."

Somehow, James had missed the three chairs near the desk. Must be because of his nerves. Following the suggestion, he walked to the nearest seat. The leather squeaked as he adjusted his position. Noisy, yet quite comfortable. The promise of a conversation remained unfulfilled, however, as a delicate snore tickled his ears before his bottom reached its destination. A smile grew on his face. Based on the smell emanating from her sleeping body, she deserved her rest. James wished her slumber lasted hours so she'd recuperate, but alas, a mere ten minutes later, the door slid open with a hiss and Rose's eyelids popped open.

A hunched senior stepped through the frame at a firm pace. He wore the same attire as his colleagues, though a large number of medals graced the fabric. Contrarily to the others, his arms crossed over a potbelly instead of a six-pack; the price of age, James assumed. The same held for his wrinkled brow, furrowed into a frown. The overall picture might not sound appealing, but at least his black hair hadn't grayed yet. An advantage he lost by sporting a comb-over from hell. Behind the elder, a pair of soldiers trailed. Despite being a good foot taller than their leader, they lacked his assurance and fidgeted in apprehension.

"Well, well, the big birdy is back!" the old man said, smirking. As a reply, Rose stretched and yawned, unfazed by the apparent insult. "The human scum too. Cuff him, boys!"

My spirit sank. Apparently, my hardships were far from over. The soldiers were gentle enough, but they made it obvious I'd regret any resistance. I didn't plan on causing trouble anyway. I figured they'd throw me back in jail, and this time, there was nothing Rose could do. That depressed me, but on a positive note, it was better than being back with Diabo, or on Wrathchild's motorcycle.

—Thoughts of James Hunter, Hocmar 28, 2134, on the Nirnivian calendar

Harsh words bounced off Rose's skin, but the order struck a nerve. Her energy returned in a rush and she hopped off the chair. Next, she brandished a menacing index finger and advanced on the senior until the appendage swayed under his nose.

"Wait! Koporal Tigh, he did nothing wrong!"

After a groan, Ron snatched her finger in midair. The brutes accompanying him gasped, and soon, they stared at the floor while they whimpered. James almost chuckled, but a question squelched his hilarity: did respect or dread trigger their distress?

"Don't you wave that thing at me, little missy. And I don't want another word out of you! What were you thinking, leaving without permission?"

Scoffing, Rose shook her head. "What?" She put her hands on her hips. The posture accentuated her frustration. By then, the underlings' palms rested on their skulls and their mouths gaped in disbelief. "I am not a prisoner! I am here by choice and free to come and go as I please!"

Tigh nodded. "Yes, that's true, but you could've at least warned us. We feared the worst! It was total panic down here. Brucie cried like a kid! He resigned three times; good thing Dan has a good temper or he'd really be out a job. Speaking of Dan, do you have any idea what you've put him through? He's been worried sick. He's got plenty on his plate already. He doesn't need this shit."

She blushed. "I'm sorry. I didn't mean to. I've been careless, but please, Koporal Tigh, don't punish Mr. Hunter for my actions. He's innocent."

"This whole country sings to your freaking tune, but don't expect me to blindly obey your every whim just because of who you are." Ron then exhaled, and his tone softened a bit. "Maybe I'm the only one who remembers, but the Melkar has no business meddling with military affairs." He gave her a pat on the shoulder. "Perk up, missy. I'm not here to punish him. I'm bringing him to Dan for a friendly neighborhood interrogation. No big deal."

"Okay." She glanced at James. "I'm sorry, but you'll have to go with him."

Deep down, I was terrified. I wanted to beg her to protect me and change his mind somehow. There was so much sadness in her eyes; so much regret. If she could've done anything, she would've; no doubt there, so I put on my brave face and pretended I didn't mind at all.

—Thoughts of James Hunter, Hocmar 28, 2134, on the Nirnivian calendar

"Thank you for understanding, Hunter."

Chapter 3

After a ride in an elevator, the soldiers guided James to a small yet elegant room. Not that he focused on the finer details: his gaze was fixed on the wooden desk in the middle, or rather the person behind it. Head bowed down, an old man sat in his chair, fingers forming a pyramid. James recognized him from earlier that day. When he'd met Rose, a group of soldiers had been present and the senior had stood among them. The elder's eyes appeared closed on first sight, but upon further inspection, James noted barely opened slits. A shiver assailed him and he attempted to step backward, but his escort blocked his retreat.

"Hello again, my boy," the senior said as a smile spread across his face. "Thank you for joining me. Have a seat." He paused for a second, then gestured toward his men. "Oh, and please uncuff him. We don't want our guest to feel unwelcome, now do we?"

The officers saluted before complying. "Yes, sir!"

"There, you're free. Don't just stand there, son, come and sit with me." Since James stayed still, he waved. "Come on, I don't bite."

Swallowing hard, James approached at a deliberate pace. As he strolled forward, he scanned the office. Along the right wall, he spotted a bookcase filled with volumes and a trophy case enclosing various items including what he guessed to be war medals. On the left wall, several pictures hung. Most depicted his host accompanied by strangers. James of course knew nothing of them, but they wore luxurious clothes and jewelry, giving an impression of wealth.

Then he almost gasped when he recognized an image of Rose. The winged woman smiled for the camera. Next to her stood a tall lady with her black hair arranged in a ponytail. Her impressive muscular mass gained his attention, and he slowed his pace while admiring the forearm thrice the size of his. Despite his interest, he chose not to delay and soon reached the chair.

Once James's bottom rested on the cushion, the elder offered his palm. "Mr. Hunter, I'm Commander Daniel Ricdeau; don't let the title impress you. We've already met, but we forgot the introductions."

James shook his hand and it proved firm as expected, though still reasonable enough not to cause pain. "It's an honor, sir!"

"Oh, now, my boy, you're only saying that because you're scared." Daniel's grin grew even wider. "It's not a bad reason! Wait, I have a gift for you." The old man pulled out a drawer and rummaged through its contents. "Uh, I've got it somewhere around here." He pulled out two rectangular objects and threw them on the bureau. Intrigued, James studied the green-and-silver metallic wrappers covering his presents. "You must be starving. I brought these as a snack, but you need them more than me. Eat up. We'll get you a real meal later if you want one."

With all the excitement, hunger had slipped of James's mind, but now his stomach growled. He seized one bar but then frowned. He had changed worlds, that much he realized. Food from this place might upset his human body, or even kill him. Why, perhaps his benefactor had deliberately poisoned the treat for his own purposes. A paranoiac consideration indeed, but given the hatred he had witnessed previously, it was still possible. He deliberated discarding the grub, only to note the torn-up packaging littering the floor. In the end, his appetite was such that he swallowed the slab as he mused. Ah well, no point fussing about it now, so he reached for the second.

In the meantime, Daniel got to his feet and walked to the cupboard. He swung the door open and lifted a large bottle containing a transparent liquid and a glass. As he observed, James tore the foil enveloping his other bar. The granola within posed little challenge for his teeth. They chopped about a fourth of the snack, and he chewed through the nuts and oats. Not bad. The satisfying crunch and sweet yet salty taste reminded him of brands he might've bought on Earth. After he finished, Daniel returned to the desk, sat the goblet on top and poured some of the fluid inside.

"It's water," he said while he nudged the glass toward James.

Suddenly, James's throat itched and burned. He hadn't had anything to drink since he had arrived, and fear suppressed his thirst no more. The rim of the glass touched his lips, and he gulped the water. Thanks to his rush, streams ran down his cheeks and neck, spreading a cold sensation and wetting his shirt. At least Daniel failed to notice his clumsiness. The senior stood, his face away from James and his hands joined in his back.

"You know, Mr. Hunter, it seems my daughter is quite fascinated by you."

The allusion lacked a name, but James shrank nonetheless. "Oh, so she's your... I'm sorry, I didn't mean to put her in danger. I—"

Daniel faced him and dismissed his concern with a wave and a chuckle. "No, no, my boy, I'm not blaming you. It's just that her behavior intrigues me. You see, Rose hasn't left this place for years, not even once. Then you show up and she disappears without a warning. That got me curious, so I decided I'd have a chat with you. I thought maybe then, I could understand what's so special about you." Daniel came back to his seat and smiled. "My boy, let me reassure you right away, I'm not like my Koporal." The mention prompted a quiver out of James. "Oh yes, I know how he is. He's a nice guy, really, but under pressure, he's all about the stick. Now that works fine sometimes, but me, I find a gentler touch is often more effective. So, Mr. Hunter, there are a few things I wish to know. I'd like this to be a casual conversation between two potential friends."

Upon finishing this sentence, the Commander leaned forward and connected his fingers in a dome. "There's no need to make a fuss of things, but if you won't cooperate, I'll have no choice but to be less pleasant." Though charming, the voice carried a subtle menacing edge, and James trembled. "It's up to you. You're a man of mystery, Mr. Hunter. You appeared out of nowhere, you escaped from a military facility and you've been associating with less-than-reputable characters. My gut tells me you've done nothing wrong, but we're currently at war, so I can't take any chances. Mr. Hunter, I want you to tell me what happened in your own words. Don't lie. If you lie, I'll know it and you'll be in trouble. I'm all ears, go ahead."

"Um, well, you see..." James caressed his jaw, and Daniel's pupils tracked the motion. "Well..." His muscles tensed. In reaction, the pupils darted around, skimming over his whole body.

And so, I told him everything. I explained how the strange man they called Stalker had kidnapped me and how I'd ended up on that bike with Wrathchild. The experience terrified me; not quite as much as Diabo, but close. It's not like he threat-

ened me or anything. On the contrary, he was very nice. He sat and listened. Sometimes he'd ask a question, but generally, he let me tell my story without interruption. The creepy part was how he looked at me. I felt like he could see every twitch; every tic. Maybe he could even see through my clothes. It made me uncomfortable. Kind of like when the doctor's examining you when you're naked, except worse. I didn't doubt that if I lied, he'd realize immediately.

—Thoughts of James Hunter, Hocmar 28, 2134, on the Nirnivian calendar

"I see," Mr. Ricdeau acquiesced once James finished. "All right, my boy, I believe you've told me everything I needed to know. Thank you for your cooperation; consider yourself a free man."

Surprised, James blinked twice. He froze for a moment and pondered the phrase's implications. Sure, it sounded simple, yet his mind insisted there had to be a trick. Did deception taint Daniel's tone or his posture? Then the adrenaline in his veins relented and the anxiousness morphed into drowsiness. James slumped forward as he relaxed. He was safe. He almost giggled at the thought, but that demanded too great an effort.

"You look dead tired, son. We can offer our hospitality, or if you prefer, you can get out of here. I suggest you stay at least for the night."

"Well, I guess there's no point sleeping in the streets."

The Commander grinned. "Glad we're on the same page. Now, you deserve your rest, but before that, maybe you'd like some explanations."

The adrenaline surged again, even if only a trickle. His curiosity piqued, James straightened. "You can say that again! I have no idea what's going on!"

Daniel nodded. "First, I think I should apologize for all you've been through. I'm really sorry, James." He gave a slight scowl. "Can I call you James?"

"Sure."

"Perfect, feel free to call me Daniel. The truth is, everyone's on edge because we're at war, but I'm getting ahead of myself." Calmed by James's account, the Commander now leaned back in his seat with his fingers laced behind his head. "You probably don't even know where you are. I doubt the name will tell you anything, but you're in a country called Nirnivia, more precisely in the city of Farson. I'll skip the details for today, but like I said, we're at war with another country, named Ostark. It gets more complicated, I'm afraid."

While the speech conveyed gravity, the senior's demeanor suggested otherwise. By then, his legs lay atop his desk. James almost gasped. The nonchalant attitude came as a shock.

"Those who kidnapped you, they're, uh"—he gave a twirl of his wrist—"like a third party in this conflict. They're Nirnivians and they fight against Ostark too, but we're hardly allies. They're part of a terrorist organization named Broken Beyond Repair—BBR for short. The red man, Diabo, he's their leader. They hate the Ostarkirans with a passion and believe Nirnivia's too weak and lacks resolve, so they fight the war we're too scared to fight ourselves, or so they like to think."

As he stopped and cleared his throat, Daniel fished out a green ball from his drawer. He flung and caught the projectile in a loop.

"In truth, they're extremists who let nothing get between them and their target. You have no idea how many innocents have died in their raids."

Reflecting on Daniel's words, James rubbed his chin. Though light on specifics, they provided a few enlightening facts. Wrathchild was a terrorist, which explained why everyone hated her; however, the bigger mysteries remained unsolved.

"Why would they go through so much trouble just to get me? They said they wanted to experiment on me, maybe even dissect me. It doesn't make any sense."

The old man shrugged. "I honestly have no idea. Whatever their reason, I assure you they're up to no good. We'll investigate and I'll keep you informed." He cackled. "Unless it's a matter of national security."

"Diabo..." James paused and frowned. "That's the lord of darkness in my religion. What's that about?"

I figured I shouldn't bring up the fact that it was in Portuguese and not English.

—Thoughts of James Hunter, Hocmar 28, 2134, on the Nirnivian calendar

For the first time since James had met him, the Commander shuddered. His lips contorted in a faint yet visible grimace. Not only that, he clenched his fist too soon and the ball struck his nails before bouncing on the floor. "Oh my, that's quite a coincidence. I don't see how there could be any more to it than that. Nobody here knows anything about your religion, and Diabo isn't an exception. That's not even his real name: they all use code names. He's Pierre Garland."

His surprise seemed sincere. I had no reason to think he might be lying. Still, I felt uneasy. First an angel, then a demon. There had to be something more there—or was I trying to find meaning where there wasn't any? At any rate, even if

he lied, he wouldn't admit it. I decided I should change the subject.

 —Thoughts of James Hunter, Hocmar 28, 2134, on the Nirnivian calendar

"Those people, uh, the terrorists, they were freaking monsters. I mean literally. And that Wrathchild woman, she did impossible things."

"Yes." Mr. Ricdeau's brow furrowed. "I'm sure you've noticed their rank includes some peculiar individuals. You might've seen other people with strange deformities. Several Nirnivian citizens are mutants. Most are unfortunate and handicapped. Many die not long after birth. A few actually have superior abilities. They can look scary, but they're as good a people as any other." He shook his head. "It's a shame so many judge them on appearance. Anyway, BBR counts several mutants among them, and not just any run-of-the-mill ones either. Wrathchild, Diabo, Stalker, and Plague are not your average criminals. They can do things a normal person can only dream of."

"Yeah, um, Wrathchild showed me some tricks with her motorcycle."

"I wish I could've seen it!" Daniel burst out in laughter. "She's my enemy, but she's talented! Well, James, I think that's enough for today. Sorry again for this whole business. I'm sure you have more questions, but I've rambled enough. My wife must be waiting for me and you're about to fall asleep."

"Oh, I'm not that tir—" A yawn interrupted James, and he covered his mouth as he blushed.

"Told you! That settles it. We'll continue our chat tomorrow. Uh, just to warn you, we're moving you to the fifth level so you're safer. I'll take you there right now; you can't go there on your own anyway."

Chapter 4

Mashar 18, 2133, on the Nirnivian calendar

The next morning, my alarm clock woke me. I didn't want to get up, I could've stayed in bed forever. Why did I even set it up? It was the freaking weekend.

—Thoughts of James Hunter, Hocmar 28, 2134, on the Nirnivian calendar

After a groan, James swung his arm in an attempt to silence his alarm but struck the air. Puzzled, he forced his eyelids open. A bookshelf filled his vision instead of the television he had installed in the perfect position for watching while lying on his mattress. He sat up in a rush and blinked twice. A few seconds of mystified silence, and he recalled the situation as the noise buzzed once more. Only then did he realize that it came not from his clock but from a doorbell. A visitor had arrived.

Flooded with curiosity, James scanned the floor and spotted his clothes. Sure, he'd worn them yesterday, but he lacked a wardrobe, so he hopped off the mattress and slipped on his pants one leg at the time. As he was zipping up, a female voice boomed, "Mr. Hunter? Are you there?"

"I'm coming. Give me a minute." James picked up his shirt and put it on while he walked. After his neck cleared the proper hole, he massaged his temples with a moan. A headache assailed him. Whenever he awakened too fast for his body's expected leisurely pace, he suffered. Despite his discomfort, James wondered who rang. He had met two women, Rose and Wrathchild, and the guest sounded like neither. Yet the voice felt familiar somehow...

He gave a press of the appropriate button and the door slid open. James almost lost consciousness, but he managed to merely recoil.

What was she doing here? She was supposed to be home. I never thought I'd see her eyes ever again, and there I was looking right into them.

—Thoughts of James Hunter, Hocmar 28, 2134, on the Nirnivian calendar

"Nadia?" James whispered as he raised his hand to caress her soft blond hair. "How did you get here?" No reply came. The woman stiffened; her lips contorted in a grimace. She gasped and traded her disgusted expression for a glare. Though James's senses warned him, his dodge failed and the slap hit him.

"Get your hands off me, you creep!"

"Ow!" Suppressing a whimper, James rubbed his cheek. The blow possessed strength, and he feared a mark might show.

Right about then, I really blamed myself for not noticing that, unlike Nadia, she wore glasses. Not only that, her hair stopped about an inch above her shoulders, where Nadia's kept going past them. And she wore a dark blue vest over a white shirt and a skirt. Nadia wouldn't be caught dead in a skirt. So, okay, I admit it wasn't my smartest moment, but in my defense, even with all that, she could've passed for Nadia's twin.

—Thoughts of James Hunter, Hocmar 28, 2134, on the Nirnivian calendar

"I... I'm sorry, miss, I... you look just like my girlfriend, Nadia. I was confused for a minute."

"Your girlfriend?" The woman scoffed. "How dumb do you think I am? Your girlfriend isn't here and you know it."

"Um, right, right, but I'm still half-asleep and I got confused."

"Just keep your hands to yourself from now on." Her tone, not to mention her folded arms, suggested disdain. "I'm Kristina Dupree, Rose's personal assistant. Rose is in a meeting, but she wants to talk to you after, so she asked me to come and get you. You've been sleeping all morning, so I've brought you this." She offered James a plastic bottle. "It's a homemade nutritional supplement I use on busy mornings. It's pretty filling. Oh, I have this too if you want something more solid. It's not much, but it should hold you until lunch."

After a bit of rummaging through the bag she carried, she grabbed a sandwich. James thanked her. The walk proceeded in silence, and he wished otherwise. Admittedly, Kristina displayed hostility, yet even an awkward chat might keep his mind off the soldiers littering the place. When they encountered one, James withdrew from his path and gawked at his uniform: how intimidating. Kristina, however, paid the officers no heed. Rather, she advanced with her head bowed down, concentrating on a tablet-like device. Every couple of seconds, she poked at the screen with the stylus. Had he not witnessed far more impressive gadgets on Earth, James might've been impressed by the technology. Why, they'd just released a touch-enabled phone. No need for a cumbersome stick either as you pressed with your fingers. His friend Patrick babbled about the gizmo constantly.

Though the tablet didn't impress James, Kristina's commitment did. She marched along the corridor, focused on her work, yet she avoided any obstacle in her way and maintained an image of pure professionalism—a far cry from the self-proclaimed all-time loser. Intending to forget this sense of inadequacy, James sampled a sip of his beverage. The fruity flavor surprised him—certainly better than what the words *nutritional supplement* implied. Pleased, he let out a satisfied grunt and considered tasting the sandwich. Before he tore open the wrapping, Kristina stopped at one of the thick metal doors.

Without peeking at him, she said, "Rose is inside. She'll be out soon."

The instant she finished the sentence, the doors opened, revealing Brucie rather than the winged lady. The muscle-bound bodyguard stood perfectly erect. He stepped forward, showcasing his massive pecs, and pointed at James.

"She wanna talk to ya. Don'tcha try anything funny, bro!"

Gulping, James flinched, shielding his torso with his palms. "Uh, what?"

A giggle echoed, and Rose's head popped out from behind the brute's shoulder. She winked. "Don't worry about him, Hunter." She circumvented her protector and shoved him back. "He's messing with you for fun. He's kind of a jerk like that."

"Hmmph..." Cross-armed, Brucie glared at his employer. "Ain't I a jerk for doing the job ya pay me for. Feeling really appreciated right 'bout now."

"Oh, Brucie, I do appreciate your dedication, I—"

"Yeah, I know. I'm just messing with ya." He stuck out his tongue. "I'm a jerk like that."

With a dismissive wave toward the giant, Rose spun around, focusing on James. "I'm glad to see you again, Hunter! Thank you, Kristina."

James blushed as he imagined the assistant mentioning his faux pas, but she only said, "You're welcome," and continued her work.

"You've already met Brucie Garland, my bodyguard, so I'll forgo the introductions. My adoptive father explained a few things to you yesterday. He meant to fill you in on the rest today, but he's busy, and I figured I should take his place. Please, join me in here."

"Um, Rose?" The blond woman tapped her watch, then immediately returned to her task.

"Thank you for the reminder. I'll be quick."

***

With every step, James's feet sank into the carpet that graced the office floor. In a rush, he scanned the environment. It seemed mostly empty, excluding a few swiveling chairs and a metal desk. On the bureau sat a computer monitor about twenty inches in size, displaying a screensaver consisting of red, green and blue balls bouncing along the edges. The orbs morphed in scope and color as they moved.

The moment she entered the room, Rose reached for a chair and sat. Then she extended her fingers and wiggled them in a manner suggesting he approach. "Come and have a seat. You can stand if you prefer, but your legs might get tired." She giggled.

After a brief hesitation where he froze in place, James acquiesced. He chose a different chair and began sitting. During the motion, Kristina passed him by. The assistant ignored both of them and poked at her tablet as before. Denying her companions even a glance, she settled for an isolated corner and kept working without interruption, except to brush aside a strand of hair when it incommoded her vision. James decided he should concentrate on Rose anyway. Her smile was radiant, a sign of kindness that helped quell his apprehension a tad. From the corner of his eye, he spotted a small bug crawling on the counter's surface. Its shape lacked definition. It was a cylinder mounted on six limbs, and so it would remain, for Brucie squashed the insect with his thumb.

Rose shuddered and fired a glare at her bodyguard. "Why did you kill it? It wasn't hurting anybody."

A muscular shrug came from Brucie. "Might be poisonous. Gotta protect ya from all threats, ya know."

"Oh God, I highly doubt it." She let out a sigh, massaging her temples. "I'll just pretend you didn't do that." Her beam returned as she looked at James. "All right, Hunter, my dad already explained about the war and who abducted you, so we can skip that part. I'd think your biggest question is how you got here. Unfortunately, we don't know exactly, but I can shed light on the matter. For a few years now, various, um, how should I put it?" Wrinkles formed on her forehead. "Let's call them 'visitors' for now. Yes, 'visitors' started appearing around Nirnivia. It hasn't happened often, but it caused major problems. These 'visitors' have little in common. Some are intelligent, others mindless animals. Several died immediately on their arrival, as if they can't survive in this atmosphere. When they do live, most of the time we cannot communicate, and it's always hard to predict how they'll react to their new situation. It seems the travels are involuntary, which complicates matters even more."

They usually couldn't communicate with the "visitors." That's logical, isn't it? What are the odds I'd not only be teleported to another world, but also that its inhabitants would speak English? I'm no expert, but I'd say close to zero. And yet, there I was. Such a sci-fi cliché. When weird things happen in fiction, we can blame the lousy writer. When they happen in real life, we can only accept them. At least this weird thing was actually helpful.

—Thoughts of James Hunter, Hocmar 28, 2134, on the Nirnivian calendar

James nodded. "Uh, I don't know about the others, but I didn't come here by choice."

"That was my understanding. We're not sure what's going on. Our scientists believe there are multiple parallel universes, some very similar to our own, others completely different. The 'visitors' come from those. We don't know why. There are several complicated theories I don't understand. We can arrange a meeting with someone more competent if you wish to learn about the hard science."

James lifted his palms as if shielding himself from the proposition. "Thank you, but that's okay. Science isn't my thing. I'm not all that smart."

"Hey, I hear that, man!" A strident pain burned James's shoulder where Brucie slapped it. "I'm in the same boat, ya know. All that science talk gimme a headache and makes me wanna get drunk. Of course, pretty much everything makes me wanna get drunk."

James disregarded the comment and rubbed his chin as he contemplated the new information he had received. He had envisaged a parallel universe before, though he'd based his guess more on TV shows. As he pondered, he asked, "If that's what's going on, why haven't there ever been any visitors on Earth?"

"I'm afraid I don't have an answer, but are you sure it's never happened?"

I remember at first, I figured that was a stupid question. Yet the more I considered it, the more I found possible examples: Yeti, the Loch Ness monster, UFO sightings, many others... I always thought those were bullshit, and I still do, but maybe, just maybe, some of them were "visitors" from other universes, like I was.

—Thoughts of James Hunter, Hocmar 28, 2134, on the Nirnivian calendar

"That's not important right now. Tell me"—a glimmer of foolish hope shone in his irises—"can you send 'visitors' back?"

The second he finished his sentence, Rose's lips contorted in a grimace. She stiffened and opened her mouth, only to waver. Despite the obvious signs, James inched toward the edge of his seat. Sweat covered his body as he crossed his fingers in anticipation. After swallowing hard, Rose bit the bullet. "I'm so sorry, Hunter, but no. We can't. I'm very sorry."

Deep down, I always knew I'd be stuck there forever. Things were so hectic until then, I'd never had a chance to think about it at a conscious level. When I heard those words, I finally realized the magnitude of what had happened, and I couldn't accept it.

—Thoughts of James Hunter, Hocmar 28, 2134, on the Nirnivian calendar

"No... no!" Enraged, he rose and clenched his fists. "That can't be. There has to be a way!"

"Maybe there is, but we don't know how."

A weakness descended on James. His family, his friends... gone. The world spun around him. With a whimper, his legs wavered. He almost collapsed but gripped the desk's edge and thus stabilized his posture. Then a crazy notion popped into his mind and he erupted in a distorted laughter. "Yesterday, your dad said something about how strange it was that I appeared here and BBR came for me right away. What if they brought me?"

Rose exhaled. "I can see what you're thinking, Hunter. You figure they brought you here and so can send you back." The winged woman shook her head. "I'm sorry, but given that neither we nor Ostark has developed a means for multiverse travel, I doubt BBR has. They don't have that kind of resources."

"But, but…"

Rose got up and touched his shoulder. "Why would they teleport you into the middle of the city rather than their hideout? Because they didn't. They heard about your arrival and arranged for your capture. I don't know why they even bothered doing that."

That was reasonable. It made perfect sense. But I didn't need reason. I needed a miracle and I wouldn't, couldn't accept anything less.

—Thoughts of James Hunter, Hocmar 28, 2134, on the Nirnivian calendar

"No! No, I can't stay here forever! I have to go back! There has to be a way! I can't… I have to go home!"

"Hunter, I'm very sorry." Her eyebrows pulled together while she tilted her neck. "I understand how you feel, but—"

"No—no, you don't!" Fists clenched, James leaned forward and glared at his interlocutor. Alarmed though remaining calm, Brucie approached. Even Kristina laid down her tablet and allowed herself a peek. "You have no idea how this is, you have no idea what I feel! I've lost every damn thing I ever had! My family, my girlfriend, my job, my possessions—all gone in the span of a second! Not only that, I'm in a place filled with freaks trying to kill me!"

An intense heat consumed James. He gritted his teeth and impulsively punched the bureau. A loud thump echoed the instant his flesh struck the steel, and a sharp ache spread through his arm. In a second, his eyes watered and his lip twisted. "Oooowwww." James crumpled to his knees, trembling.

Still shaking, he examined his fingers. Fearing they might be broken, he debated twiddling them, but his nerves betrayed him. Then Rose kneeled and reached for them. With a gasp, James recoiled, and she offered a smile.

"It's okay, I'll be careful." Another sob and James forced himself immobile, though he averted his gaze. Rose grabbed his hand and patted it, moving the fingers. In spite of his condition, he barely felt it. "At least you didn't break anything."

James started weeping. "Listen to me! I have to go back! I have to! I want to see my family. I want to see my girl-friend. I... I want to see Nadia. Please, I'm begging you. Shit, Nadia..." He gulped. "She saw me disappear into thin air and must think she's going insane! I have to go back!"

"Hunter, it's all right. She'll be fine, okay?" She stroked his arm. "She's safe back at home. Probably confused, but safe. I'm sure there are people taking good care of her. You're safe too. We'll take good care of you here. Hunter, look at me. Look at me, please." A warmth flowed across James's cheek. The red-haired woman caressed it and posi-tioned his face so he'd see her. "Everything will be fine, I promise."

It wasn't her words. They didn't mean anything—just ba-nalities she hoped might comfort me, but how could they? Nothing was fine; she knew that as well as I did. There was no going back, she said it herself. No, it wasn't her words. It was her eyes, or rather what I saw in them: sorrow. So much sorrow she desperately tried to hide. She did understand, she really did. I could tell. Yeah, she'd never changed universes, but she'd lost people before. Hell, I shouldn't have been surprised when she said Daniel was her adoptive father. Whether in this world or mine, I didn't have a monopoly on pain.

—Thoughts of James Hunter, Hocmar 28, 2134, on the Nirnivian calendar

"I... I'll be okay. Thank you," James mumbled, blushing. "Sorry about that. Um, I'm kinda embarrassed."

The bodyguard failed to realize his own strength, and his tap on James's back almost propelled him forward. "Ah, come on, man, ain't no need fo' that!" He grinned. "We get it, anyone else would bawl like ya, or worse. Well, not me 'cause I'm a real male, but ya know." The playful mocking earned him an elbow in the ribs, courtesy of Rose. "Ow! Come on, I'm joking, geez!"

"Well, please stop! You mean well, but now is not the time."

James faked a chuckle. "It's okay. I, um, remembered something. I wanted to ask about this before; it's important. Where I'm from, we sure as hell haven't heard of Nirnivia, but people here mentioned humans and—"

Kristina harrumphed. "Um, Rose..." Suspicion crept inside James. Might she be interrupting his question on purpose? A bit of pondering and he rejected the impression as mere paranoia. "I'm sorry, but if we don't go, you'll be late."

The Melkar presented an objecting index finger, only to exhale. "I'm sorry, Hunter. I'll be back in about an hour and we'll have lunch together; we can talk more then. Kristina will take you to the clinic so they can do the required tests. Don't be scared, Hunter, it's a formality for staying in

Valardir. Security reasons." She smiled again. "Don't worry, we'll take good care of you."

With that, the winged woman walked toward the door with Brucie in tow. A groaning Kristina waved for James to follow. Complete silence accompanied her gesture. He strolled beside her in the corridor and she remained focused on her device and nudged the screen. Once in a while, James peeked at her for a fraction of a second. She ignored his glances, perhaps even didn't notice them. Halfway there, he stared at the beautiful assistant for longer than usual. He opened his mouth and then closed it again. Then he took a deep breath and gathered his courage. "Um... can you... can you tell me why people here know about humans?"

Kristina sneered. "I don't know! Maybe because when you go around groping everything that moves, you make a reputation for yourself."

James flushed for the umpteenth time and resolved he'd keep quiet for the rest of the trip. At least he finally ate his sandwich.

Chapter 5

The sun shone down on Janice, but compared to the powerful rays up north at her previous post, there was no need to break a sweat. Still, her shades served their purpose well. She pushed them up as she observed Valardir in the distance. The main door stood about twenty steps away. If she went there and swiped her card, it'd open easily. Freak, a salute at the camera and they'd let her in. Security was lacking at the first level, but that changed the deeper underground you descended. Though her destination waited inside and entering demanded little effort, she stayed immobile and watched with crossed arms. A few minutes passed before she marched forward with a grunt.

Once the locking mechanism disengaged, she entered the premises. Two familiar faces manned a desk inside. They hammered on their keyboards, oblivious to the arrival. Such a disgraceful behavior from the receptionists: the duo not only ignored Janice, they failed to spot her on the camera. A smirk forming on her face, she prepared a snarky quip for Vince and Peter, but to no avail. They finally lifted their necks, avoiding the rebuke by a second. Seeing Janice, they both jumped to their feet as their mouths gaped. Shocked exclamations echoed while she advanced toward her colleagues.

"Janice, you're back!" Peter said as she high-fived him.

"We didn't know you were coming!" For Vince, she reserved a fist bump. "How's life at the border?"

"Hot and boring."

Vince chuckled at the pleasantries but, by his forced expression, only out of politeness. "I hear that! It's pretty cool down here, but with you around, I can feel the temperature climbing already."

"Careful, you sure you want another harassment complaint?" A wink accompanied the threat.

Perplexed, Peter frowned. "Another?"

Janice raised an incredulous eyebrow. "Wait, you haven't heard about that?" The shrug he offered confirmed his ignorance. "Ah, man"—she glanced at Vince—"I thought we told everybody!"

"Me too! We better fix our oversight!" His own giggles muffled Vince's words. "It happened a few years back, like a couple of months before the war. It was the annual Valardir picnic—you know, the last one. Well, me and Janice we were on the same team for the Hudrad match and we won, so I towel-slapped her and everyone else. It's like tradition! Professionals do it all the time. Janice got all fake pissed and accused me of sexually harassing her. She said she'd get my ass fired, and if they didn't fire me, she'd sue."

"You know me, I was just kidding around! But anal Mike overheard me."

"Oh shit!" a face-palming Peter mumbled.

Janice sneered. "So you know the asshole, huh?"

"Yeah, sure!" He gave an empathetic headshake. "Who doesn't? Let me guess, he didn't get the joke."

"Bingo!" Vince brandished his index finger at Peter in a congratulatory manner. "He filed a formal complaint in Janice's name."

After the sigh, she said, "I tried to explain I was only messing around with an old buddy, but it's like he didn't understand what I meant."

"He didn't. Anal Mike's a pile of bones, but there's not a single funny one in there." The trio burst into laughter. Soon, Peter leaned against his bureau on the verge of collapsing while Vince smacked his thigh. "What the freak happened to him anyway?"

"He stepped on a landmine during the war." The instant Janice finished her sentence, the hilarity vanished. Embarrassed, Vince scratched the back of his skull as Peter fixated on the floor. Both men blushed, and judging by the warmth spreading around her visage, she guessed the same held true for her. The remark killed the party. Why had she answered the question? She should've remained quiet, or lied and pretended she had no idea. The awkward silence lasted about a minute, while she rummaged through her brain for a comeback that might lighten the mood. "Um... hey, by the way, you two are really slacking off! You didn't even notice me on the camera. You lazy bum, I should report you to Dad!" The duo exchanged a peek. "Oh, come on! Don't make me call you anal Vince and Pete!"

Vince swallowed hard. "No, it's not that. It's just, we really should've noticed. The bigwigs are hot and bothered about security since yesterday. Koporal Tigh himself came here and ordered us to be careful. Actually, he said if we screwed up again, he'd jam his foot up our asses so far we'd need a proctologist." The soldier wiped a pearl of sweat. "I don't think he meant it literally, but with the Koporal..."

"You're scared of Uncle Tigh?" With a wave, Janice dismissed the notion. "Ridiculous! He's like a cute pissack in a morglar's costume." A smile graced her lips as she recalled the pissack living near their backyard. She had been no more than nine then, and after she'd spotted him scurrying along one day, she'd left various nuts and snacks on the ground. At first, the twin-tailed rodent proved suspicious, but eventually, he sampled the treats and approached his benefactor closer and closer. Once, he even let her run a finger through his soft auburn hair. She remembered his delighted squeals as she caressed him. Too bad he chewed through one of their window screens and her father had stipulated she stop the feedings. Had he been the princess's pet, however...

"Yeah, he's nice to you all right; he's a jerk to everyone else except your dad."

"That's only the morglar's costume. Why is he worried about security anyway?"

"They all are." Peter groaned. "Since Stalker got in, they've been acting crazy."

Confused, Janice creased her brow. "What? BBR Stalker? He got in here?"

A nod came from Vince. "Well, yeah. You didn't know? I guess we shouldn't be surprised. The bigwigs hushed the press. But, yes, the weirdo somehow slipped inside, and with Her Holiness living here, the Commander and the Koporal are freaking out."

"He got down to level five?"

"No, only level one. He went for the human, not Her Holiness."

Suppressing a chortle, Janice shrugged her concern away. "Level one? Who cares? Level one is like a rusty padlock on a high school locker compared to five, even three. I could break into level one, it's not... wait! The human was here?" Her frown intensified. Of course, she had heard about the human visitor on the news, but nothing concerning keeping him in Valardir. Why? A military prison or even a normal one would serve better.

Peter acquiesced. "Uh-huh, Her Holiness insisted he stay here under her protection."

"Ooh la la..." A clap resonated as Janice clasped her hands together. "The princess is worried about the poor little human. How cute." Vince and Peter both gasped and glared at each other while Janice shook her head. "Oh, you're such cowards! Two big armed soldiers terrified. I repeat: not just scared, but terrified of a woman half their size who wouldn't hurt a flesh-eating bacterium. Not even if it infected her. Her immune system would shut down."

"But, Janice, proper respect must be shown to the Melkar."

"Psht, don't give me that crap. I—" A swoosh interrupted her rebuttal. The trio turned toward the door leading further into Valardir. As anticipated, it slid open. Less expected, the Commander appeared through the gap, fingers joined behind his back. Each soldier straightened and saluted the moment they identified their superior.

The gray-haired elder beamed. "At ease, men. At ease." They complied, apart from Janice, which prompted a giggle out of the Commander. "And lady too." Then he walked to her and patted her arm. "Good to see you, sweetie. It's been a while."

"Almost five months, and it should've been eight." In her mind, Janice added, *I wish it had been.* Out loud, she continued, "I was surprised when you asked me to come back for a special assignment."

Daniel nodded. "Ah yes, it's a most important matter. Speaking of which, we should head for my office and talk about it." A wrinkled hand wrapped around Janice's shoulder. "Great work at the border, by the way, I'm proud of you."

***

Metallic clinks echoed from the father and daughter's rhythmic footsteps. As they marched toward his office, Daniel studied Janice's arm. The corner of his lip twitched a little when he realized it had grown even bigger in the past months. Something must've weighed on her mind back at the border. Whenever she endured anger or frustration, she coped by pumping iron at the gym—not a bad method compared to some others.

"You look like you're in great shape, sweetie." A noncommittal shrug served as the lone reply. Daniel resisted a sigh. "We thought you'd come for a visit last evening. Your mother was disappointed when you didn't show up. She missed you a lot."

"Sorry, I traveled the whole day, and when I got to my house, I sat on the couch and fell asleep. I only woke this morning. I didn't even have a chance to set the alarm; that's why I'm late."

"Yes, I put you in a rush. Sorry about that, but it's important. Thanks for coming this quickly. I'm in a jam and it can't wait."

Janice crossed her arms and frowned. "This is about my special assignment, right?" He acquiesced. "So, what's going on?"

"I think it's better if we wait until we're in my office. We'll be there soon anyway." As if to prove his words true, they reached an elevator. Both entered the small cubicle, and Daniel pressed the button for level two. A prompt appeared on a screen above the keys, asking him to swipe his card. He performed the requested action, and the message changed. The camera identified two persons, and he needed to input his PIN confirming the other passenger's authorization. Before he had the opportunity, Janice swiped her own pass, saving them a few seconds.

"Thanks, sweetie."

"No problem."

With that, a rumbling resonated and the elevator began its descent. Five underground levels comprised Valardir, each more secure than the last. Daniel himself spent most of his time on floors four and five but also possessed an office on the second floor. He often received guests lacking the clearance for the lower tiers, such as minor politicians, and so the office ended up useful. Since going further below required fingerprints, scans and biometric tests, he decided the higher office would be sufficient for their chat, much like when he had met James Hunter. At any rate, they soon reached their destination and proceeded along a new corridor.

Janice stifled a snicker. "By the way, how's the princess?"

A shiver ran down Daniel's spine. He straightened, then spun around, facing Janice and stopping their progress. "Don't start. Enough with the jealousy already."

"I'm not jealous, I—"

Daniel interrupted by poking at his daughter's sternum. "The poor girl needed a family. Why do you always blame me for taking her in?"

"I don't!" Her face reddening, Janice threw her hands in the air. "I'm glad you took her in! You gave an orphan a home—great! I applaud you!" A few claps complemented the remark. "It's the one thing in your shitty life you can be proud of! No, I blame you for chasing my brother away!"

The rebuttal flushed the air out of Daniel's lungs. He recoiled. In his brain, an image of his son's clear blue eyes popped. A heavy blow of shame struck his heart. "I... Laurence chose to leave. I didn't throw him out."

"Yeah, well, you didn't exactly encourage him to stay."

Prey to a sudden headache, Daniel massaged his brow. "I made a lot of mistakes as a father, I admit that. I apologized again and again; I'm not perfect. I wish you'd finally settle down and have kids of your own so you'd understand." He moaned. "Sweetie, I haven't seen you for five months. Can't you drop it just this once?"

Janice gritted her teeth only to exhale. "Fine, whatever. Seriously, though, how's Rose? I heard she got herself a human." She chuckled. "I couldn't even keep my pet pissack, and she gets pretty much the biological equivalent of a Nirnivian person!"

"That pissack wasn't a pet, it was a wild animal. You're lucky it didn't bite a finger off. And you're leaving out an important part of the story: we bought you a dog. Not jealous, my wrinkled tush."

"Yep, and he had to stay outside. Rain or snow, it didn't matter."

"Inside dogs are too much trouble. They leave slime everywhere. It's too messy."

An incredulous gasp escaped from Janice's throat. "Oh, and the human isn't trouble?"

Daniel patted her shoulder. "Sweetie, you have no idea."

Chapter 6

Standing behind the podium, Nicky rearranged her notes. Complex technical details littered the papers, jargon far too dense for her to memorize everything in the short time her superiors had granted. Alas, the crowd would have to tolerate an orator reading her speech. Not that it mattered, as they'd resent the message no matter how eloquently put.

Ready to begin, Nicky surveyed the crescent-moon-shaped seating inside the auditorium. A couple minutes and she'd be able to start. Most chairs sat occupied, though late arrivals still scrambled for their seats. Bronze-skinned Brigs formed the majority of the audience, which was not surprising given they accounted for more than half the remaining Nirnivians. Despite their relative rarity, she recognized a few Zargs, Perz and even a Jonilan among the faces. Perhaps a little silly, but the fact that Perz attended put her mind at ease, even if they'd likely prove hostile regardless of their shared racial heritage and dark complexions. As for the Zargs, while far paler than her, she considered them kindred spirits after a fashion. Both peoples had suffered through a war brought upon them by other cultures. But that was neither here nor there. They'd all had to forgive the mistakes of the past long ago to survive.

"All right, everyone, my name is Nicky Standford"—she cleared her throat—"and I'm from NISDA. Ms. Constance Prim, the liaison between High Command and the technical department, is indisposed today, so I've been sent to give you instructions. I'm sure you've all heard about how Stalker from BBR infiltrated Valardir. This would be unacceptable under normal circumstances, and with the Ostarkiran threat and Her Holiness living here, we must be even more vigilant." That said, she went on and listed a number of security improvements the technicians in attendance were meant to implement. They fired incredulous glares toward her. Disgruntled whispers even reached her ears. She ignored them and kept talking.

Once Nicky finished, a thin man wearing a white dress shirt and a blue tie raised his hand. Based on his almond-shaped eyes and long black hair arranged in a ponytail, she judged him to be a Jonilan. Nicky resisted a sigh and signaled he could speak. "Hi, I'm Jonathan Rivers. I'm concerned about some of what you proposed. Frankly, I don't think whoever made the decisions thought it through, and I can't blame them. The Stalker incident happened yesterday!" The technician caressed his chin and lowered his volume. "The new measures aren't practical, and—"

"Practical or not, it's necessary. Sometimes good security means we have to sacrifice convenience. We'll have to adj—"

"Fair enough, but is the Commander aware we'll need experimental technologies?"

Various gasps echoed while a scowl materialized on Nicky's brow. The insolent man had interrupted her. True, she'd treated him the same, but most of his colleagues lacked the nerve to cut off an NISDA officer. "Of course, Mr. Rivers. It's a concern for him, but he came to the conclusion that the Melkar's safety is paramount." A smirk graced Nicky's lips and a slight mocking tone followed. "If there isn't anything else, I—"

"Ah, but there is! The deadline's unrealistic. We're already overworked and understaffed. Under this workload, it'd take us a year to install and test everything properly. You're giving us four months. There's just no way. It'll be a disaster."

Nicky rubbed her forehead and exhaled. "Mr. Rivers, let me be clear, I'm only the messenger. These orders come from my superiors and were approved by the Commander himself. There's nothing I can do except report your reservations and recommend you share your concerns directly."

A nod came from the Jonilan. "Thank you, I will."

Chapter 7

From his seat, James observed Dr. Greenberg pick up an object on a nearby counter as he whistled a tune. Thanks to the angle, he had a good view of the physician's brown hair arranged in a mullet; few members of the medical profession he met chose such a coiffure. At any rate, the doctor spun and faced him, wiggling the syringe he'd obtained. James gulped and nibbled his lip.

"Hey, buddy, perk up! I only need a little blood." To illustrate his point, he presented his index finger and thumb, separated by a minuscule gap. Dr. Greenberg's speech sported a different accent compared to everyone else. Every word trailed a tad, just enough to notice. "You won't feel a thing."

"Uh, is it really necessary?"

"'Fraid so!" He walked toward James, the stethoscope hanging from his neck bouncing with every step. "We do DNA tests on everyone periodically, and we need a baseline."

Realizing what the words implied, James scowled. "So, uh, I better get used to this?"

Like before, Kristina focused entirely on her tablet while in the clinic. The instant they'd arrived, she'd leaned against the wall in a corner, and she'd continued poking the screen with her stylus ever since. Still, when she heard the question, she glared at James and answered in Greenberg's stead, "Don't be a baby! If you don't like it, you can always go live in the streets."

Resigned, James let the physician roll up his sleeve. Afterward, the medic wrapped a tourniquet around his arm. The pressure made James wince. "All right, then. Madam Vein, meet Mister Needle!" As warned, the metal prong plunged into his skin and a sharp pain assailed him. Though he gritted his teeth, the sensation proved less intense than expected. "Okay, you did very well." That said, the doctor traded the plunger for tweezers. He squeezed the spines together, resulting in a clink. "This might hurt a bit too." He plucked a hair off James's skull.

"Ow!"

"That's the worst of it, I swear." The doctor reached for a cotton swab. "Open your mouth for me, please." James complied and Greenberg rubbed the gauze against the inside of his cheeks. Once done, he removed the white stick. "Okay, that's 'bout it! Only one last thing—please come over here, buddy!" Greenberg gestured toward a large gray cylinder. A few button presses later, it opened with a hiss, revealing a cavity in the top part and a small mattress in the bottom. "Just lie here, please."

James swallowed hard. "Uh, what is it?"

"This baby?" The medic tapped the device twice. "There's a country called Ostark out there, and they're masters at plastic surgery. This scanner here checks for micro scars to make sure you're really who you look like."

A frown appeared on James's features. "Don't the DNA tests do that?"

"Sure, as long as no one messed with the data on file. You can never be too careful!"

"All right..." Filled with apprehension, he headed for the machine, only to withdraw at the final moment.

I didn't mean to be difficult. It's just that thing reminded me of a tanning booth, so it screamed cancer.

—Thoughts of James Hunter, Hocmar 28, 2134, on the Nirnivian calendar

For the second time, Kristina glanced at him. The blond woman moved a lock of hair, blocking her vision. "Listen, we all go through the scan every two weeks. It won't kill you. Get on with it, please."

"Oh, speaking of which"—the physician snapped his fingers—"you're due in three days."

"Yes, I'm aware of that. It's in my schedule."

Despite my reservations, I lay on the mattress. Dr. Greenberg put a mask over my eyes, and I heard the cylinder closing. I didn't feel anything. If it wasn't for the low-pitched rumbling, I wouldn't have known it was on. The whole process lasted maybe five minutes.

—Thoughts of James Hunter, Hocmar 28, 2134, on the Nirnivian calendar

***

Rose said about an hour, but even after going to the clinic, I waited in my room for at least two. When the buzzer on my door rang, I was so happy. I mean, I had nothing to do except walk in a circle. I guess I could've read, but I couldn't focus at all so... anyway, we went to the cafeteria and, well, let's just say I had a new problem.

—Thoughts of James Hunter, Hocmar 28, 2134, on the Nirnivian calendar

What an unusual predicament James found himself in. He stood near the counter and studied the menu plastered on the wall above. The letters he had learned as a child appeared on the canvas, yet the food items turned out to be anything but familiar. What in the name of hell was Sherblob pie, let alone what it tasted like? To the best of his knowledge, he suffered from no allergies, but when it came to this new cuisine, how could he be sure? It might even be poisonous for a human.

If the incoming decision made him sweat, the various glances coming from the crowd only exacerbated the effect. Thanks to their tardiness, relatively few patrons filled the tables in the room. However, most were soldiers dressed in imposing uniforms, and even worse, many were armed with visible guns. They glanced toward James and even pointed at him while they mumbled among themselves. On occasion, James averted his eyes from the menu and discreetly peeked at them. Soon, he began trembling and swallowed hard. Memories from his assault upon arriving in this new world crept back into his mind, and the bump on his skull flared. Suddenly, his hunger more or less vanished. He considered excusing himself and returning to his room when Brucie wrapped his arm around his shoulders. The strong embrace ended up too constricted for comfort, though not to the point where it brought physical harm.

"Hey, dude, why the long face? Gotta be confused by all the stuff on there, ain't ya?" The bodyguard winked. "Don't worry, pal, I got ya covered! Ya trust me, don'tcha?"

James's cheek reddened. "Uh..."

A soft giggle emerged from behind the two men. Rose walked before Brucie and smirked. "Not if he has any sense left in him, he doesn't. I'll order for him."

Brucie then tightened his hug, and James gulped. "Come on, I got good taste, ain't I?"

"Um..."

"That's enough, Brucie. Give him a break! It's his first day, you'll have your fun later." The redhead rested her right hand on her hip while, with the left, she formed a fist minus the thumb, which pointed out in a manner suggesting the brute should step away. "I'll take care of Hunter, you stick to your job description."

Brucie sighed and shook his head in disappointment. "Fine, fine, whatever."

"Okay, now that you're safe, how about we find you something to eat?" She marched next to James, taking Brucie's place, though she refrained from touching him. "You're not a vegetarian, are you?"

"N-no..."

"All right, that gives us more choices. How well do you handle spicy foods?"

James bit his lip. "They're not really my thing."

"That's fine." A gentle laugh echoed as she patted his back. "Why are you so tense? It's just lunch, we'll find you something." She gestured toward her bodyguard. "You're past the danger, so relax! Maybe you have more of a sweet tooth?"

She tried hard, but I was still trusting a complete stranger. I mean, she seemed very nice and all, but there's no way she could be sure I'd like what she'd pick, no matter how many questions she asked. Still, compared to Brucie, following Rose's advice felt like a sure bet.

—Thoughts of James Hunter, Hocmar 28, 2134, on the Nirnivian calendar

***

Their meal acquired, the trio carried their trays to a table near the edge of the cafeteria. Rose and Brucie sat on the side opposite James. The few soldiers around them still fired a few random stares toward James, but he tried to ignore them. He focused on his plate instead. A small chunk of white meat rested in the middle. God only knew what kind of animal it came from, and James favored not asking. On the side, he found a green salad. Red pieces peppered the leaves. Nearby lay a loaf of what seemed to be bread. Next to his dish stood a glass filled with blue juice from a fruit Rose called druikinaka, a familiar name, but he failed to remember why. The color both unsettled and mesmerized him. Despite his apprehension, James satisfied his curiosity and sampled the beverage. He almost dropped the goblet in shock: the flavor proved sweet like candy.

Several minutes of silence flew by. James barely touched his food; he played with it more than ate, a fact that did not escape his companions. The winged woman stopped her own munching and pointed at his tray. "Are you all right? I'm sorry if my choices aren't doing it for you. I'll try to do better next time."

"No, that's not it. It tastes great." James groaned and forced himself to gaze into her eyes. "I'm not all that hungry. There's so much going on."

I wasn't completely honest: the food tasted pretty bland. It wasn't bad, just... not that good either. Don't get me wrong, I've had far worse, and I would've gladly chowed it down, but... like I said, my heart wasn't in it.

—Thoughts of James Hunter, Hocmar 28, 2134, on the Nirnivian calendar

Rose swallowed a morsel of her own lunch before proceeding. "I understand, but you should try. Your body needs nutrition even if the mind doesn't want it."

"Yeah, ain't that right?" Grinning, Brucie waved his fork toward James in a lecturing manner. "Look, ya scrawny thing, you gotta fill up with proteins if we're gonna build ya up."

The Melkar emitted a soft giggle. "Not everything's about muscular structure, Brucie."

"Yeah, it is!" After hopping to his feet, the bodyguard pumped his biceps, showing off his prowess. "Come on, tell me you don't want this."

Rose's laughs only increased, and she covered her mouth. "You're such an idiot."

"Yeah, a freaking sexy idiot!"

James ignored his companions' jests and lowered his head once more. A few seconds passed, and then he looked up and fixated on Rose. He hesitated, recoiling, only to gather his courage again. "Rose... can you... never mind."

The woman smiled and stretched her arm, touching his right hand. "Hey, don't be shy. If there's anything I can do for you, let me know."

"It's just... I was wondering if you'd tell me why people around here hate humans so much. How do you even know about us?"

Rose's complexion grew a touch paler, and she averted her gaze. "It's... a sad story." She exhaled. "You're not the first human visitor. I never met the other guy, but he appeared a while ago. He was traumatized, as you can imagine." The creases on her brow grew deeper. She closed her eyes. "Apparently, he took a child hostage." She whimpered. "I'd rather skip the details if you don't mind, but in the end, both the child and human died."

I wasn't sure what to think of her explanation. I agree the death of a child is appalling, but I felt it didn't justify the rage I witnessed back then. To judge humanity as a whole based on the action of one crazed man was hardly fair. Then again, I guess it must be easy to discriminate against people from another universe. I have to admit that if something like this happened on Earth, we might react in a similar way. More concerning was that Rose glossed over the incident. It was difficult to tell if that was because she preferred that I didn't know or because it was gruesome.

—Thoughts of James Hunter, Hocmar 28, 2134, on the Nirnivian calendar

"That's horrible, but, uh, they tried to kill me. Isn't that a bit much?"

Rose acquiesced. "Of course it is, but please understand, the situation here is unstable. With the war, everyone's on edge, and don't forget, a child died. People don't react well when children are put in danger, and with all the stress and panic we face daily, it doesn't take much for them to overreact. I'm not saying that excuses their actions, and I can't ask you to forgive them, but they did what they did out of misplaced fear and anger. I'm sure most regret what they've done."

"Yeah, um, you're probably right." He paused. "Are you sure it's okay for me to stay here? I mean, it's a military facility."

"It's a little strange, but it's all right. I have connections with the Commander, remember? It's not exactly a four-star hotel, but we'll take care of you without charge and you'll be safe here."

"I guess I don't have many other choices. Thank you."

"You're most welcome. Once we're finished here, I'll show you around."

Chapter 8

Under James's watch, Rose and Brucie placed their empty tray on a multicolored stack and he followed their example. A *plock* echoed as plastic collided. The deed done, the winged woman then gestured toward the exit. "All right, I don't have much time, but I'll show you around as promised. Before I forget, here, take this." After a bit of rummaging, she presented a gray key card. "You won't go far without it."

"Thanks." James picked up the "gift" and twisted it around. The material proved cold to the touch. He detected no particular feature except for a NISDA logo. "Hey, I've been thinking... why aren't the doors using a retina scan like the elevator your dad brought me down in?"

"Actually, the doors on the lower levels require those scans in addition to the card."

A blush reddened James's cheeks as he remembered Rose had had to scan her retina to open the cafeteria's door earlier. To hide his embarrassment, he continued without missing a beat. "So, why bother with the card?"

Rose shrugged. "No idea. I guess they figured it'd increase security a little. Anyway, Valardir is underground. Right now, we're on level five, the lowest and most secure."

"Isn't it a risk having me here?" James winced. "I won't cause trouble or anything, but, um..."

"Don't worry, I understand." She giggled. "Well, in theory, you're right, but since I moved here, they made special arrangements. They separated level five into two parts, one consisting of my living quarters and the other the military stuff. Neither of us have access to the other without permission." She caressed her cheek. "Back then, this arrangement took a lot of work, and it was so rushed too. I feel bad for the workers, but they didn't even complain."

The moment she said that, an obvious question entered my mind. Why did she live here? Not that I didn't appreciate the hospitality, but it was kind of a dreary place. And claustrophobic. If I had any other choice, I'd have left right away. But she had stayed here for years, according to her father. Was it for protection? From what? Everyone showed her such respect, I couldn't imagine. I almost asked, but something, maybe a twinkle in her eyes, gave me the impression I shouldn't.
—Thoughts of James Hunter, Hocmar 28, 2134, on the Nirnivian calendar

"Uh, so they moved the cafeteria to the fifth floor? Isn't that a problem for the soldiers who don't have clearance?"

Waving his comment away, the Melkar laughed. "Oh no, the cafeteria was already here. In the beginning, they had only one on the upper level, but because it was such a hassle to get up there from down here just to eat, they quickly added some on the third and fifth floors." She gasped. "Look at us chatting. It's fun and all, but we must start the tour before my next meeting."

As suggested, they exited the cafeteria and reached a corridor. Despite being different from the hall James had explored earlier, it appeared quite similar: the same metallic walls, the same dark domes concealing cameras, and the same soldiers patrolling.

"So, our living quarters are arranged in a square. If you're lost, keep walking in either direction and you'll find your room sooner or later." Rose pointed at the men in the distance. "As you can see, there are plenty of soldiers around. They're on guard duty and will assist you should you need help, but don't bother them with idle chitchat. They take their job seriously and hate useless distractions. Right across is a recreation room. Like the cafeteria, they put one here for convenience long before my arrival."

After she completed the safety procedure, the door slid open and they went inside. On the right, James spotted a TV stuck in the corner. The screen depicted pure blackness, yet a woman sat atop a sofa watching. Further inspection revealed she slumbered with her mouth gaping. That was when an interjection distracted him. Intrigued, he skimmed the other side. Two men wielding sticks laughed and boasted near an octagonal table. Though not in the anticipated rectangular shape, James deduced they played pool, or rather the Nirnivian equivalent. Behind the duo, he noticed two arcade cabinets. The pixelated graphics they presented might've been advanced in the eighties.

"It's nothing too amazing, but it's the place to be for company. The soldiers in here are on break, so by all means, talk to them when you're lonely. They can be intimidating, but they're a very nice bunch. As you can see, there are various games available, but I'm afraid you'll have to refer to Brucie for the rules."

Yeah, I was afraid too...

—Thoughts of James Hunter, Hocmar 28, 2134, on the Nirnivian calendar

"'Fraid, Rose? What are ya afraid 'bout? I'm the freaking champ at these things, ya know." Brucie slapped James's shoulder. "Ah, bro, you wanna learn, ya come to me and I'll show ya how to ace those games Brucie style!"

Rose leaned toward James's ear. "That means he'll teach you how to cheat."

While she reduced her volume in a mock whisper, the words remain distinct enough for the bodyguard to hear. "Cheat?" He gave a crossed-arm sneer. "Psst, don'tcha start rumors. Ain't gotta cheat to beat these losers."

The two soldiers spun and faced him. "Hey, screw you, Brucie!"

"Yeah, screw both o' ya too!" The blond bodybuilder showcased his fist in a most offensive manner.

James swallowed hard as he recoiled, expecting a fight, but the others dismissed the insult via their middle fingers and focused on their business. After a deep breath, James aimed at the television, more to distract himself from his stress than anything.

"So, I can watch TV here?"

Rose nodded. "Normally, yes, but right now it's broken, sorry. They'll put one in your room eventually. It'd be there already, but there's a technical issue."

With the explanation finished, they returned to the corridor and strolled forward. Five minutes later, the winged woman motioned toward a double door. "That's an elevator. You can't use it on your own, but I swear you can leave Valardir anytime you wish. You're not a prisoner. Every soldier patrolling the area has been informed about you, so if you ask, they will escort you to the exit. I can't do it myself because I'm not supposed to go to the top level unless there are special circumstances, such as when you arrived. If you do go outside, remember there's a procedure to get back in. It's nothing to be scared of, but personnel are limited at night and they might hold you in a cell until the next day. They don't call it that, but it's pretty much what it is." A pearl of sweat dripped down James's brow and she offered a smile. "Spending a night there wouldn't be the end of the world, but your room is a lot more comfortable, so I recommend always returning before eight p.m. if you can."

And so they proceeded to the next door of interest. The instant his pupils landed on the entrance, the bodyguard rubbed his hands together. "Ah, bro, this here's like the freaking best room in the whole place!"

Rose scanned her card as well as her retina as demanded. The first detail James discerned ended up being a blue mat. Several pieces of equipment populated the chamber. Most he failed to identify, but he noted a treadmill and a stationary bike as well as several weights of different sizes spread around the place.

"This is my personal gym, more or less. Dad set it up so I could exercise. It's basic, but it serves its purpose. I'm mostly here early in the mornings. A few soldiers train here for convenience, but it's rare, and usually they don't dare come if I'm there. I wouldn't mind really, but they don't want to bother me. Of course, you're free to use it too."

"Thanks..."

The bodyguard then wrapped his arm around him and squeezed him against his massive pecs. Poor James grunted under the strain. "Ah, freak yeah, dude! Gimme a chance and I'll build ya up like crazy huge. What do ya say, bro?"

"Um..."

A chuckle came from Rose. "You can discuss this later, I'm in a hurry." James exhaled in relief, though discreetly, and they pursued the guided visit until the following door. He expected they'd stop, but to his astonishment, his guides kept walking. Rose said, "That leads to the second part of level five, so you can't open it. If you try by mistake, that's fine, but don't do it three or four times in a row or Koporal Tigh will use it as an excuse to mess with you."

Without catching her breath, she gestured toward the next door. "Over there's my personal library where I do research for my work. It's mostly filled with books, but I also have a GlobalNet connection in there. You have no idea how much trouble it was setting that up. We put a whole lot of pressure on the poor techs." A frown wrinkled James's forehead. "Oh, sorry, Hunter, of course you don't know what I'm babbling on about. It's a gigantic computer network that spreads all over Nirnivia. We can use it to access a tremendous amount of information in the form of pages and—"

"Oh, I get it. We have one of those too, I think. We call it the internet." In a polite move, he chose not to mention their version covered not a mere country but the entire planet.

"I begged Dad to give you access to this room so you can use the GlobalNet, but he refuses. Security risks and all. I don't get it. My connection is isolated from Valardir's system. Even if you were infected by a virus, there wouldn't be any serious danger. In any case, it's off-limits and I'm strictly forbidden from cheating and letting you in."

"That's okay. I understand."

The Melkar tapped a small box from which protruded a speaker and a button. "You can use the interphone to check if I'm there and talk to me, though. Let's move on." Soon, they reached the next entrance. "Ah, now this is by far my favorite room."

Brucie pouted. "Yeah, it's good, but it ain't gym good, ya know?"

Through the opening James went. Inside, the brightness blinded him and he squinted as he sheltered his eyes with his hand. Unlike in the other chambers, the light originated not from fixtures mounted on the ceiling, but rather from the opposite wall near the left corner. The lamp responsible took the shape of a yellow orb.

It was... warm. The light, I mean. I guess they all are, but this one...
—Thoughts of James Hunter, Hocmar 28, 2134, on the Nirnivian calendar

As James's pupils contracted, he remarked the cyan paint covering the wall—a far cry from the silver color bathing every other location. White blotches randomly stained the blue in several spots, yet he sensed a pattern. He stepped forward, and the ground sank a little under his weight. And the smell... a fresh odor surrounded him, akin to grass and dirt with a touch of humidity lingering in the air. Perplexed, James lowered his gaze. Indeed, plants and multicolored flowers decorated the room. Near the center, he glimpsed a pool, and a tanning chair rested beside it.

Rose joined his side. "It's my garden. It's silly, but give it a year and you'll almost swear you're outside."

"No. It's not silly at all."

"That's great, because you can come here as often as you wish. We have to continue."

His mouth still gaping, James trailed his hosts, though not without a final peek at the improvised park. For several minutes, the trio marched. Whenever they encountered guards, the soldiers withdrew a tad, leaving them greater space than required. James gritted his teeth as he studied Rose's wings. Somehow, he doubted they intended the reverence for him. At any rate, he put his uneasiness behind until they encountered a wooden door. Rose and Brucie continued, but James paused. Twice the size of every other, it caught his attention, especially given the uncommon material. Curious, he walked toward it and stroked the surface with his finger. Cold as steel, yet visually a convincing imitation. Shivering, he grasped one of the golden ring-shaped handles. It wouldn't budge.

"Hey! You ain't got no business here!"

Busted. Damn, that guy surprised me so much I jumped in shock. I stopped breathing. I tried to think of an excuse... anything. "I got lost" was the best I could do, but if Rose contradicted me later on... would she? I swallowed hard and turned around. Brucie was there, laughing his ass off. Rose, however, patted my shoulder with a worried look on her face.

—Thoughts of James Hunter, Hocmar 28, 2134, on the Nirnivian calendar

"It's just us, Hunter." She glared at her bodyguard. "Don't scare him like that!"

"Just a joke, geez!"

"Yes, but he's nervous enough as it is." Rose smiled. "Forgive him, he acts like a child. He's technically right, though—this is another restricted area and you need a proper key card to open it."

James gulped. "I'm sorry, I... I..."

"No one's mad at you, Hunter. You didn't do anything wrong, so relax. Come, we're almost done with the tour." Once she finished her sentence, she seized his hand and slowly pulled him away.

I wanted to ask why the door looked so different, but again, something told me I shouldn't.

—Thoughts of James Hunter, Hocmar 28, 2134, on the Nirnivian calendar

The trio kept going until they arrived in front of two more doors. "These are our bedrooms, mine on the left, yours on the right. Your card won't open my door, but like the library, there's a buzzer and an intercom, so you can check if I'm there and all that. But please don't buzz after 10:00 p.m. unless there's an emergency as I may be sleeping. I'm usually not busy when I'm in there, so feel free to drop by."

"Sure thing."

"And finally, right across is my office, where I spend most of my days. Again, you don't have access, but there is an intercom. This one won't buzz because I'm often using video conference. Let me show you." They approached the contraption. "You see there is a green button and a red button? Well, the green one means you'd like to talk to me, but it's nothing too important. You can press it anytime you want for any reason, and if I'm available, I'll answer. If I'm busy, I'll ignore you. The red button means it's an emergency that requires my immediate attention. I can't imagine you'd ever need to press it, but if I end up being wrong, do so. I stress again that it's for emergencies. Don't push it just because you're bored."

James twitched. "Um... of course, I'd never do that."

"I'm sure you won't. Since I'm here and my meeting starts in two minutes, I better go inside. Your room is right behind us. You should be fine. Or, if you'd rather go somewhere else, Brucie can show you the way."

The cross-armed bodyguard grumbled. "I'm s'posed to watch over ya, remember?"

The woman waved his concern away. "Psst, I'll be all right even if you leave for a few minutes."

"Thanks for the offer, but I think I'll go lie down. I'm still kind of tired."

"All right, then, we're off." Rose walked toward her office. At the last second, she snapped her fingers. "Oh, I almost forgot—if you're awake at six thirty, we can have breakfast together tomorrow. If you're an early bird and can make it for five thirty, we can hang out for an hour or so."

"Uh, sure, sounds great."

For a brief moment, the door stood open and James snuck a peek at Kristina Dupree. The blond assistant swiveled in her chair while poking her tablet as usual. She shook her head. "Rose, you're late. The meeting's about to start. We were supposed to review the—" The closing door cut off her lecture.

Now alone, James looked around the hall pondering what he should do next. Resigned, he sighed and returned to his quarters and lay down like he'd claimed he would.

Chapter 9

The short man exited his office and the door slid shut behind him. Half a smile formed on Janice's face. Even at full height, the senior's bald spot passed well below her chin, and his chronic hunch only accentuated the contrast. Ron Tigh took a few steps forward, then stopped and rummaged through his pocket for something. Perhaps his keys? Janice had no idea, and she'd never discover the truth, for she chose that moment to approach him, crossing her arms. "Uncle Tigh, you're a hard man to reach. I've been looking for you all day."

With a grunt, Ron turned and glared at her. "Yeah, I'm a busy guy." The elder advanced toward her, his paces echoing on the metal floor. Once close enough, he pointed a menacing index finger at her sternum. "And I'm not your uncle, young lady!"

She gave a groan, accompanied by a headshake. "It's called a term of endearment, you old idiot."

"Well, I don't like it, all right? You sure aren't a niece of mine, you whippersnapper"—though his mouth twisted in a sneer, his lips quivered—"and you remember it or I'll—" Unable to keep up the charade, Tigh burst into laughter and Janice wrapped him in an embrace. "Ah, Janice, I've missed you!"

"Same here, Uncle!"

"Your dad told me you'd show up. I'm glad you caught me. How was your trip?"

"Oh, fine." She shrugged. "A bit rushed, but okay."

"It's been months!" A slap on her shoulder and then he gestured toward his bureau. "Come in, we'll talk for a while."

"Weren't you going somewhere?"

"Bah!" The senior dismissed the notion with a wave. "They'll wait, it's not important. Come on, I'll serve you a drink!"

"A drink?" Another snicker came from Janice. "You're being naughty."

"Nah, kiddo"—Ron faced the door he had sealed moments earlier and swiped his key card, followed by a fingerprint test—"it's druikinaka juice." He satisfied the retina scanner next. "Now your dad, he stashed priceless uisge in his secret drawer." The door swung open and they entered the office. "Breaks all regulation, of course. He'd be screwed if the Council caught him."

Janice stood near the entrance while the Koporal sprang for a mini fridge along the left side and rummaged through its contents. As he spoke, she skimmed the room. All in all, it shared a comparable layout to her dad's office, though a little smaller, perhaps due to his lower rank. More telling than the similarities, however, were the differences. Pictures littered Daniel's walls, but his remained bare. She remembered in the past, he had kept a photo of his wife atop his desk, but it had since vanished.

"I'd like to offer you something like that, but I can't touch the stuff." Ron shook the transparent bottle he produced from the shelves. The azure liquid within splashed against the container. "This'll have to do!"

"Well aware of that, Uncle Tigh, and juice will be great, thank you." Janice flopped in the chair designated for visitors. With her hands linked behind her head, she poorly resisted a chuckle. "By the way, I meant to warn you that if you jam your feet up both Vince and Peter's asses, they'll drag you to their proctologist!"

"Ha!" The Koporal rolled his eyes. "Yeah, I didn't think it through, but it was still effective." Without further ado, Ron put down his flask on the desk. "I had to make it clear I wasn't messing around." Then he dropped the two glasses he carried upon the surface. A sharp *pwok* resonated. "We can't let those two buffoons goof off on the job."

"Oh, you were pretty damn clear. They're both scared shitless."

"Good! That was the idea." Wrapping his fingers around the jug's cap, Tigh attempted twisting it off, but it refused to budge.

"Sure, I'm familiar with how threats work." Janice leaned forward and squinted. "Speaking of which, I've been hearing stories about you and Dad pimping up security."

Ron paused his struggle for an instant. "Yeah, so?"

"Some of those rumors are rather extreme. I'm wondering if the techs are exaggerating, or..."

"It's probably all true." He sighed and he resumed his efforts. "Hey, it's a military complex." He moaned. "We can't have a two-bit terrorist sneaking inside."

"Fair enough, but don't pretend this is about NISDA." Janice smirked. "Dad's worried about his princess, that's why."

"Yes, yes. Okay, I admit it." More grunts peppered Tigh's words. "It's not a big secret. And it's not just him— we're all worried." Pearls of perspiration formed on his brow. "Maybe Daniel's pushing the caution a little farther than I would, but I support him a hundred percent on this." His cheeks reddened. "We have to keep her safe. You know what would happen if he got to her. I can't imagine you'd want that to happen."

"Of course not!" In a nonchalant gesture, Janice reached for the bottle. She expected he'd resist, but Tigh let go without complaining. "Blood-related or not, Rose is my sister and I'd die to protect her. Still, you guys already pushed the techs damn near their limits." A flick of her wrist and the cap came off. "They're getting... agitated."

The elder's lips parted as he admired her feat. "We're only asking them to do their jobs." His gaze fixated on the container before lingering on her arm and then his. "If they don't, they'll have to drag me to their proctologist too."

"Fine, but I think you better be ready to do your job too, just in case."

"What are you insinuating?" Ron reclaimed his jug and began pouring juice in her glass.

"Nothing, but if things get crazy around here, don't let it escalate to a Tabarar vote. NISDA doesn't need the Council on its ass."

"Oh, freak no, we don't!" Since the fluid almost reached her goblet's rim, Janice signaled for Ron to stop. After a nod, he focused on his own. "Those pencil pushers don't understand the cold hard truths of the military world. There's no way it'd come to that. Dan has a good head on his shoulders, and if that changes—well, I'd do my duties as second officer and get him in line. There's hasn't been a Tabarar vote in almost fifty years, and there won't be one on my watch!"

"Oh, I dunno, you're a big softy with Dad. Shit, man, you let him keep a human in Valardir!"

"That's complicated, and don't worry, there's a good reason why I said yes."

"Me, worry?" She shrugged. "Nah, I'm messing with you, Uncle Tigh. How else is a woman supposed to have fun around here?"

"Ah, you rascal, pulling an old man's leg, for shame! Shame!" He gave a wink and lifted his glass. Dutifully, Janice grasped hers and they clinked. "Enough silly talk, girl, how was life on the frontier? Meet some new guys?"

"Nah, but I found an old buddy from the battlefield." Janice sampled the blue beverage. Sweet, and so gratifying...

"Tell me all about it!" And so she did. Since her exploits at the border proved dull, they soon traded old war stories. Both being soldiers, they recounted several bloody tales. Of course, the elder had survived many more fights, but Janice provided plenty despite her age. Not even forty and she had almost died on numerous occasions. Such were the realities of war.

Chapter 10

Mashar 19, 2133, on the Nirnivian calendar

For once, the winged woman changed her outfit. Ever since James had arrived in this world, she'd always worn the same white dress no matter the day or the hour. On this morning, at last, she broke the rule and instead sported a combo made of a purple T-shirt and black shorts. James sat on the floor with his hands wrapped around his bended knees and observed her. The Melkar joined her fingers behind her back while stretching her arms at an angle. As she warmed up, James inspected her immaculate clothes. He caressed his skin through one of the many holes in his sweatpants. That and the stains on his shirts filled him with a sense of inadequacy compared to his friend. Such was the fate of those who relied on charity for their wardrobes, he supposed.

"Hey, Hunter, you're not very chatty this morning." Rose flashed him a smile. "Too early for you?"

A grunt came from James. "That and... well—" Frustrated, he gestured toward the dumbbells, treadmill and other equipment. "When you said we could hang out before breakfast, you forgot to mention we'd be doing this."

"Oh..." Rose's extended arms now pointed straight ahead of her. "Sorry, I thought you knew. I told you I train early in the morning. I'm rather busy and never go outside. That's not healthy, especially since my job involves a lot of sitting. I need some exercise."

"Yeah, you did tell me, but I kind of forgot. I'm not an athletic person."

That was putting it mildly. I never did anything like this back home; I'm more of a couch potato. And I'm so uncoordinated. I was sure I'd fall and generally look like an idiot. Don't get me wrong, I'm used to looking like an idiot with my friends, but... these were new people, and I still had some sense of self-respect.

—Thoughts of James Hunter, Hocmar 28, 2134, on the Nirnivian calendar

"Listen, Hunter"—a palm rested on his shoulder as Rose sat beside him. The delicate touch brought a measure of comfort—"I think you should exercise with me—for health reasons. It doesn't matter whether you're good at it or not. We won't mock you." She paused and rubbed her chin. "Okay, Brucie will, but I won't and I'll make him shut up." All the occasions when he'd tripped during gym class or unintentionally bumbled into a classmate popped into James's mind. Warmth spread across his cheeks as he blushed. "Fine, you don't have to. Just stick around and we'll have breakfast after. It won't be so bad. We can still talk and have some fun."

"Brucie seemed thrilled to, um..."

Rose giggled. "Oh, don't worry, I'll handle him."

Right on cue, the door slid open accompanied by a swoosh. The bodyguard strolled inside carrying a rolled blue mat on his shoulder. Brimming with enthusiasm, he whistled a dissonant tune as he arranged the pad next to the other one that was already present. The space provided by the old one proved lacking for two people: a detail they'd missed. Due to this, Brucie had gone and fetched another. Infuriated by the idea of delaying his beloved exercises, the muscle mass had grumbled when he left, but his joviality had since returned in force. Once the task was done, Brucie faced his trainees, smirking.

"Get off your asses, maggots!" Both obeyed, though James offered numerous groans in the process. "I'm gonna give ya both the workout of a lifetime. Shit, when I'm done with ya, you might sweat blood." He aimed at James. "'Specially you, little man!"

Daunted by the stare, James swallowed hard. Rose stepped forward. "Brucie, Hunter won't be joining us."

"Wha?" With his mouth gaping, the blond bodyguard threw his hands in the air. "Dude! Ya got the chance o' your life! Don't let me down, bro! What's wrong? Too much of a wuss fo' Brucie's extreme hard-core challenge? Look at ya, weakling! Just skin and bones! What are ya gonna do if BBR comes back for ya? Huh? Piss your pants and cry?"

James shrugged. "Probably."

"Wiseass. Ya shouldn't kid, dude. You're so outta shape, Rose got twice the muscles and she ain't got no muscle."

Two times zero is zero, so I guess he was kind of right. Well, except in that case, we both have no muscles, so his comparison was pointless, but... wait, why am I wasting my time on Brucie's math skills?

—Thoughts of James Hunter, Hocmar 28, 2134, on the Nirnivian calendar

"She could kick your ass." The bodyguard shook his head in disgust. "But I'll fix ya. I'll turn ya into a real stud, like me." He stroked his jaw. "Well, almost like me. Can't do miracles, ya know. The gals will jump on ya. Come on, what do ya say?"

"Thanks, but, um"—James bit his lip—"I'll pass."

"You don't want gals, huh?" Brucie snapped his fingers. "Got it. No problem, I'll have ya swimming in guys." With a yelp, James found himself dragged against the brute and trapped in a hug. "Brucie's all 'bout equal opportunity fer everyone, bro!"

Thankfully, he set the coughing James free. "No, that's not it. I already have a girlfriend and, uh, well"—he gulped as he recoiled—"I don't really want a relationship with a woman who's so superficial she only cares about my body. I'm sure she'd feel the same way. I mean, there's more to—"

"Fine! Have it yer way!" Reddening from rage, the bodyguard dismissed his argument with a wave. "Rose, she'll get all the gals fo' ya!" The winged lady tilted her head and scowled. "I know, I know. Could ya pretend ya want the gals? Ya know, make him jealous... motivate him." Her lips parted as she lifted a contrarian index finger. Before she had the possibility to utter her objection, Brucie continued. "Ya ain't gonna help me out, are ya?"

"No, Brucie. I don't really want a relationship with a woman. Period. Especially not if she only cares about my—"

"'Nough said. I get it." He glared at James. "Fine, ya baby, be a wuss, I—"

"Brucie!" Rose advanced between him and his target with her palms on her hips, leaving him no hope of finishing his sentence. Though she was normally of gentle demeanor, the posture accentuated her frustration. The bodyguard looked down at the floor while scratching the back of his head. "That's enough! Stop bullying him and apologize."

And he did. It was the most forced and insincere apology I ever heard, but he did. Watching a woman like Rose intimidate a monster three times her size was quite fun, and a tad scary. I mean, sure, she was his boss, but... I sensed there was more to it than that. And it's not like it was just Brucie. Everyone feared her. No, that's not the right word. Anyway, Brucie didn't lie when he said his training would be difficult. Jumping jacks, sit-ups, push-ups, weightlifting, and so on. Shit, the push-ups alone... I haven't even thought about doing a push-up since school! Good thing I chickened out or I would've ended up half-dead and retching on the ground.

—Thoughts of James Hunter, Hocmar 28, 2134, on the Nirnivian calendar

***

And so, the trio took their trays and went in search of a table. James noticed they skipped the register, a detail he'd missed during his first meal. When probed, Rose explained her bill and Brucie's accumulated on their tabs, and being their guest, James ate for free. Satisfied, he followed his friends as he studied his dish and salivated. The fluffy yellow pancakes covered in a golden syrup smelled great, and he assumed them to be delectable. Brucie settled for eggs along with toast and a type of meat alien to an earthling. As for Rose, she carried a bowl of what seemed to be gruel and pieces of various fruits. Though sure each breakfast tasted fine, James believed he had made the superior choice.

Once James grew bored of studying his food, he concentrated on the winged woman. Rose had returned to her white dress. The gown complemented her features—no question about that—but still, three days of wearing the same clothes: how strange. In comparison, even the simple outfit she wore for training provided a breath of fresh air.

Speaking of which, thanks to their intensity, she had finished the exercises drenched in perspiration and emanated a less-than-pleasant odor; not that James blamed her for biology. A fast shower solved the issue, however. She'd even rearranged her red hair to perfection after the workout had left her hair in a damp mess. The makeover had required a minimum of time; no doubt she'd learned to spruce herself up under pressure.

At any rate, their quest for a table came to an end soon. The three of them set down their plates and took their seats. From the corner of his eye, James spotted a familiar face. Next to them, Kristina Dupree poked at her tablet and, on occasion, sampled a morsel from a half-eaten omelet. Rose soon recognized her assistant.

"Kristina?" She smiled. "Why are you here so early?"

Surprised, the blond woman hopped in her seat before glancing toward her employer. "Oh, Rose! I had a lot of work to do, so I figured it would be quicker to have breakfast here."

"Why not join us?"

James tensed as the Melkar uttered her suggestion. In a rush, he twisted his neck, hoping the angle concealed his slight scowl from Kristina.

It's not that I hated her; it's more that I thought she hated me. I mean, she certainly didn't give me the impression she wanted to ever talk to me again and, well...

—Thoughts of James Hunter, Hocmar 28, 2134, on the Nirnivian calendar

The assistant opened her mouth, but Brucie interrupted her. "Hey, yo, Kristina, you're a hot gal, right?"

She blushed a little, then glared. "Pardon me? I'm aware of your reputation, Brucie Garland. Don't you dare try your dirty tri—"

"No, no, I ain't hitting on ya. Just sayin', you good looking, right, so I wanna ask ya." Stretching his arms, the bodyguard touched both his companions' backs. "Like, you wouldn't date James's scrawny ass, right? You'd pick Rose over some lazy punk, right?"

Kristina's already flushed cheeks turned pure crimson. "Uh, excuse me, Rose, I have to go." Without delay, she jumped to her feet and scurried away, abandoning her breakfast, though she seized her device.

Oh God, I never saw anyone that red. I didn't even know it was possible.

—Thoughts of James Hunter, Hocmar 28, 2134, on the Nirnivian calendar

Thrilled by the aide's discomfort, Brucie burst into a chortle. The hilarity proved so intense that he literally fell off his chair and rolled on the floor laughing.

"Brucie!" Rose shook her head in disgust. "Why did you say that? You know she's shy!" More chuckles served as the lone reply. "Stop it! It isn't funny!"

"Ha, ha, ha, ha, ha! I beg to differ!"

"Oh, Brucie, you're a jerk sometimes."

James's gaze alternated between the two of them. An embarrassing argument he'd rather avoid, but he'd discovered at a young age how to deal with such circumstances. He merely focused on the important matter: pancakes. Curious, he prodded his pancakes with his fork. The metal prongs squished the fried dough, promising a soft and spongy treat. James licked his lips and grasped his knife. The blade cut a piece and he popped it into his mouth. His teeth crushed the pancake, spreading the delightful taste to his tongue. An almost perfect texture—perhaps a tad dry. Nothing a boatload of syrup couldn't fix! James snatched the carafe and spilled the sweet nectar over his grub before sampling another chunk. How sublime: an ideal combination of sugar and wheat!

"Look, Brucie, not everyone appreciates your sense of humor, so please be more sensitive! I don't care if you mess with me, but Kristina is—"

"Even wussier than the human dude!"

"Oh, shut up, Brucie!"

Ah yes, pancakes... so delicious; so scrumptious, even. Bliss for the senses. What else mattered compared to these heavenly creations? So gulp them he did. Only one problem: after a while, they were gone. Poor James stared at his empty plate, pondering the concept of seconds, even though another bite might rupture his stomach. Not that the situation justified the injury. By then, the conflict had been resolved. Brucie wolfed down his eggs and Rose also attacked her breakfast, though at a leisurely pace. As she swallowed a bit of her cereal, she glanced at James's bowl.

"Whoa, someone was hungry."

"Uh, yeah... ha ha."

She leaned forward. "I'm not sure if I'll be able to check on you later. I might not be available for lunch or dinner. You'll be fine either way. Just come here and choose whatever you like. The staff knows about your special arrangement."

"Okay..."

She gave a wink. "And don't mind us. We bicker, but we don't hold grudges."

Chapter 11

After breakfast, Rose explained to me that she needed to go to her office. Since it was on the way, she and Brucie escorted me back to my room. After that, it'd be goodbye for now and I'd have to entertain myself somehow.

—Thoughts of James Hunter, Hocmar 28, 2134, on the Nirnivian calendar

With his hands folded over his stomach, James walked alongside the others. A scorching sensation spread through his chest. Grains often gave him heartburn, and since he'd gulped down those pancakes in record time, the acid reflux proved intense. On his side, Rose asked if he'd be all right on his own. He assured her, attempting to conceal his discomfort with what he assumed to be little success. Next, she proposed he visit the rec room and met people. James played along and mumbled a "maybe," but inside, he rejected the notion. The soldiers resented him. Oh, they kept their distance and addressed him in a polite tone, no doubt because of Rose's influence, but he felt their glares on his back. They'd rather not have him here, and he supposed it'd be best if he made his presence small, especially given...

"James, my boy, what perfect timing!"

Startled by the interjection, he jumped and straightened his neck. A few meters away stood Commander Daniel Ricdeau. The old man stretched his arms outward in a welcoming gesture as a beam drew on his wrinkled visage. James acknowledged his greeting with a wave and forced a smile despite his pain. A second later, he noticed the woman strolling beside the Commander. Like him, she wore a deep blue uniform, though it lacked the senior's numerous medals, and the stripes on her shoulders numbered two instead of six. If the relative lack of decorations implied a lesser rank, her physique displayed superior strength. At over six feet, her stature dwarfed her senior's, not to mention James's. Only Brucie sported a greater height by a quarter of an inch. Spotting the trio, she offered a grin, revealing two rows of immaculate white teeth.

"I meant to introduce you to my other daughter, Janice." Daniel motioned toward his companion.

Right on cue, the gigantic female stepped forward. Based on her size, James expected a powerful stride, yet her movement conveyed a delicate grace that implied a subtle femininity that her muscles had masked on first sight. Her brown eyes, the same color as her father's, glared at him— probably because of his status as a human—and his cheeks reddened while he shrunk a little.

"Ja... Janice?" Astonished, Rose gasped as her eyebrows flashed. "You're back? I had no idea... I thought it'd be a few more months."

"Oh?" For a fraction of a second, Janice's slightly dilated pupils darted to her sister and then returned to James. "There's been a last-minute change of plans. Dad must've forgotten to tell you." On that note, she extended her hand for the visitor's sake.

"Yes, yes"—the Commander snapped his fingers and nodded a couple times in rapid succession—"I'm sorry, P— uh, Rose, with all the fuss over the recent security breach, my mind is scattered all over the place."

Anxious, James grasped Janice's palm as he resisted swallowing hard. Due to her impressive mass, he anticipated a crushing grip, and his body contracted as she squeezed. Against the odds, Janice's handshake possessed a gentle touch. Her soft skin barely tickled his own. James relaxed and almost let out a relieved sigh.

"Nice to meet you, James."

"Um, nice to meet you too." Thanks to their proximity, he studied her features. On further inspection, she indeed shared a family resemblance with the Commander. The spiky nose, the general shape of their mouth and even ears. Their faces differed, however, as hers was round and his was elongated.

Janice's lips pursed, and she leaned forward a little. "I heard about—"

Before she finished, Brucie waltzed beside her and, in a nonchalant motion, wrapped his arm around her hips. Then the bodyguard tightened his squeeze, pulling Janice closer. The deed done, he pointed his free index finger at James.

"Don't ya think 'bout messing with my wife, buddy!"

No chance for James to react. The words failed to even register when Janice said, "Come on, Brucie, lower your hand." A glacial sense of menace tainted the once-sultry voice. "I dare you, lower it just one inch..."

The instant she uttered her sentence, Brucie withdrew his limb and recoiled. "It ain't like that, babe; I'm just messing 'round with the little dude, I swear." A strained giggle escaped his mouth. "Guy can't take no jokes; he thinks it's real and gets all nervous. It's funny as shit, I tell ya. Didn't think you'd mind."

"You're lucky I like you, Brucie; God only knows why." Janice smirked. "If you try that again, I'll rip 'it' off."

"Oh, you won't have to worry about his wandering hands, Janice." A cross-armed Daniel Ricdeau advanced at a determined pace. He stopped half a foot away from Brucie. Though he was diminutive compared to the bodybuilder, his glower radiated with confidence. None could question who wielded the true power. "He'll be too busy searching for a job." Brucie flinched, and the elder chuckled. "What? You're surprised? What did you think would happen when you groped the Commander's daughter when he was standing right there?" He sneered. "I don't like your boorish behavior, son. I never have. I've tolerated you because of Rose, but you crossed the line."

By that point, Brucie's cheeks grew crimson and perspiration drenched his brow. "But, sir..." He twitched. "It was just a freaking joke! Rose, help me out, won't ya?" A begging glance was fired toward the winged woman, but she merely shook her head. "Uh... ah shit."

Satisfied, the Commander turned and peeked at his daughter. "Well, look who doesn't get jokes now?"

Janice acquiesced. "Yep, you shouldn't dish it if you can't take it, Brucie." With that, the duo burst into laughter. A clap echoed as they exchanged a high five.

That's when I realized I liked Janice and Daniel.

—Thoughts of James Hunter, Hocmar 28, 2134, on the Nirnivian calendar

Brucie groaned. "Whatever, dudes. Whatever..." Defeated, he retreated next to Rose.

Freed of distraction, Janice's focus reverted to James and smiled. "I heard about you. It's so sad."

"Yeah, it's rough." That was putting it mildly, but he preferred not venting his frustrations to a stranger. "I don't know what I'd do without Rose."

"Ah yes, you're in good hands with my sister. She's very dependable, and with her connections, she's the best friend you can have in this universe, so you better be nice to her!" From the corner of his eye, James caught a glimpse of the Melkar blushing. "I can't be nearly as helpful to you, but I figure you need all the 'allies' you can get." Janice patted James's shoulder. "You should drop by the rec room sometimes. I usually hang out there after work. I'd introduce you to a few pals and we could play a game of Rubarg or two." She inclined forward and lowered her volume in a mocked whisper. "Rose is great for the serious stuff, but I'm more fun."

"Hey!" The adopted sibling frowned. "That's true, but don't rub it in."

"Um..." James scratched the back of his head. "I don't know... I never played, and..."

"So what? I'll teach you!"

"Uh... maybe? I'll think about it."

"What's that?" The soldier formed a cone around her ears with her fingers. "Is that how humans say 'yes'? Dad's looking at his watch, so we have to go, but don't think this is over! You can't say Janice without saying perseverance! Unless you're good at spelling."

"Janice, wait!" Rose said. "I haven't talked to you in months! We should get together too."

"Oh, yeah..." She shrugged. "I'm sure I'll see you around."

Rose gazed at the floor. "Yes, of course..."

They traded goodbyes and the duo departed. As she went, Janice accorded James a final peep and winked. Rose waited until they were out of earshot, then beamed. "Aw, you made a new friend. She thinks you're cute."

Blood flushed James's cheeks. "Uh, no. I mean, we just met."

"I didn't say she wants to marry you, I said she thinks you're cute. Trust me, I know my sister, and—"

Brucie chose that moment to step between them. "That's bullshit!" he screamed while he jammed his right fist into his left palm. The other two stared at him, shocked by the interruption. "Brucie can't take a joke? What's that shit? Their stupid joke ain't funny!"

"Ah, Brucie"—giggling, Rose tapped his back—"I can't believe you fell for it. After all these years, do you really believe Janice would've threatened you if she had been mad?"

"Nah, she'd punch me in the dick and..." He gave a frustrated grunt. "Shit! I shoulda seen it! Damn, she'll never let me live it down, ya know?"

"No, she won't." Rose spun around and faced James. "Anyway, back to our business. It's your choice, of course, but you should drop by the rec room with her. It's true: she's the fun one."

I knew I should. It's not like I had anything better to do and Janice did seem nice, and yet... I mean, Rose suggested I hang out with someone who punches people in the dick. Okay, so yeah, I guess Brucie kinda deserves it sometimes. And technically, I'm not so sure he's a person; maybe he's like some sort of intelligent ape that... never mind. And really it wasn't the dick-punching thing that put me off, or anything about Janice. It's just, well, I felt I should steer clear from of the soldiers, even with her there. Besides, how much "fun" was fun? 'Cause I wasn't sure Nadia would've appreciated too much of it. Cute or not, I didn't think it'd go that far, but still...

—Thoughts of James Hunter, Hocmar 28, 2134, on the Nirnivian calendar

Chapter 12

Mashar 22, 2133, on the Nirnivian calendar

The checkered pattern harkened back to chess. Such ended up being the first thought to enter James's mind when Rose laid the board on the folding table, and it gave him hope. Sure, he'd never mastered that particular game—not even close—but he understood the basics, and he anticipated similar rules. How wrong he turned out to be. He wished he could just enjoy Rose's garden. The gentle wind simulated by the strategically placed fans blew the winged woman's ginger hair and the surrounding flowers' perfume tickled James's nostrils. These normally pleasant sensations distracted him from his current task, and he suspected he'd have a hard enough time with his full attention.

The whole ordeal had started in the morning. Having an uncommon day off, Rose had showed up at his room and proposed to teach him how to play Kuhard: her favorite game. He figured why not? Any hobby requiring no involvement with the soldiers helped to avoid boredom, and when bored, he tended to remember his family, Nadia, Patrick—Earth, in short—and those memories brought only sadness in this universe. In retrospect, he should've realized his error immediately: Brucie bit his tongue so as not to burst into laughter.

Over an hour had passed since they'd started, and still, Rose explained the various figurines' roles. Depicted in red and blue depending on the player's side, they ran a wide gamut of shapes and functions. Their style baffled James. The majority sported realistic proportions, but a few exceptions adopted a cartoonish design instead, displaying features such as gigantic eyes or extraordinarily long and deformed noses. Not only that, but their names shared the duality. Most pieces depicted members of the military—for example, the commander or the infantries—while a couple hardly fit the setting, like the berserkers or the cooks.

"So, that's about it for the koporal," Rose said as she rested the azure-uniformed senior brandishing his index finger in an imposing gesture. Next, her fingers lifted a strange fellow wearing a protective mask and a trench coat. In his arms, he held a bundle of what appeared to be sticks of dynamite. "Okay, now for the bomb expert. He can move as many spaces as you wish per turn, but only diagonally."

A concept reminiscent of the bishop—the lump in James's throat diminished thanks to the familiarity.

"Oh, for the first ten turns. After that, he moves in straight lines."

And the discomfort returned. What a mess...

"When it comes to fighting, the bomb expert is rather frail. He'll always be defeated in short-range combat, his only means of attack being that he can lay down a bomb, though there can only be one on the board at any time. After three turns, it explodes and kills anyone nearby, friend or foe, except for the bomb expert himself. You understand?"

"Uh, yes..."

"Great! So, let's switch to the berserker." The Melkar caressed a bare-chested warrior holding an axe in each hand. The snarl on his face suggested an intense bloodlust, and the horned helmet accentuated the impression. "He's not very mobile. By default, he can only move one space forward. However, he can move one space in any direction if you're willing to lose the next turn. It's a big sacrifice, so it's usually done when necessary to correct a mistake. Berserkers are extremely aggressive and cannot be defeated at close range. Any foe who somehow gets in a square next to a berserker is automatically decapitated, so you must take them out with long-range attacks." Rose smiled. "Like a bomb! Are you still following me?"

Oh God, no! But I pretended I did so she wouldn't repeat herself. Yeah, it's not very nice, but I have my limits.

—Thoughts of James Hunter, Hocmar 28, 2134, on the Nirnivian calendar

And so it went on and on. Everything had to be so complicated. A variety of triggers, some quite arbitrary, changed the rules as the game progressed. Nothing stayed fixed. After she finished her lecture about the pieces, Rose switched to victory conditions. Turned out that in the beginning, the goal was to assassinate your opponent's commander. Twenty turns later and it became reaching the opposite side and only got more maddening from there.

Two more hours disappeared and Brucie groaned. "Had enough of this shit." He shook his head. "I'm gonna guard the door on the outside. That's fine, right?"

The winged woman giggled. "Yes, of course, if that's what you prefer."

"Cool, thanks." The bodyguard left at a determined pace. Rose waited until he cleared the door and chuckled.

"I'm surprised he lasted this long." She raised her glass and sampled a sip of the light green beverage she'd served both James and herself upon arrival. He had tried it earlier. The acidic taste reminded him of lemonade, though, considering the color, he expected a different fruit, if any, acted as the base ingredient. "I tried teaching him once, and not even fifteen minutes later he ran out of patience and wiped the board clean with his arm. Poor Brucie isn't the intellectual type."

James forced a snigger. "Um, yeah, this doesn't seem like his thing." His inner voice added, *Or anyone else's.*

"Okay, then, so back to winning conditions. We covered everything, except for one obscure case. It's so weird and rare, there's no real point bothering to explain it, but for completion's sake, if it's a weekend and the date is odd and it's between 10:15 and 10:27, you win by killing your opponent's cooks. If they're already dead, you also win, unless you fail to notice. I've never seen it happen, but hey, you never know, so try and remember!"

Like always, I said I would but had no intention to. What a drag. I mean, where was the fun? And there were so many rules! Five hours in total and she couldn't cover everything. She lent me a book so I could revisit what I'd learned, and promised we'd pick up where we'd left off when she had a chance. I hoped she'd forget. Then again, I guess I didn't have anything better to do...

—Thoughts of James Hunter, Hocmar 28, 2134, on the Nirnivian calendar

Chapter 13

Mashar 27, 2133, on the Nirnivian calendar

I don't know why I kept going back there. It was just... alluring for whatever reason.

—Thoughts of James Hunter, Hocmar 28, 2134, on the Nirnivian calendar

To the eye, the material resembled wood—no question about it. James touched the simulated grooves with his own hands. Of course, he realized metal formed the door and not lumber, yet the illusion implied considerable workmanship. Even the fake handles seemed so real. They begged for a pull, but no matter how much strength one applied, the door never budged. Thanks to further observations, he discovered a card reader concealed within the door frame. Not that it surprised him, as Rose had suggested that much during their previous talk. Still, why bother hiding the mechanism? Probably to retain a rustic charm, yet for what purpose? None he could fathom. The winged lady insisted the door blocked a restricted area, but that failed to explain the reason for the custom appearance. After all, the other door provided a standard facade.

Though on the surface banal, the mystery fascinated James. The simple truth was, he grew bored in his new environment. Rose, for all her hospitality, spent most of her time on her job, whatever it might be, and Brucie followed. On occasion, James went days without seeing them. Stuck on his own, he lacked activities. The gym offered little entertainment value for him, and the same went for the rec room, since the TV remained unfixed and most games demanded at least two players. Often, he went to Rose's garden and loitered beside the pool. He understood why it turned out to be her favorite room, but even that became dull. Prey to unparalleled monotony, he thus visited the strange door and wondered what lay behind it. No doubt his imagination dwarfed reality, but he fantasized anyway. Perhaps a squadron of robots, ninjas, or a sentient computer...

Despite James's enchantment, Rose's warning resonated deeply into his mind. He stayed distant and only gazed upon the door when no guard lingered nearby. On that day, however, his courage proved greater than usual. He stood next to the door and caressed one of the many furrows on the exterior until footsteps echoed. Gritting his teeth and cursing his curiosity, he jumped backward, hoping to put distance between himself and the forbidden entrance. A futile endeavor: the soldier saw him. Stupefied by the visitor's behavior, the watchman scowled and tilted his head. James swallowed hard as his legs trembled. A sickness filled his stomach. How could he get out of this bind?

Without thinking, he said, "Sorry, uh... I'm not..." He gulped. "Um, I just think it looks cool. I'm not trying to sneak into the restricted area or anything."

The guard scratched his head while his frown intensified. "Restricted area? What are you talking about? It's a chapel."

"What?" Confused, James blinked twice. "But... Rose said..."

Before he finished his sentence, the man's blood drained from his face. White as snow, he gasped and recoiled a bit. "The Melkar... she's right! I mixed up the doors, ha ha ha." He pointed a menacing index finger at James. "Get out of here, and don't let me catch you around restricted areas again!" Then he spun and darted away.

Okay, so it was a chapel, so I guess the special door made a little more sense, but... well, why did she lie? That opened a whole new can of worms.
—Thoughts of James Hunter, Hocmar 28, 2134, on the Nirnivian calendar

***

I wasn't even planning on seeing her. It was evening, and I got bored in my room. I figured maybe I should go and relax in Rose's garden. I didn't feel like it, to be honest, but better than lying on my bed staring at the ceiling. For a minute, I thought about bringing a book to read in the "sun." I checked the bookshelf, but there wasn't anything interesting to me. I considered picking up the Kuhard manual—I did say I'd study— but in the end, I just didn't have the courage.
—Thoughts of James Hunter, Hocmar 28, 2134, on the Nirnivian calendar

The instant James entered the corridor, melancholic wails caressed his ears. He frowned. Thanks to superb isolation, the sound had failed to penetrate his chamber. Curious, he advanced, intending to locate the source. A few steps later and he noted the door to Rose's room was open, a most unusual occurrence. Inside, she stood tall, violin positioned under her jaw. With quick but precise movements, her bow tickled the strings. Two soldiers guarded their post and hummed, enthralled by the song. Upon spotting James, one of them walked away, swallowing hard. James assumed he had stopped during his rounds and dreaded being busted.

It was beautiful, yet so sad... a slow, haunting melody that made my soul cry. She played with such grace that it humbled me. I didn't want to disturb her, so I stayed outside and watched. When she finished, I applauded. She was surprised. She hadn't noticed me before. Surprised, but not angry: she smiled.

—Thoughts of James Hunter, Hocmar 28, 2134, on the Nirnivian calendar

A giggle came from Rose. "Be careful now, Hunter, you don't want me to become overly proud of my limited musical abilities."

"Limited?" James shook his head. "That was great! You're by far the best violinist I've ever met."

Flattered, Rose blushed at the compliment. "Oh, it's because you haven't met many violinists. The guards seem to agree with you, though, so I let them listen whenever I play." She invited him forward with a wave. "Since you're here, why don't you come in for a chat?"

"Yeah, sure!" He'd never visited her quarters. On first sight, they proved to be a similar size to his. The furniture also came in the same variety: a queen bed in the corner next to a small table, a dresser in another followed by a bookcase, a mini fridge and a desk in the front. Scuff marks covered everything, revealing their age. Frankly, he'd expected grander living conditions for someone clearly venerated by the populace. At any rate, near the back, Brucie slumped into the lone chair. Though the bodyguard remained quiet, he greeted James with a nod.

"Just sit on the bed," Rose said.

"Okay." And so James approached the mattress and rested his bottom against its soft surface. A doll lay on Rose's pillow. It possessed two eyes, one bigger than the other, and a curved line served as lips, but it lacked a nose. Painted-on dark hair completed the grotesque visage. As for its torso, it consisted of a white egg shape decorated by three black buttons, and four nondescript blobs, missing toes and fingers, formed the arms and legs. James suppressed a shiver and averted his gaze.

"If you enjoy my violin, Hunter, you should hear my piano." She sat beside him. "That's where my true talent is. Too bad there's no space here for something so large. I had to abandon it when I moved."

"Um, so you play several instruments?"

"Only those two. When I was a kid, my mother—well, adoptive mother—insisted I learn music. Music is the voice of the soul, she always said." She curled a lock of hair around her index finger as she remembered. "My mom has an affinity for culture, and she showed me a whole new world: theater, museums, music... not always the things a kid wants to do, but she felt it was important for me to become a well-rounded person. I can still hear her say, 'There is more to life than toys and games, young lady.' It's funny—as a child, I hated playing, but I had all the time in the world to do so. Now that I'm an adult, I love the violin, but I'm so busy that it spends weeks, even months, gathering dust in the closet. I still try to take it out on occasion, so I don't forget."

"That'd be a waste," James said. He discerned an oval mirror mounted above Rose's bureau. Banal in appearance, a cheap product surrounded by a fake gold frame, the glass nonetheless demanded one's attention. The crack in the lower left particularly attracted his interest. Intrigued, he pondered how it had become damaged and why Rose hadn't replaced it. Perhaps concerned by his silence, the Melkar glanced at him, tilting her neck, and he resumed the conversation.

"Uh, don't take this the wrong way, but I can't imagine your father at the opera."

Rose chuckled as she fixated the floor in a futile attempt to hide her amusement. "Not so much. How can I put this—his tastes are less refined than my mom's. He'd prefer a demolition derby to the opera." She stroked her chin. "It's a little weird seeing them together, actually. They don't share the same hobbies, but they manage somehow. In a way, they balance each other." A crease drew on her brow. "Some people think my mom and dad had an arranged marriage. He's NISDA's commander, and she's the head priestess, the highest rank in the clergy, and that's just too much of a coincidence for some. Mom and Dad say it's not true, that it's only a ridiculous rumor. I hope so. It sounds horrible. Can you imagine marrying someone you don't love?"

James contemplated the idea for a moment. "No... but then again, many couples marry for love and don't last."

"What do you mean? Love isn't a good reason to get married?"

"No, that's not my point." James gulped. "I guess I'm saying that, unfortunately, love isn't enough. Love tends to fade away."

And that's a fact I knew very well. I've had a fair amount of relationships. They all started wonderfully, but sooner or later they soured. Same for pretty much everyone I know. Even with Nadia... oh, we kept up appearances, but deep down I could tell there was trouble ahead. It's not like she complained openly, but there were small signs. Not that I blamed her; she could find a better guy than me, and she would. It was inevitable. Still, before I vanished on her, we had a few good months, at least, and I would've given anything to live them.

—Thoughts of James Hunter, Hocmar 28, 2134, on the Nirnivian calendar

An appalled laughter parted from Rose's lips. "Love isn't enough? What happened to you? That's so cynical."

"Maybe. It's not a romantic way of thinking, but that's how it's worked out for me so far."

"Maybe you're right. I can't deny many marriages fail. I don't have enough personal experience to judge myself, since I've only been in love once." As she uttered her sentence, Rose grasped the ring on her left hand's fourth finger. She twisted it around in a gentle motion. Frowning, James studied the jewelry. He'd somehow missed the green gem she wore, and by the tremendous girth, he shouldn't have.

What a stone. Really stunning, but not good for my self-esteem: I'd never be able to afford that kind of rock for Nadia.

—Thoughts of James Hunter, Hocmar 28, 2134, on the Nirnivian calendar

"Rose, are you married?"

The winged woman blinked twice and tensed up. Away in his chair, Brucie leaned forward. "Yes."

James scowled. "Why didn't you mention it before?"

"Well..." Rose shrugged. "There's been so much going on, I didn't think of it."

"You should introduce us. I'd like to meet him."

A clap echoed as the bodyguard slapped his forehead. Rose looked in the opposite direction, but despite her effort, James glimpsed her watering eyes.

Ah, crap.

—Thoughts of James Hunter, Hocmar 28, 2134, on the Nirnivian calendar

"He died during the war." Her voice broke, strained and distorted by emotions. "He was a civilian. He shouldn't have been a casualty, but they killed him anyway."

"Oh, Rose, I'm so sorry." James recoiled a bit. "I should've kept my trap shut."

"Don't be silly, Hunter, it's fine. You didn't know." With a trembling hand, she wiped the tears tumbling down her cheeks. "By the way, I've had an idea. The chapel isn't big enough for an organ, so they have a keyboard in there. I could use that as a piano. It's not the same, but it's something, right?"

Shocked, James froze as his mouth gaped. The chapel... she'd brought up the chapel, thus compromising her lie. The discussion about her dead husband must've shaken her to the point that she'd forgotten having concealed its existence. What should he do? If he held his tongue, she'd become suspicious. Fearful of her potential reaction, he decided he'd act dumb.

"Uh, there's a chapel here?"

"Of course. I wouldn't be able to perform my duties as the Melkar if there weren't—" The second she spoke those words, Brucie jumped to his feet and yelled her name. Blood drained from her face as she masked it with her palms. "Oh God!"

James feigned obliviousness. "You never even told me what the Melkar is."

"That's right, I haven't been completely truthful. Remember the wooden doors?" She exhaled. "It's not a restricted area, it's a chapel."

"It is?" He scratched the top of his skull. "Um, I don't get it. Why lie about that?"

"Because if you knew it wasn't restricted, you might've wanted to see it. And once you did, you would've asked plenty of difficult questions about my position. It's nothing bad or secret. I planned to tell you eventually, but it's complicated, and you've already been through so much that I was scared I might overwhelm you." Rose groaned. "No, no, I despise lies and I won't pile them up anymore." She patted his hand. "I lied because I didn't want to explain to you what the Melkar is. Most people would have insisted, but you're so shy, I thought I might be able to get away with it. I swear it's nothing bad, but I... well, I was afraid that once you knew, things wouldn't be the same between us."

"Um, you don't have to tell me if you don't want to... it's not really my business."

Yeah, I said that, but trust me, I didn't mean it. I wanted to know so badly I could've exploded. From the moment I'd met her, I'd wondered what the hell the Melkar was. Now I could find out, but I was terrified because she didn't want me to know. I could see myself back in the cell, or executed. Hard to imagine Rose going that far, but still...

—Thoughts of James Hunter, Hocmar 28, 2134, on the Nirnivian calendar

She sighed. "No, if I don't tell you, you'll imagine something even stranger than what it is. We're past the point of no return." A deep breath Rose took. "All right, then, the Melkar is... well..." She flushed. "It's so hard to explain... I'm like—" She grunted. "I'm asking a lot, but would you mind giving me a rain check until tomorrow? I'm tired, and I can't figure out where to start. But tomorrow, I can show you what the Melkar is directly."

"Uh, all right... I guess."

"Thank you, Hunter. I appreciate your patience." Rose smiled. "For now, since you enjoy my violin, how about I play some more for you?"

Questions filled my mind, but they disappeared when she started playing again. I liked the first song better, but this new

one had its own charms. I could've listened for hours. In fact, I did. Sometimes, when I close my eyes, I can hear her violin in my head. It's the one good thing I received from all this. I wish I could forget everything about Rose and her universe—everything except her music. And I do hope I don't forget it. My memories are all I have now. Without a miracle, I'll never hear her play again. The crazy thing is, that miracle is within reach, but... ah, goddammit, what should I do?

—Thoughts of James Hunter, Hocmar 28, 2134, on the Nirnivian calendar

Chapter 14

Mashar 28, 2133, on the Nirnivian calendar

The script in Rose's hands served no purpose. Twenty minutes had passed since she'd opened the binder and still, she scanned the first page. A sentence or three she read, perhaps a paragraph at most, and her focus vanished. Instead of the sheet, she fixated on Logan positioning the cameras. The bearded man fiddled with the equipment, whistling a tune. It wasn't that Rose had any interest in his task. Technical details bored her, and yet at this moment, the cameras proved more appealing than her text. Noticing her inattention, Kristina harrumphed, and Rose returned to her duty until her wandering gaze betrayed her again—a backstabbing that took far too little time. Speaking of her faithful assistant, the blond woman paced around the chapel, clutching her trusted minicomp tight.

"Rose, finish it." She gestured toward the Melkar's paper cup. Rose peeped at it and, imagining the dark liquid inside, she grimaced. "Yes, I know you hate coffee, but you need it. It's bad enough you're not allowed makeup, so we can't hide the bags under your eyes. I don't want you yawning like a morglar on top of it."

"Fine, fine." Rose glared at her beverage. In truth, Kristina panicked for nothing. Sure, her physical appearance telegraphed her lack of slumber, but she didn't feel tired. Quite the opposite: adrenaline flowed through her veins at the mere thought of what she'd soon do. Her mind boomed with alertness, to the point of being scattered—

hence her poor concentration. However, Kristina meant well, and if it pleased her...

Rose held her breath for an instant before gulping the remaining coffee. The bitter acidic taste assailed her tongue and sickened her stomach. A retching sound echoed. She covered her mouth, hoping it stayed down, and despite her apprehension, it did.

"Good girl." The assistant poked at her folder. "And since you played the violin until three a.m., you didn't get the chance to rehearse."

"It'll be okay, I've been doing this since I was six. It's not the sermon I'm worried about."

Kristina shook her head. "Of course not, you're worried about him." She groaned. "The human is so much trouble."

Rose stepped forward and rested her palms on her hips. "Don't blame him, it's not his fault. I played for him that late by choice. He didn't ask me to." With a wave, Kristina dismissed the argument. Her lips parted as she planned a rebuke, but swallowing her reply, she spun and resumed her walking. "I'm sorry, Kristina. You worked so hard so I'd look good, and I messed up."

"I'm not mad. I just don't want you to make a fool of yourself on national TV."

"That can't happen. If I did the show in my underwear, I'd start a new fashion craze." She giggled.

The comment finally loosened Kristina a tad. A smile formed on her visage. "Probably, but—"

The sliding door interrupted her. From the gap, a trio emerged, consisting of Rose's mom, her dad and Janice. Daniel and Madeleine advanced toward the altar while Janice lingered behind and admired the paintings hanging on the wall. Exhaling in relief, Rose marched in her parents' direction and met them midway.

"Mom! Dad! Thank you so much for coming!" She reached for her mother's wrinkled fingers. "Especially you, Mom! I'm so sorry for putting you on the spot at the last minute! I meant to call you yesterday, but I lost track of time!"

"Now, now, my dear, it is not a problem. I was already attending your sermon today—a too-rare treat—and so it poses no inconvenience for me to lecture James about the Melkar while I am here."

"Still, you've only had a few hours to prepare."

A shrug came from Madeleine. "Oh, I do not need preparation. As head priestess, I am more than familiar with the material, a fact you are no doubt aware of." The old lady rubbed her chin. "Though I admit, I do not understand why you did not simply explain who you are by yourself."

Rose shuddered. "I should. It's silly, I'm so terrified of how he'll react that I can't bring myself to."

Daniel patted her shoulder. "I'm sure he'll be fine. Where is he anyway?"

"He—" A sensation of being observed invaded Rose, and she paused. In the distance, Janice stared at her, deep in thought. She glanced back, almost said hi, but the second she moved, Janice turned away and pretended she studied the portraits. Rose suppressed a moan. "He went to bed late. I figured I'd let him sleep as long as possible. I suppose we should get him." She peeked at Kristina. "If I send you, will you slap him?"

"Only if he molests me."

Rose touched her brow, exasperated. "You're exaggerating, Kristina. He didn't molest you."

"Ooh la la, so much drama..." Cross-armed and smirking, Janice approached a bit. "Looks like Kristina's allergic to humans. Have no fear: Janice is here! I'll get him." On that note, she began to leave. Brucie chose that moment to rise from the bench where he sat.

"Hey, wait up, won't ya? I'll go with ya!"

"Nah, you're not my bodyguard." She winked. "Stay here and do your job, you slacker!"

***

Complete silence filled the room except for his rumbling stomach. Hunger assailed James, yet he lingered on his mattress. His eyelid morphed into stones too heavy to budge. Any attempt at lifting them ended in instant failure. The last couple hours, he'd spent between slumber and wakefulness, switching from dream to conscious random thoughts again and again. Due to his appetite, he considered starting the day, but he lacked the strength: his lone attempt at rising left him lying on his side instead of his back before snoozing on.

James hadn't felt this tired since... he had no idea, probably during high school, when some of the party animal once residing within his body had still remained. If he really wished to, he could blame Rose. The winged woman had played her violin until three a.m., quite inadequate for an early bird like him. In all honesty, however, the fault belonged to him. He had chosen to listen, and besides, when he had finally gone to bed, sleep had eluded him. Curiosity invaded his mind, given Rose had promised she'd reveal the truth about the Melkar, and as such, an intense excitement mixed with fear poured through his veins. Questions entered his brain, only to leave without an answer. Wild scenarios he imagined, each more ludicrous than the previous, while he twisted and turned. By the time he dozed off, his blankets fell on the floor.

I was so messed up, I figured hungry or not, I'd stay in bed until way past noon. That's when I heard the buzzing sound. Someone at the door... I wondered who it might be for a second or two. Then I realized it had to be Rose. I was late for our "appointment." I groaned, trying to stretch a bit, and my spirit sank. Maybe she'd sent Kristina. That'd be unpleasant to say the least. I reminded myself that no matter what happened, I should avoid physical contact. Well, maybe not if she somehow choked and needed the Heimlich maneuver. No, no, I take it back. Even then, I'm pretty sure she'd rather I let her die.

—Thoughts of James Hunter, Hocmar 28, 2134, on the Nirnivian calendar

James's struggle to reach the door resulted in him staying immobile but moaning. The strident ring echoed relentlessly piercing his ears. The visitor grew impatient and a voice came from the speaker. "Wakey-wakey, James!" The voice was lower-pitched and sultrier than Rose's or Kristina's, so it couldn't be them. "Come on! They're waiting for you!" Janice! Relieved, James sighed. No angry blond assistant for him today. With a grunt, he rolled toward the bed's side. "Hurry up, it's time for the thrilling tale of the Melkar!"

"Yes, I'm coming!" Of course the insulation padding the wall prevented her from hearing.

He hopped off the mattress and his knees bent upon impact. A swirling gray haze accompanied by colored stars obscured his vision. Head spinning, James rubbed his brow and took a few deep breaths until the malaise subsided.

"You'll love it, I swear!"

He stepped forward with his neck bowed down and peeked at his naked thighs.

"There's intrigue!"

Stifling a curse, James spotted the clothes from yesterday on the nearby chair. Better than nothing...

"And action!"

He grasped the pants, put one leg in, stumbled and crashed on the floor.

"And a whole lot of self-loathing."

In pain, James sobbed as he slipped the jeans on properly and zipped up.

"Hey, two out of three isn't that bad!"

Next, the shirt. Desperate, he advanced toward the door, blinded by the fabric.

"Okay, James, I don't want to pressure you, but the whole thing is live, so they can't wait for y—"

At last, the door slid open, cutting her off.

James kept walking and, thanks to Janice's impressive height, almost collided face-first with her breasts. A gasp, and he straightened so he'd look her into the eyes. The soldier's lips formed an amused grin.

"We're not in that much of a rush. Come on, let's go." She wrapped her arm around his shoulder and pulled him. "And keep your wandering hands to yourself." With a closed fist, she waved beneath his nose. "Me, I don't slap."

"Um..." James's cheeks reddened. "Well, that's..."

Janice burst out in a welcomed hilarity as she freed him. "Oh God, Brucie's right! It's so easy!" She winked. "And so much fun! No need to explain, I know the whole story. Kristina can be... uptight sometimes. Besides, it's my wandering hand you should be worried about."

On that note, she swung, aiming toward James's delicate bottom. Gulping, he tensed and straightened, dreading the blow. The palm stopped its motion an inch from the target, and a giggle swerved through the air.

"Yep, too easy indeed!"

Oh God. Another one! No, actually, that's not fair. I like her a whole lot more than Brucie.

—Thoughts of James Hunter, Hocmar 28, 2134, on the Nirnivian calendar

She offered a pat on James's back. "Consider that revenge for ignoring me!"

"Huh?"

"Don't pretend you don't understand. Every time I see you, I say you should come hang out with us at the rec room, and you're like, 'Yeah, sure, that'd be great!' but you never show up! What's wrong? Do I have bad breath?" As a joke, she covered her mouth and exhaled. "Nope! So, I guess I'm that unlikable, huh?"

"No... um..." Blushing, James scratched the back of his head. "I'm, well... it's not..." He lowered his gaze. "Those guys, the guards, they hate my guts and they're kind of intimidating."

The moment she heard those words, Janice halted and spun toward him. "Don't let them get to you. They'll leave you alone. You're under Rose's protection and they won't go against her will."

"Yeah, I figured that out myself. It's, well... I don't want to hang around the rec room if they don't want me there, you know?"

"James, stop admiring the floor and look at me." Despite her demand, he fixated on the ground. "Come on, look at me." She grabbed his upper arm. Though it required work, he suppressed a growl and obeyed. "Don't let those idiots push you around. You live here now, and they'll have to deal with it. Don't lock yourself in your room for their sake." She smiled. "Besides, they can't hate you. They don't know you! They just don't like having you around because you're not supposed to be here. Freak, I'll admit it, I don't understand why Dad's keeping you here, but he is, and if the Commander's fine with it, that's good enough for me, and it'll have to be good enough for them too! So, you listen now—tomorrow I'll bring you to the rec room, and if anyone has a problem with it, I'll handle their complaints. You better come willingly or I'll drag you by the ear! I will!"

He swallowed hard. "Yeah, sure."

"All right, it's settled!" She offered another amicable tap on his shoulder. "Come, we'll be late." And so they resumed their march and chatted along the way. Soon, the duo glimpsed the infamous wooden door. Janice seized her key card and almost scanned it. "I should warn you, Rose is very nervous and the chapel might be a shock. It'll be a big deal for you, but try not to let it show. For her..."

"Uh... maybe it'd be easier if you told me what's going on before we go in there?"

"I could..." Janice caressed her chin, deliberating on the possibility. "Nah, it'll be funnier if I don't!" She laughed. "I can just imagine the look on your face."

Geez, how nice, Janice.

—Thoughts of James Hunter, Hocmar 28, 2134, on the Nirnivian calendar

Chapter 15

All the mystery surrounding the door vanished in an instant as it slid open before James. Anticipation weighted heavily upon his mind, to the point that he hardly reacted. Twice he blinked. The narrow doorway revealed little of the room's contents, so he advanced forward. A thick red carpet ornamented by a golden border cushioned his steps. Rows of wooden pews ran perpendicular to the rug's sides. Rose waited in the front, talking to Kristina, with Daniel Ricdeau and some other people he'd never met. Next to them, a cross-armed Brucie smirked at him and winked. Behind the bodyguard lay a white altar followed by two immense stone statues. Right on cue, the Commander spotted his daughter's arrival and walked toward James, waving for an old woman in a purple monk's robe to come along.

Janice warned him not to panic, but the notice made no sense. Overall, the effect mimicked chapels on Earth except without the recognizable symbols. Nothing to make a fuss about...

And then he looked up and saw the sculptures' upper bodies. The one on the right depicted a lady in a dress. None of the facial features tickled his memories. No doubt a stranger, yet the hairstyle seemed familiar, especially the braid, and the wings even more so. The one on the left, in spite of lacking color, clearly represented Rose herself. For a beat or two, James's heart stopped, only to rush in frenzy afterward. He gasped for air and stepped backward.

Fingers patted his back as Janice whispered, "It's okay, buddy."

She told me I'd be in for a shock, but it didn't help. Why was there a statue of Rose? Who was that other woman?
—Thoughts of James Hunter, Hocmar 28, 2134, on the Nirnivian calendar

Amidst James's confusion, Daniel Ricdeau extended his hand. James shook it out of pure reflex. Doing so, he studied the paintings on the left wall more attentively. They immortalized a tall black-haired winged woman in various situations, such as addressing a crowd or praying. In the last one, she rested in a coffin.

"Hey there, my boy! Nice to see you again. I haven't been able to check on you much lately; the joys of being the Commander, I guess!" The old man gestured toward the woman next to him. "Here, I'd like to introduce you to my wife, Madeleine."

The dame offered a little bow and a wide grin, though perhaps a tad forced. Her round face reminded James of Janice, though far more wrinkled, and age had rendered her hair gray instead of black. In addition, the somewhat cylindrical purple hat she wore struck him as something her daughter would never wear. Not that he could be sure of that fact, since he barely knew Janice.

"It is a pleasure to meet you, Mr. Hunter. I am Head Priestess Madeleine Ricdeau, and Rose's adoptive mother."

"The pleasure's all mine, I assure you." James spun toward her and gave the appearance of looking into her eyes. Reality proved otherwise, however, for in truth, his gaze ventured a touch sideways, focusing on the portraits gracing the right wall. The first picture displayed a man holding a baby girl with tiny wings on her back. The second illustrated a young red-haired child lecturing a mob. In the others, James recognized Rose as an adult.

"Mr. Hunter, due to my area of expertise, Rose asked me to explain to you about the Melkar. She is, of course, more than qualified to do so herself, but she felt it would be better if she showed you through a demonstration while I supplied the details. She will soon address the nation in a sermon. In order for you to understand her role, I shall offer a primer on both our history and religion. We will retire to private quarters soon so we can talk without interrupting the broadcast"—she pointed toward the furthest bench—"but first, how about we take a seat and enjoy her performance for a few minutes?"

"Good idea, dear. My boy, I realize this isn't your faith and don't worry"—Daniel chuckled—"I don't expect you'll convert, but Rose's speeches lift people's spirits, and you need all the cheering up you can get. There are only a few who can be here in person, but most of the country watches on television or listens on the radio. Come on, let's sit at the back."

Unsure how else to react, James acquiesced. They sat together. The firm wood hurt his spine a little, but he had endured worse. A few soldiers littered the room, but for the most part, the pews sat empty. Before long, Rose took her place behind the altar.

"Good evening, people of Nirnivia. I hope you are feeling well. As you must know, this is Rose Ricdeau, the Melkar. If I may, I would like to start in a rather unusual way. As many of you have heard, we received another 'visitor' recently of a kind we have already met and most would prefer never to see again. It is true, we have another human among us. The previous human caused a tragedy, and I understand why some of you fear this new 'visitor' and hate him, but please, give him a chance. I believe he is different, and I am hopeful that Mr. James Hunter is a good man. Besides, Ulgorack would never condone judging a man for another's fault."

"Rose is doing you a big favor," the Commander murmured in James's ear. "Now that she 'approves' of you, most will leave you alone. But don't let your guard down, my boy. There might be exceptions."

"Hatred is a sin," Rose went on, "and so those who have reportedly attacked Mr. Hunter without provocation have sinned. But I forgive you as Ulgorack forgives you, and I am sure that, eventually, Mr. Hunter will find it in his heart to do the same. But enough about that. Last time we began an analysis of the Multafas's scroll, and today we will continue."

I had no idea what she was talking about. She mentioned things like Ulgo-whatever and Tima-something. Lots of mumbo jumbo I was unfamiliar with. Despite that, I hung on to her every word. Rose was an incredible orator; her charisma was phenomenal. She used simple terms, simple sentences; nothing special in that regard, but there was something about her. Something that made you pay attention. She could take the most poorly written speech and turn it into gold. Her enchanting voice played a part, but there was more than that. It's hard to explain. I could've stayed there and listened for hours, but my curiosity got the better of me.

—Thoughts of James Hunter, Hocmar 28, 2134, on the Nirnivian calendar

Mesmerized, James turned toward Madeleine and muttered, "Who... who is she?"

The priestess smiled. "She has many names. The official term is the Melkar. However, sometimes we also call her the holy prophet, or the Voice of God. Perhaps those names are more meaningful to you."

"Yeah, I guess…"

"If you are ready, perhaps we should retire so we can converse at our leisure?"

That sounded fine to me, so I nodded.

—Thoughts of James Hunter, Hocmar 28, 2134, on the Nirnivian calendar

***

Following Madeleine, James, Daniel and Janice headed for the chapel's back room. The group tiptoed along the wall so they'd remain silent and out of the cameras' view. The small chamber contained few pieces of furniture: a chest of drawers in a corner, a table and a couple of chairs. Attached to the ceiling, a speaker spread Rose's voice. Even from here, they could catch the lecture should they so desire. By now, the Melkar had left the sacred texts behind and in their stead shared letters sent by viewers.

"Very well, let us begin." Madeleine inhaled and selected a seat. "If you are to learn about the Melkar, Mr. Hunter, I must give you an overview of our religion. We believe that in the beginning, there was only the original god, Ulgoron, creator of the universe and everything we hold dear. The act of creation was exhausting and required more power than Ulgoron originally thought. As the necessary energy flowed through him, he found himself divided into two entities: Ulgorack and Timagoron. Ulgorack received Ulgoron's joviality while Timagoron inherited mostly from his pessimistic side." She cleared her throat.

"Now, it is important to realize that because neither of them is truly whole on their own, neither Ulgorack nor Timagoron fully understand Ulgoron's intention. Together, sharing what unique knowledge they possessed, they came to comprehend almost everything. Only one mystery remained—the species who calls itself Gorumars.

"These creatures acted in a contradictory manner, sometimes being honorable, other times vile beyond vileness. Neither knew whether the Gorumars were a mistake due to the unexpected division or part of the original design. In time, Ulgorack came to see the best of them while Timagoron focused on the evil and became consumed by hatred. The gods attempted to settle their differences with their fists, but they were evenly matched.

"In the end, they came to a compromise: the Gorumars would decide their own fate. The ones who lived righteously would be granted access to an afterlife that realized Ulgoron's initial vision. Those who failed to do so would be banished into nothingness. Though they cannot control us directly, the gods can influence us, and so Timagoron attempts to lead us toward treachery and evil deeds while Ulgorack spreads kindness and love."

The priestess paused to gather her thoughts before proceeding. "Thousands of years ago, Ulgorack helped his followers by sending a very special person to this world. She was a winged woman. We call her the Melkar. The statue and paintings on the left side of the chapel depict her."

***

Rose's fingers trembled as she held the sheet of paper. In all probability, the tremors remained invisible on the people's televisions, but she couldn't deny her nervousness. Stage fright she had vanquished ages ago: public display no longer posed a challenge for her. Yet on this day, her old jitters had come back. How would he react? she wondered.

"I received a letter from an eight-year-old girl who recently lost her mother. She wants to know why Ulgorack makes her suffer like this if he loves her."

Eight years old. Childhood memories filled her. Young and hopeful, she strolled in the schoolyard during recess. By pure luck, she stumbled on a group of children. They played with a ball, pushing and shoving each other while they laughed. Envious, she observed when a girl smiled at her, chuckling. "Hey, Rose! Wanna play?"

Horrified gasps echoed from the others. A boy stepped toward the speaker. "You crazy? If she gets hurt, we'll get the strap." The gang returned to their game and ignored Rose.

She had grown used to such treatment; it happened often. Exclusion due to reverence: a bitter irony. Even now, her heart sank a bit at the thought. Her eyes watered, but she had a lecture to finish, so she resisted her sorrow and struggled along like always.

"It's important this little girl understand that God does not wish her pain, and he isn't the cause of her suffering. Life is a cycle: we live, we die and we are reborn. We bring our own sorrows. All the trials we face, we choose of our own free will. We simply don't realize it. We do this because pain teaches us how to better ourselves and live a better next life. Eventually, the cycle ends, and there can be two outcomes. Those who overcame their ordeals and improved themselves in the process go on to the afterlife. Those who failed to do so and succumbed to the darkness of their heart disappear into nothingness..."

***

A headache assailed James while Madeleine kept babbling about gods he'd never heard of, bearing impossible names like Timawhatever and Ulgosomething. His own religion proved an elusive mystery more often than not. He hadn't set foot in a church since he was a kid, and the little scripture he'd studied had left him confused and skeptical. Compared to that, a faith from another world was baffling beyond reason. Desperate to comprehend, James's mind frantically sought any detail that might recall familiar lore.

"This Melkar"—he rubbed his chin—"was she like the daughter of your god, Ulgorack?"

"My dear, no!" The priestess dismissed the ridiculous notion with a wave. "In fact, such a claim would be blasphemous!" She frowned. "The Melkar was merely a person born of a normal mother and father like everyone else. Ulgorack simply arranged for her to receive three very special gifts—four if you count the wings." The elder paused as she moistened her lips.

"The first gift was a great charisma and a way with words so she could easily spread her message of peace and love. The second and most important gift was that Ulgorack communicated with her through visions and other cryptic means. The last gift was a defense mechanism so she could protect herself from harm. Using these powers, the Melkar was to enlighten her people and guide them toward the lofty goal that is the afterlife."

"So, um... the words of the Melkar are somehow like the words of God himself?"

"In a way, yes, but nothing is ever so simple." Madeleine sighed. "The Melkar was a regular person in most respects. She could make mistakes, she could misinterpret the visions—she could even let her own selfish desires blind her like anyone. Worse of all, even she was not immune to the corruption of Timagoron. Despite all this, she accomplished miracles. She brought her followers closer and closer to the afterlife. But as I said before, things are never that simple. Some, influenced by Timagoron, refused to believe in the Melkar. At first, they tried defamation. When that failed, they started a brutal war. Even war could not stop the holy prophet, however, and so her enemies used deception instead."

The senior's voice trembled. "The Melkar had a pure heart. She had faith in the goodness of people, and her detractors, in an act of cowardice and treachery, used her optimism to their advantage. They called for peace. They proclaimed they had made a mistake and came to realize that different religious beliefs were no reason for war and that with understanding and respect, there could be coexistence. The Melkar agreed to meet their leaders for negotiations, but it was a ruse."

Madeleine clenched her fist. "The infidels murdered her in cold blood," she sneered.

As Head Priestess Ricdeau told me this, it came to mind there are always two sides to a story. How could we know the truth wasn't twisted by the passage of time? How could we know the Melkar wasn't a fraud? After thousands of years, it's hard to judge facts accurately. Then again, I realized I could say the same of my own or any religion. At any rate, pointing this out to Madeleine would have been a terrible idea, so I didn't.

—Thoughts of James Hunter, Hocmar 28, 2134, on the Nirnivian calendar

***

It demanded an effort, but Rose resisted peeking toward the door to the back room. By now, Madeleine must've reached the part about the Melkar. James had learned about her role. A bead of sweat rolled off her brow as she pondered his reaction. Her dad assured her that her worries were futile, and he might be right. A person from a different universe shouldn't care about a Nirnivian prophet, and yet... from a young age, she'd discovered precious few remained impartial when exposed to her alleged heritage.

"Life is sacred." According to her followers, her own life most of all, ridiculous though the notion might be. "That is one of our fundamental principles. This is true for not only so-called intelligent beings but all life: from animals to insects and even bacteria." Yet people worshiped the ground she walked on. She received special treatment beyond measure, against the doctrine she preached, without asking for it, let alone wishing it. And for what?

"Are we then to let diseases kill us so we don't harm the germs invading our bodies?" She shuddered, remembering the time when her third-grade teacher had annulled a test's results because she had failed. Too difficult and thus unfair, he'd argued. In truth, the kid she used to be had spent the evening with a novel instead of studying. Simple childhood irresponsibility. Madeleine had raised her to be honest—it was imperative for the Melkar to be honest. Still brimming with innocence, Rose admitted her guilt, but the teacher ignored her pleas.

"Of course not. Our lives are also sacred. We have a right to survive, so when we are in danger, we can in good conscience defend ourselves. In the end, such a case consists of two hallowed life forms battling for their right to exist, and who wins, though important to us emotionally and personally, is of little consequence in the grand scheme of things."

***

"Nevertheless, the Melkar's followers did not take her death lightly." The priestess shook her head. "They demanded blood, which admittedly went against everything the Voice of God taught them. In the end, not only did the infidels kill the Melkar, they helped Timagoron corrupt her believers. The war resumed, and it was far bloodier than before."

"That's true, my boy." Mr. Ricdeau bit his lip. "We still feel the effects of that war, believe it or not. They used dirty weapons that left deadly particles behind. The poor fools almost destroyed the world. Most of the planet became unhabitable. The least affected areas could support life, but not without a price. Many babies were born with strange deformities. Facing extinction, the people finally stopped their madness. The believers in the Melkar and the infidels each formed their own country in the habitable territory, separated by a neutral zone: Nirnivia and Ostark. We forbade all contact. The state of the world slowly improved. Today, life's coming back to places that haven't seen it in a long time, but large stretches of wasteland remain. The mutation rate is decreasing, but it's still a problem, as you've seen for yourself."

Those dirty weapons Mr. Ricdeau mentioned reminded me of our nuclear bombs. Those people actually waged a nuclear war. Except the bombs they used were even more destructive than ours, or so it seems to me with my limited knowledge. The thought of such a war was chilling.

—Thoughts of James Hunter, Hocmar 28, 2134, on the Nirnivian calendar

"Are there still"—James whimpered—"dirty weapons around?"

"Yes." Daniel nodded. "Both Nirnivia and Ostark have some. Fortunately, my boy, it's unlikely they'll be used. It'd mean our mutual destruction." He shrugged. "Besides, it'd be pointless: IML technology's lost." The old man's mouth opened as he realized the term lacked meaning for James. "Oh, that's short for International Missile Launcher. Without one of those, our missiles can't reach Ostark and the same for theirs. That's part of the reason for the neutral zone."

Good; at least there was that. Unless, of course, one of the countries managed to build a new one. I almost said that to Daniel, but really, I didn't want to think about the possibility; just too scary.

—Thoughts of James Hunter, Hocmar 28, 2134, on the Nirnivian calendar

***

"War puts a bitter twist on the principle of sacred life." Rose exhaled. As she finished her sentence, a picture of a stomping robotic leg popped into her brain. "In war, survival sometimes demands radical actions. Does anything go?" She imagined his torso, shining metal replacing the flesh. "Of course not." Regrettably, he disagreed. "We have a right to defend ourselves, but ideally, we should not use more force than necessary. A murder attempt should be stopped nonlethally if possible." A burst of flames consumed her daydream; Rose shivered. "Our opponents, though misguided spiritually, have a right to exist just like us." Finally, his face—scarred beyond repair, a speaker for a mouth...

"Despite our faith and good intentions, in war, it can be hard to see when enough is enough. It's easy to go overboard. We have done so in the past and we will likely do it again in the future. When that happens, we must repent and beg for forgiveness."

***

After the reveal about the dirty weapons, there was an awkward silence. Unsure what to do, I noticed a picture of Rose on the wall. As I looked at the photo, it became clear. I guess it wasn't that hard to figure out, but I've said it before: I'm not all that smart. She was the new Melkar, a reincarnation of the previous one. The proof was her wings. If that wasn't enough, Ms. Ricdeau's reaction when she mentioned the original's murder added credibility to the idea. And they were at war. Suddenly, this holy war, the cause seemed so obvious and I didn't want to believe it.

—Thoughts of James Hunter, Hocmar 28, 2134, on the Nirnivian calendar

"It's because of her." James swallowed hard. "Rose was born with wings, which means she's the new Melkar. Ostark found out, broke the no-contact rule and restarted the war."

"Very, very clever!" For the first time since their discussion had started, Janice spoke. She gave him a thumbs-up. "And probable, but you're wrong, sorry." The soldier rubbed her chin. "Actually, you're kind of right about breaking the no-contact rule."

"Indeed..." Madeleine Ricdeau smirked. "Oh, the people of Ostark heard about the Melkar's return despite our efforts to hide it. We briefly hoped the holy prophet's second coming would convince them we were right about her. That did not happen, but neither did our worst fears. We were contacted by their leader, president Tamar. He explained to us that his people believed the original Melkar hadn't even existed—that the old war's real causes were long forgotten. Our new Melkar was, as far as they were concerned, a simple mutation like so many others. However, they did not want conflict. President Tamar swore that as long as we let them be, we could worship our Melkar as much as we desired. This alone proved how little the fool understood. The Melkar is not a deity to be worshiped; it is a guide to be followed. Admittedly, many, perhaps most of our own followers make the same mistake, but I digress."

"Let me tell you, my boy, Tamar had to jump through hoops just to give us that message." A chuckle came from Daniel. "Back then, there wasn't any easy way to communicate between Ostark and Nirnivia; that was the whole point. Either he really worried about a new war, or he planned some nasty trick. As you might've guessed, my boy, we were a bit suspicious"—he scowled as he joined his hands in a pyramid—"but the president remained true to his words. The new war started around five years ago, under President Laforge. Rose was twenty-eight at the time, and there's no reason to believe she was their target. I'd go as far as to say there were no reasons Ostark attacked, they just did! A place called Chestnut Park was destroyed in the process, and that started the Chestnut War." The senior grunted.

"They never explained why. Oh, I'm sure they have a motive, but I'll be damned if I know what it is. The best guess I've heard is territorial expansion, but there doesn't seem to be any need for that. Ostark's population is a fraction of what their land can support."

That wasn't quite right. There was something... something implied Rose was somehow involved with the war. I couldn't remember what at first, but then it came back to me.

—Thoughts of James Hunter, Hocmar 28, 2134, on the Nirnivian calendar

"When I was outside, I saw a bionic man on TV. Um, he said... he said Rose wasn't the real Melkar. That she was a fraud manipulating people."

The Commander clenched his fist. His muscles tensed as he sat there gritting his teeth. An intense rage shone in his eyes. Unsettled, James recoiled in his seat a tad, but Madeleine patted his shoulder in a comforting gesture, assuring him it would be all right.

***

"I will now answer a final letter for today, sent by a fifteen-year-old boy." Rose's fingers trembled as she reached for the paper. All her fears about Hunter had left her nerves rattled. "This poor soul has suffered his share of sorrows, and he is now considering killing himself. If he's listening today, I urge him not to."

In the distance, she noted Kristina lifted her gaze from her minicomp every few minutes to glance at her boss. The blond assistant remarked Rose's twitches and worried about her. Rose fired a discreet smile that she hoped was reassuring.

"I know life isn't always easy, that it can feel like it's not worth it. We are weak; sometimes the challenges we bring ourselves seem insurmountable."

When it came to popularity, Kristina lacked ability. People deemed her cold and distant, judging her interested only in her work.

"Maybe we are so eager to learn that we occasionally take on more than we should, but despite our weakness, we have strength." Why, her dear bodyguard himself often joked about what he perceived to be a lack of genitalia on her part; however, Rose suspected the tasteless jest resulted from Kristina's rebuttal of his advances rather than her actual demeanor, though Brucie insisted otherwise.

"If you persevere, things will improve, and you will be closer to the afterlife. Closer to perfection." So unfair, really. That woman cared; no question about it. Her shyness concealed her inner warmth, but it lay under the surface. How many times had she delivered food unprompted when Rose's hectic schedule precluded a meal, or risked her job by reprimanding her own employer about her sleeping habits? Those weren't the acts of selfishness most assumed of her. Unfortunately, people based their opinions on appearance. They never dug below the skin.

"But if you commit suicide, then all you will find is a direct way to nothingness. No more reincarnation, no more afterlife... only nothingness."

***

"That bastard!" Daniel Ricdeau slapped the table before him, and a loud thump spread through the air. Surprised, James recoiled. "That'd be Doctor Death." The Commander's tension diminished as he relaxed after a deep breath. "He's a mysterious man, the new leader of Ostark who took over when President Laforge died. We don't know who he is. He appeared out of nowhere one day and became very popular in Ostark. Rumor has it that he's a genius in many domains, particularly medicine. He saved many lives and became a legend. Or at least that's what our spies tell us. He hates Rose, but we have no idea why. Before he appeared, the Ostarkirans never even mentioned her name. They didn't go after her in particular. They attacked our city, caused death and destruction, but she clearly wasn't a priority. This all changed when the Good

Doctor, as they call him, came to power. Rose is his target, and he uses the Ostarkirans' hatred to help him get to her."

"The really messed-up part"—Janice leaned forward—"is that the mechanical freak kinda did us a favor." Daniel aimed a dark stare at his daughter while Madeleine preferred an inquisitive, though still harsh, one. "Come on, don't pretend you don't know what I mean! Before he came, this was a normal war—attack after attack; constant bloodshed. And what's worse, it was a complete disaster for us."

The old man crossed his arms. "I'll admit we were losing, but I wouldn't go that far. We still had a chance."

Janice dismissed her father's rebuttal with a wave. "Don't kid yourself. The Ostarkirans slaughtered us like animals. We were finished. A month, maybe two and it'd have been over. Dad, you're a great commander, but we were impossibly outgunned. It's as simple as that."

"That is enough." The priestess rolled her eyes. "How about you two agree to disagree and move on?"

"Yeah, fine, whatever." A shrug came from the youngest Ricdeau. "The point is, when Doctor Death became president, he scaled down the war effort big-time. He called for a truce right away and organized peace talks. He even arranged for a direct line of communication between our Council and his cabinet. It's mostly used for threats"—Janice sniggered—"but, hey, there's already more collaboration than ever between our countries. When we refused his demands, he still removed his forces. We say we're at war, but it almost feels like peace time. That's why we call it the uneasy peace. Sure, there's been some incidents. Sometimes one of us makes a bold move and there's retaliation, but minor stuff all in all. I've never seen anything like it. It's like, I dunno." Frowning, Janice snapped her fingers twice in rapid succession. "Like a cold war. Just came to me. Not bad, eh?"

Daniel winked. "Yeah, pretty nice. I'll have to steal it."

I could've been an asshole and spoiled her moment by mentioning we had one of those, but nah.

—Thoughts of James Hunter, Hocmar 28, 2134, on the Nirnivian calendar

"Don't get me wrong, though." Janice winced. "I don't trust that freak. Besides, he's after my little sister. To him, it's like a sick game where the goal is Rose. That's why we couldn't agree to his demands: he asked us to deliver her to Ostark. Since we said no, he tried to capture her, or get her to surrender. We can't prove Ostark is behind the kidnapping attempts, but who else could it be? The really scary thing is, he wants her alive. No idea why, but it can't be for cookies and tea if you catch my drift."

James was hanging on to Janice's every word when a sob reached his ears. Shocked, he jumped in his seat and wriggled around. Tears ran down Madeleine's cheeks.

"Oh, Janice, my dear, please do not remind me. I do not dare imagine what perverted acts that man would perform on my poor daughter."

Silence fell over the group, enough for Rose's voice to echo from the speaker. "Now, I would like you all to pray with me, for all the people who died protecting us, for the sickly in our hospitals, for our lov—"

"Janice is right, to a point." The Commander shook his head in disgust. "The war has calmed down since Doctor Death has been in charge, but the man's twisted." His volume grew louder and louder. "We're not safe. If he captures Rose, who knows what he'll do next?" He rose, clenching the table. The muscles in his limbs tightened.

"Even if he were to leave us alone once he got her, we'd never sacrifice the Melkar, never! We lost the original. Ulgorack in his mercy finally sent another one—it took thousands of years. We won't give her up! And even if we lost our faith"—furious and red-faced, he punched the table, resulting in an echoing thud—"I won't let him hurt my daughter! Never! Not while I breathe!"

Wide-eyed, James stepped back, more from instinct than a conscious choice. He peeked at the door and swallowed hard. No serious intention of leaving entered his mind, yet the fury he witnessed made the exit appealing. Sensing his anxiety, Madeleine offered a smile.

"Please forgive my husband's outburst. He is passionate about our family's safety."

"Um, yeah, sure"—James scratched the back of his skull—"I understand."

A blush reddening his chin, Daniel pushed a benevolent chuckle. "I'm sorry, I got carried away. Well, my boy, I'd say we covered the basics."

"Why, yes, I assume you received more than enough information for one day. The priestess concurred. Besides, it appears Rose is about to finish. We should join her."

Indeed, the angelic voice flowed from the speaker: "...wish you all a good evening, and may you all go in peace."

Chapter 16

One after another, the group within the chamber exited the small quarters and entered the main chapel. James trailed them all, dragging his feet along the carpet. Behind the altar, Rose and the cameraman exchanged a few inaudible pleasantries. The prophet stood with her hands joined behind her back. Madeleine advanced toward her daughter at a greater speed than her cohorts. Filled with pride, she extended her arms as if intending a hug that never came.

"That was a great performance, Rose, as usual." A round of approval resonated through the church while Daniel and Janice nodded. As for James, he attempted to formulate a congratulatory message, but his eloquence, should it deserve the term, failed him.

Rose bobbed her head appreciatively. "Thank you!" A grin spreading across her face, she faced James. "So, Hunter, getting an idea of the big picture?"

"Um, I guess so." His voice remained a mere whisper, and he averted his gaze.

A chuckle came from Daniel. "Oh, the poor boy is overwhelmed." The old man patted James's shoulder. "We gave him an overload of information."

"I can imagine!" The alleged Melkar gulped. "It must've been an intense history lesson. It's about lunchtime, so how about we clear your head with a good meal? I can answer any questions you have while we're there."

"That's nice but, uh, I'm not feeling too good." Still refusing to lift his head, James scratched his neck. "I... it's a lot to process and I haven't slept much. Sorry, but I think I should lie down for a while."

Madeleine leaned forward. "My dear, you are indeed pale. Perhaps you should consider a visit to the clinic."

"Oh no, I just need a quick nap."

A concerned expression came from the winged woman. "You're sure you want to skip lunch? You haven't eaten yet."

"Yeah, I'm not hungry. I'll grab a bite later."

"Okay, then, Brucie and I'll walk you to your room."

Daniel smiled at Janice and nodded toward James and his companions. "How about you go with them?"

Unconvinced, the biological sibling shrugged. "Nah, they know the way."

Though the angle obscured his vision, James discerned what he imagined to be a slight scowl forming on the Commander's brow. It only lasted a fraction of a second, however, soon replaced by his traditional grin. Waving at those left behind, the trio departed. James dragged his feet along the way, staying a few paces behind the others. Undeterred, Rose pursued small talk, but his replies were brief and noncommittal. Soon, she understood the implied signal and hushed. At least until they arrived at their destination.

Before James opened his door and retired, she fired an apprehensive glance at him. "You're okay, Hunter? You seem troubled—I guess it's normal, but I do worry."

I couldn't even look her in the eyes. After all I'd learned, I didn't know what to think of Rose. She was a holy prophet; I was nothing but a loser, an all-time loser. I felt so... inadequate.

—Thoughts of James Hunter, Hocmar 28, 2134, on the Nirnivian calendar

"I'm tired, that's all. I'll be all right."

A sigh echoed from Rose as she rubbed her forehead. Though barely audible, James could swear she muttered, "Not you too...," before saying, "Hunter, look at me. Look into my eyes, like you did before... please, look at me. It's only Rose. I'm just a woman, like any other." A request that clearly meant a lot to her. As much as James wished to comply, the gesture proved impossible. Rose groaned. "Not again. Not this again..." Disillusionment dripped from her words. "It's always the same thing: people can't see me as a person. I'm the Melkar and nothing else. I thought you might be different."

"I'm some random guy." James covered his face. "You're a holy prophet. It's kind of intimidating."

"You want to know something, Hunter?" The normally suave voice grew tense, and the posture she adopted confirmed the sentiment. Her hands now rested on her hips. "What my mother told you about me is a fairy tale. I'm not a prophet. I'm no voice of God. I'm a simple woman with the misfortune of having been born with wings. Sometimes I wish I could rip them off and be rid of all this nonsense. People infer too much."

"Not this shit again, Rose!" He had stayed uncharacteristically silent so far, but now Brucie grunted as he shook his head. "Come on, stop denying your fate. It ain't cute no more, ya know."

"Shut up, Brucie, I'm serious!"

"Hey, I've seen ya with the mirror—speaking to it, and you acted like it talked back. Weird crap. Either ya were talking with God or you're crazy."

"Then I'm insane, lock me up." While sarcastic, the tone conveyed a touch of seriousness. "Brucie, I know you want to believe, but don't do this to me, not now! James, I mean it." She sounded as if she begged. "I'm not the Melkar or a prophet of any kind. I'm only Rose."

"So, you don't believe in this religion?" James asked.

"No, I do believe in the religion and in Ulgorack. I believe there once was a Melkar, but I'm not the new one."

"Then what are you, Rose? Why are you deceiving all those people?"

I bit my tongue, but too late. What Doctor Death had claimed on TV, that Rose manipulated her people for her own interest, popped into my mind and I blurted out something stupid. I cursed myself, but no way could I take it back.

—Thoughts of James Hunter, Hocmar 28, 2134, on the Nirnivian calendar

"That's cold." Was that a tear in her eye? "That's freaking cold. I saved you, Hunter, and that's how you repay me?" She glared at James, and he almost recoiled. "I told them, Hunter. I told them thousands of times. I still do on occasion. They don't listen. I can't convince them. They say I'm testing them, or that I don't realize what I really am or some other excuses. They want to believe—no matter what happens, they twist it to fit their fairy tale. I can't stop it. After a while, I figured maybe I can use this to make Nirnivia a better place." The anger left her visage, ousted by sorrow. "More and more, I think this was a mistake, but I'm in too deep now. I can't stop—there would be consequences. Oh God, what did I get myself into? I just... I just want a friend. No one sees me as a friend... I guess it can't be you."

She seemed so furious; it was a little scary. Yet it wasn't rage I saw in her, but rather disappointment, sadness. I'd hurt her, I couldn't deny that. I knew she told the truth: she'd ex-

plained to her people she wasn't the Melkar. Either that or she was the best liar I had ever met.

—Thoughts of James Hunter, Hocmar 28, 2134, on the Nirnivian calendar

"Rose, I... I'm sorry, you've been nothing but good to me. It's all so confusing, all so new... I'm... uh, I don't know, maybe I'll be able to deal better tomorrow."

"Yeah, go rest, Hunter. We'll talk again later."

***

I don't know why I did it then and not before. I thought about it all the time, especially when I was alone. I'd lie on my mattress, caressing my belt buckle and remembering what I read online about how that guy used his... images from my previous life popped in my mind—all the people I'd left behind: my mom, dad, Patrick, Nadia...

Each of them seemed to ask the same question: Why keep going? I'd lost everything. There was no point. Rose had told me I'd never go back home, and this world... well, it didn't take long to realize it was batshit crazy. Somehow, I resisted the temptation, but that day I...

Maybe it was exhaustion; I was tired as hell. Maybe everything I'd learned from Madeleine overwhelmed me. Or maybe it's simply because I'd pissed off the only person who actually cared. Whatever the case, I unbuckled my belt and...

—Thoughts of James Hunter, Hocmar 28, 2134, on the Nirnivian calendar

A rhythmic beeping brought James's clouded mind back to reality. Darkness surrounded him due to his closed eyes. He struggled to open them, but the battle proved too much. Where was he? No memories remained except... yes, an argument with Rose. He'd returned to his room. What had come next he failed to recall.

After a brief rest, he tried lifting his eyelids once more. They obeyed, but only for a second. Pure haze greeted his vision—not very informative. A few extra attempts and they stayed up. Little by little, his sight cleared. He lay in a bed, though not his. James wished to survey his environment, but restraints limited his movements. A tube ran to his wrist, an intravenous line, he guessed. In the distance, a man dressed in white bent over a desk. James meant to call him, but his voice was muffled. Then he understood that a plastic mask covered his face, probably for oxygen. That explained it: the clinic—he had to be in the clinic. And thus, that person...

Indeed, perhaps hearing his plea, Dr. Greenberg rose, revealing his mullet and turned around. "Oh, buddy, you're back!" Smiling, the medic rushed to his side, footsteps echoing along the way. "You gave us a scare! But you'll be fine."

James couldn't tell whether that was true or not, but soon, his energy levels improved considerably, confirming the prognosis. Before long, the physician removed the needle in his skin and the mask. About an hour later, a nurse supplied some food consisting of meat and vegetables accompanied by a green gelatinous substance for dessert. James suppressed a sigh: even in another universe, hospitals served gelatin. At first, his appetite was lacking, yet he forced himself to eat. A few bites swallowed and his stomach grumbled for more. He'd barely rested his fork when Greenberg announced a visitor. Undoubtedly Rose, he figured, unless the Commander or Janice had beaten her to it.

In a matter of minutes, the door slid open and a woman wrapped in a familiar white dress appeared, corroborating his deduction. Rose ventured a couple steps forward, paused and offered a hesitant wave. Behind her, Brucie followed, staring at the floor while he nervously scratched his head, an act he copied from James.

"Hunter!" The prophet swallowed hard. "I'm so glad you're okay, I was so scared!"

"Yeah, um, sorry... I can't even remember what happened."

"Oh... well..." There was another gulp. "I had a bad feeling, so I returned to your room. I found you hanging yourself in your closet with your belt. I've never seen anything like it."

Encouraged by the account, pictures surged in James's brain. His lungs on fire, he'd choked as the bodyguard lifted him in an effort to lessen the strain on his neck. Meanwhile, Rose reached for the buckle with her trembling fingers and wrestled to unclip it while shouting for help.

"You saved me again. Thank you."

"You're looking me in the eyes." A large smile appeared on her face, in contrast to her previously apprehensive expression. "That makes me happy. Listen, Hunter, I beg you, don't do anything stupid like that again, okay? I am very sorry about our fight. I overreacted. Your reaction was justified, but in a way, that made it more hurtful. I'm not mad at you, but rather my general situation. I don't want you to—"

"Rose, stop. I didn't do this because of the fight. I've been more depressed than I let on. This whole thing has been..." He sighed. "I can't even describe it."

I have no idea if that was true or not. To this day, I'm still not sure why I tried to kill myself. It felt like she needed to hear those words, so I said them, and I think I made the right decision.

> —Thoughts of James Hunter, Hocmar 28, 2134, on the Nirnivian calendar

"Hunter..." The alleged Melkar advanced, closing the gap between them. She caressed the back of his hand. "It's natural to be depressed given the circumstances, but suicide... don't ever let it get to this point again. I'm there for you should you need it, and I'm not the only one. Maybe we should arrange for you to meet a professional."

"Rose, I'm sorry. I said some things back there that I'm not proud of."

She made a dismissive gesture. "It's fine."

"No, it isn't." James grunted. "You've been nothing but kind to me, and you've even saved my life twice. That should be proof enough that you're a good person and I can trust you no matter what."

"I'm not that good. I wondered why I risked my life to save you." She exhaled. "I think it's because in my heart, I hoped I might've finally found someone who'd judge me not for what I represent, but for who I am. People tend to have strong feelings about me: they see me as either a holy prophet or a treacherous dictator. It's hard to have normal relationships in this situation. It's foolish, but I pretty much saved you because I hoped someday we might be friends. See? I'm selfish, like I said before."

"You're too hard on yourself. Besides, I really need a friend too!"

"That's good. I should go now. You need your rest. I've been here too long already. Dad sends his regards. Dr. Greenberg wouldn't let him in. He said too many people might overwhelm you. He only tolerated Brucie because he's my bodyguard."

Speaking of which, Brucie waggled an interrupting index finger. "Uh... ya know 'bout all the sorry mushy stuff." He looked at James but averted his gaze. Standard brazen Brucie could be a trial, but unexpectedly shy Brucie annoyed him even more. "I, uh, I'm kinda hard on ya, ya know. Mess around with ya, make all kind o' super funny jokes. Just wanna let you know, you're a cool dude. Didn't mean to make ya feel like I don't want ya here, right?"

A chuckle came from James. "Hey, big guy, no worries. I get you." He presented his fist. With a chortle, Brucie provided the requested bump.

***

With his hands joined behind his back, Daniel paced along the corridor. Despite his insistence, Dr. Greenberg maintained that he must stay outside. At least he'd let Rose in. His daughter had grown attached to the human boy in a short time, and his suicide attempt had traumatized her. The moment she'd discovered him choking, a panic had overcome her, and the same held true for Daniel—though in his case, more for Rose's sake than James's. Several years of self-imposed sequestration had left her in a depressed state. Of course, Rose put on a brave face for the populace, but deep down...

As much as he loved her, nothing Daniel did helped, and Brucie had also struck out. A psychologist remained out of the question; if the public found out, it would create a scandal. Normally, Daniel placed his daughter's well-being before such concerns, but the people needed their faith at the moment. He doubted it would work, anyway. Still, the last few days, her mood had improved a lot and that had brought him hope. Taking care of her new human friend chased the dark clouds away. Somewhat ruefully, he conceded that a perfect stranger had managed to help his own daughter better than he could. Great, except if he died now...

The clinic's sliding door interrupted his pondering, and Rose emerged, trailed by the bodyguard.

"He'll be okay, Dad," she said before he opened his mouth.

"What a relief!" Reassured, Daniel exhaled. "We don't know much about him, but he seems like a nice boy. I'm glad he's all right. You were the first on the scene, despite the security cameras. It's a real miracle you saved him. God must've spoken to you."

The prophet shrugged and turned her head, thus concealing her eyes. "God had nothing to do with it. I knew there was something wrong with him, but I wasn't sure what. As I left, I realized he was considering killing himself, so I went back." Rose walked away, and Brucie followed. "It's easy for me to notice the signs. I see them every time I look in the mirror."

Stricken, Daniel recoiled. "Rose..."

He debated going after her and having a talk, but it'd be useless. Her demeanor made it clear she'd rather be alone, and forcing the issue would only exacerbate her somber thoughts. Instead, he gazed at the clinic, and his lips formed a weak smile.

"Can you help her, James? Or will you end up adding to her misery? I do like you, my boy, but I swear..." Daniel clenched his fist while gritting his teeth. "If you ever hurt her, you'll have to answer to me."

What Matters Most

Chapter 1

Mashar 28, 2133, on the Nirnivian calendar

He was always so focused on his work. He didn't hear me enter his laboratory, as usual. Sometimes I felt like I was invisible to him. His science: that was his world, his passion, and he excelled at it. In appearance, nothing else mattered to him, but the real passion wasn't so much science; it was helping others through it.

—Thoughts of Evelyn Losier, Hocmar 28, 2134, on the Nirnivian calendar

Evelyn Losier, the Ostarkiran vice president, entered the small yet well-furnished laboratory. As expected, she found the cybernetic man they called the Good Doctor, a moniker the Nirnivians had corrupted into Doctor Death. Against her hope, he engaged in a video call at that very moment, standing before a screen. Not wishing to interrupt his conversation, Evelyn stayed behind and waited. Despite the distance, she recognized two peculiar Perz women on the monitor. The brilliant duo was composed of Anya and Tania.

Born identical twins, the sisters must've grown sick of sharing the same appearance, as they'd both adopted extravagant yet singular styles. Anya dyed her hair a bright cyan, sported a ponytail and corrected her nearsightedness with glasses. On the other hand, Tania chose a pink tint, let her hair flow free and preferred contact lenses. None could deny their duplicate facial features, but it'd be impossible to confuse their identities.

"We're finally approved for Gorumar trials!" a beaming Tania said, shaking her fists as she hopped around. "It's a huge opportunity and a major step forward for medical science!"

Calmer than her sibling, Anya adopted a half-smile. "And a better life for the patients."

"Yeah, sure..."

The mechanical man nodded. "You both performed admirably. Consider my high expectations met. You deserve your reputations as the top experts in nanotechnology. This project would never have succeeded so quickly without your collaboration."

Anya waved the notion away. "Oh, you're too modest, Good Doctor. You drafted the theory; we only followed your instructions. We didn't do anything you couldn't have done yourself."

The cyborg had lost an eye during the incident responsible for his current physique. An electronic replacement had taken its place. In a clever twist, it consisted of a group of blue lights arranged in a smiling face. Even cleverer, the smiley could change expressions, which allowed him to express emotions that had become difficult to convey after his disfigurement. As if to prove this capability, the smile changed into a shocked open mouth. "Nothing could be further from the truth. I suppose you are correct in a small way, though. With enough time, no doubt I would master nanotechnology. Yet you are currently far more advanced in that field. Given my lack of proficiency and the number of presidential tasks I must attend to, it would have been at least another two years before the skin reached this stage."

At the mention of the word *skin*, Evelyn noted the conversation's subject, displayed on a nearby counter beside the Good Doctor. She took a few steps toward the rectangular cases, roughly three inches wide by two inches high, containing the twins' labor. The overall effect reminded Evelyn of small picture frames, except displaying flesh instead of photos. She counted over twenty in total, representing each of Ostark's races. Brigs, Zargs, Jonilans and Perz—all would benefit from day one. The president never tolerated discrimination. Now closer, Evelyn gasped at Anya and Tania's workmanship. The membrane mimicked biology to perfection, including blemishes. They'd spared no expense for authenticity. Each skin tone matched its biological counterpart's, and the various examples showed an ability to adapt to minor color variation between individuals. A few samples even sported body hair.

On the videophone, Tania pouted. "Still, it took waaaay too long! I told them we were ready for trials months ago, and they did a bunch of tests for nothing!" She shook her head and threw her hands in the air. "The skins were fine, like I said."

"Always in such a hurry, dear sister." Anya sighed and waggled a reprimanding finger. "We're talking real-life patients. Their safety must be guaranteed."

"Yeah, yeah, of course. But I already guaranteed it." She scowled. "Bureaucrats try slowing down progress with their red tape, but they can't win! Nothing stops science and..." The tirade continued for a moment, and Anya kept rolling her eyes. Once her pink-haired sibling finished, the blue-haired one almost retorted, but the president proved faster.

"Be that as it may, you succeeded, and I suggest you celebrate." He lowered his head and tapped his chin. "However, Tania, there are chemical compounds I would like you to synthesize, if the request is not too onerous."

"With pleasure! It'll be a ton of fun!" Tania exclaimed, rubbing her hands together.

"Excellent, I shall send you the criteria by the end of the day." The conversation ended soon after, and the mechanical man reached for a beaker filled with a yellowish liquid.

"They did this?" Evelyn asked, pointing toward the tissues stretched on metallic racks for display.

"In a manner of speaking, yes. Technically, nanomachines synthesized the replacement skins. However, the twins built and programmed the nanomachines and thus were essential to the process."

"It's incredible." Evelyn's finger approached a Perz-mimicking membrane, only to stop at the last moment. Biting her lip, she fired an inquisitive glance at the president, who acquiesced. Her fingertips caressed the dark skin. A quiver ran down her spine. So soft, and yet she sensed the minor imperfections anyone possessed. "It's just like the real thing!"

"Because it is the real thing." Evelyn frowned at his remark. "No, do not misunderstand. It did not come from a person. The twins formed the skin by synthesizing cells that are exact duplicates of yours or mine. Give one of these to a dermatologist along with a so-called real sample, and they would fail to identify which is which."

"Well, that's wonderful. So many people will benefit from this. The burn victims alone... uh..." She blushed at her faux pas. In response, her superior's smiley displayed the emoticon for laughter.

"I am aware of my deformities, no need to sidestep the issue," the cyborg said, reaching for a dropper. "You are, of course, correct. Burn victims such as myself will benefit from the twins' work. Why, I could rebuild my old face."

"You sound like you're not going to."

"I am not. Time is precious, and I will not waste it on a mere cosmetic improvement." He plunged the dropper into the yellow liquid, collecting some. "The people of Ostark have accepted my appearance so far. I assume staring at my disfigured visage shall remain acceptable for the foreseeable future."

Surprised, Evelyn frowned. "But, we're talking what? A few days, maybe?"

"I have many important ongoing projects. I will not interrupt them for a trivial matter, not even for mere days."

Half-satisfied, she offered a couple of weak nods. "I see. Still working on an Alcharia cure?" He gave no answer. Instead, the Good Doctor seized a pack of microscope slides and picked one. "I don't understand why you're so interested in that virus."

"Because it is deadly and without treatment."

"But it's so rare."

"Indeed it is"—the president dropped a minuscule drop of yellow fluid on the glass slab—"but every year, people lose their lives to this disease. The fact that they are few does not mean their deaths are insignificant. I spent years seeking a cure, without any success. The solution eluded me for far too long. I suppose it is an unsolvable puzzle, and I relish its challenge." By then, he had inserted the slab into the microscope and peered into the device. "As much as I appreciate your interest in my work, I know it is not the reason you are here. What can I do for you, Evelyn?"

Evelyn closed her eyes and sighed. These discussions never went well. "We had a meeting concerning the war effort scheduled next week. I've heard you canceled it, and I wondered if you'd be willing to reconsider."

"Please do not take offense. I do not mean any disrespect." The cyborg grabbed a bottle and a specimen.

Deliberately, he measured a few millimeters of the greenish substance. With such precision in his movements, you might presume the material to be dangerous, but he was a man who displayed equal caution whether pouring water or diffusing a bomb. "However, such a meeting is currently unnecessary. The war is progressing exactly as I wish."

"It's just..." Evelyn's mouth twisted. "Some of the cabinet members are getting wary. They know you have a plan, but you've been so vague about it. They trust you, but it would do them good to be reassured."

"Please be honest, Evelyn, you are the wary cabinet member."

"Good Doctor, I—"

He shrugged. "You disapprove of how I have been handling the war." Evelyn almost said something, but he interrupted her. "Do not apologize. You have a right to your opinion and are welcome to share it." The mechanical man resumed his work and poured the green liquid into the beaker containing the yellow one. That deed done, he stirred the mixture. Seconds later, a putrid chemical scent caused a slight burning sensation in Evelyn's throat. "I do not ignore other people's points of view."

I had a lot of respect for the Good Doctor. Disagreeing with him hurt. But all we did then was propaganda and information gathering. There was no doubt we had the upper hand, but how long before Nirnivia struck back? At least we were more aggressive with BBR, but they were just some bothersome flies.

—Thoughts of Evelyn Losier, Hocmar 28, 2134, on the Nirnivian calendar

"I..." She whimpered. "I trust you with all my heart, Mr. President." She gave a sob. "It's Nirnivia I don't trust."

"A diverging opinion does not imply a lack of trust, Evelyn, and I appreciate your candor." Again, he began the procedure he'd performed earlier and reached for his dropper. "Do not be sorry for performing your job adequately. As for the Nirnivians, they are not enemies. They are simply fooled into believing it is so. While we could destroy them, that would be unfair and cruel. Once we have Rose as our prisoner, I will show them the truth with such proof that even they will have no choice but to accept reality."

There was no doubt for me that Rose was a fraud. She was a menace, a dictator, and had to be stopped. But over time, I had slowly lost faith in whatever plan the Good Doctor had devised. Rose was out of reach, and anyway, what would he do if he got her? When those thoughts came to my mind, I felt shame. I knew I shouldn't be so skeptical. He did so much for us, and he was a genius. He never appeared to pay attention to his surroundings, yet he never missed a beat. Even more impressive was his gift for predicting how people would react when faced with a given situation. That skill had served him and all of Ostark well in the past. If he said all was under control, it had to be. But still...

—Thoughts of Evelyn Losier, Hocmar 28, 2134, on the Nirnivian calendar

"But, Mr. President"—her voice trembled—"I don't want Nirnivia destroyed, not if it can be avoided. But our attempts to capture Rose have failed, in large part because we couldn't send our best men. Since most of them hold such grudges, they might kill her instead. Now she hides in Valardir at all times. We can't get to her." She groaned. "I still don't understand why killing her is so out of the question, anyway."

The smiley in his eye morphed into a sad face. Rarely would the president interrupt his research for the sake of a conversation, but he did so then. "Oh dear, Evelyn, how many times do I have to repeat myself?" He patted her shoulder. "If we kill Rose, she will become a martyr. Achieving peace will then be impossible. It would be a tragedy—a reprisal of the events that ravaged this world thousands of years ago. I cannot accept such a reckless course of action. Please have faith in me, Evelyn. I know I ask for a lot without proof. It is true we have failed so far, but our victory is imminent. Through pure chance, I now have a deus ex machina up my sleeve."

He was always so cryptic. I usually found it charming, but sometimes it was just frustrating.

—Thoughts of Evelyn Losier, Hocmar 28, 2134, on the Nirnivian calendar

"What do you mean?"

"It does not matter. I will reinstate the meeting with the cabinet as you desire. I cannot let my vice president grapple with such stress and anxiety."

On the surface, he was so cold. For instance, he didn't glance at me once during the conversation. Yet I knew in my heart he did care about me and everyone else. The Good Doctor had devoted his life to his people. He had slaved to improve our lives, and the results were undeniable. I was curious about his so-called deus ex machina, but despite some occasional minor doubts, I trusted him. I have to admit, he didn't always make that easy.

—Thoughts of Evelyn Losier, Hocmar 28, 2134, on the Nirnivian calendar

***

When his vice president left the laboratory, the Doctor stayed behind, continuing his experiment in silence. Less than a minute later, another presence filled the room. With all his strength, the cyborg resisted the urge to look. He came back, the laughing fool. Had the mechanical man still possessed his old flesh, no doubt goose bumps would have covered his body. Confirming his suspicion, a low-pitched voice said, "Wha ha ha. Ain't that swell work by the twins? He he, I wonder, do they know the real reason you had them synthesize those skins? Gwa ha ha ha ha!"

Don't show any reaction, avoid replying. Any interaction might suggest a desire to continue the exchange. The Doctor gazed through his microscope, concentrating on his subject more than usual. Soon, the unwanted guest vanished. The president then closed his lone remaining eye and exhaled through the nose.

Chapter 2

Mashar 29, 2133, on the Nirnivian calendar

The heat proved so intense that the blanket ended up useless, so James sat on top of it. On his knees rested a plate containing his breakfast. James picked up a piece of toast and took a bite. Bland, even by bread standards; how could you mess up eggs on toast? Somehow, they'd managed. He'd changed universes, and still hospital food lived up to its poor reputation.

In the distance, a nurse wiped down a counter with what James assumed to be a bleach solution, or rather this world's equivalent. She applied considerable elbow grease, far more than some of her peers he had observed back home. Despite her toiling, she aimed a discreet peep at James every few minutes. Once she scowled at him. He had grown used to such attention, since he had endured it throughout his stay, and not only with this particular woman. He caught many worried glances and derogatory whispers. No doubt having a visitor around made the staff anxious. Other than the discomfort brought by their suspicion, James couldn't complain. The caretakers catered to his needs and responded to any request as fast as possible.

His stay should be brief. Dr. Greenberg assured he'd be released tomorrow. Remembering that promise, James eyed the inactive heart monitor. The fact that they'd disconnected this contraption meant the medic told the truth, or so he assumed. Frankly, they could've discharged him earlier, Greenberg said. They kept him for two reasons:

protection against himself, and extra tests. The physician had subjected James to a bunch of blood and urine samples, various X-rays, and other procedures useless for his condition. A precaution in case James required further medical attention, he was told. Humans possessed a similar physiology to Nirnivians, but differences existed, and the more Greenberg knew about his body, the better he'd perform his job. That explanation seemed logical, so when asked for consent, James had agreed without hesitation.

Before long, a single piece of egg remained on James's dish. He felt full, yet he stuck the remaining food with his fork and brought it toward his lips, only to drop it instinctively the moment Commander Ricdeau entered the room. The senior advanced at a brisk pace, emanating confidence with every resounding step. Surprised, the nurse froze as she spotted the old man. James detected a slight tremble in her hand. Then she attempted a nervous military salute. Daniel offered a smile and a nod.

"No need for that. You're not under my command. Please, ignore me and continue what you were doing."

The caretaker acquiesced. "Yes, sir!" With that, she returned to her scrubbing.

The Commander approached the bed with his fingers joined in a pyramid until he stood beside James. His grin widened. "Hey there, my boy, I thought I'd check on you. You gave us quite a scare."

"Sorry about that, sir, I don't know what I was thinking." James blushed. "Thank God Rose was there."

"Yes... the doctor said they'll release you tomorrow. I can see why, you look great! Careful, ladies, there's a new hunter on the prowl." He gave a wink. "Ah, I kid, I kid. But I don't have much time, so I'll cut to the chase." Then Mr. Ricdeau turned sideways, but the motion failed to conceal his slight frown. "I didn't just I come here to chat. I want to talk to you about Rose."

James's muscles tensed. "Really? What about her?"

"Well, I've heard there was a fight between you two." He gave a shake of the head and waved his own words away. "No, that's too dramatic... it was more like an argument."

"Oh, that was nothing, sir. I, uh—it was stupid of me. The whole Melkar thing freaked me out and..."

"No need to explain, I get it!" He patted him on the shoulder. "You don't learn your friend is a prophet every day. It's heavy stuff." There was a short pause, then he opened his mouth, only to hesitate a second longer.

"Listen, James, you're not the only one who feels intimated by Rose's special gift. She's always been isolated as a result. Because of this, she enjoys your company"—Daniel adopted a half-smile—"and if you enjoy hers too, that's great. And I hope it's the case, but you don't have to feel the same way she does, if you catch my drift." The senior cleared his throat.

"Look, I know you're thinking you better get along with Rose given your living arrangements, but if you'd rather not deal with the Melkar business, go ahead and say so. If you pretend to be her friend, she'll only get hurt. People are always kissing her holy butt, pardon my language. She can smell phonies a mile away. Don't worry, we'll take care of you either way. We'll move you out of Valardir, somewhere safe, and we'll protect you. I'll have to figure out the details, but no biggie."

"Well, uh..." Shaking, James scratched the back of his head. "I've enjoyed the time I've spent with Rose so far. It's awkward right now between us, but I'm hoping we can get past it. I'd like to stay. Uh, unless you think I should go."

"No, no, my boy. I'm not trying to get rid of you. You're welcome to stay. I'm only a father looking out for his daughter. She's an adult, so I shouldn't be doing this, but... well, you'll understand when you have children." Daniel faced James again. "There's one last thing. Since the... let's call it 'incident' happened, we decided to take precautions. We don't want you to end up here again, my boy. There'll be people checking in on you regularly, and you'll meet a military psychiatrist, Dr. Nigel Crane." The Commander waggled a warning index finger. "Don't even try to get out of it. It's mandatory. He's great. I consulted him after a disturbing mission. Anyway, that's about it for me." He gave another tap on the shoulder. "Take care, James!"

My body relaxed as he walked away. He seemed like a nice guy, but he had an intensity to him. Maybe it's just because he was in charge and I knew it.

—Thoughts of James Hunter, Hocmar 28, 2134, on the Nirnivian calendar

Chapter 3

Crumpled in his chair, Jonathan Rivers stared at his computer screen. He reread the email he'd received over and over again, slapping his brow each time he finished. No matter how often he studied the text, it remained the same nonsense he had witnessed earlier. Logical as that fact might be, he kept hoping his eyes deceived him, only to end up disappointed. After countless attempts, he grunted. What were the bigwigs smoking? He'd warned them, yet he suspected they might claim otherwise once the dust settled. The fools asked the impossible and, unsatisfied by their stupidity, they threw additional monkey wrenches in his path, which further complicated the task at hand.

Interrupting his inner monologue, the sound of the door sliding open behind him echoed. "Oh boy, I've seen this posture before. What's got you so glum?"

Though his guest faced his back, Jonathan recognized the firm yet paradoxically soft voice. Brian, his good friend and colleague, paid him a visit. "The shit's about to hit the fan." Jonathan adjusted his glasses. "Remember how they want us to do a year of security 'adjustments' in four months?"

A forced chuckle came from Brian. "How could I forget?"

"Well, just when you think they can't screw us any deeper, they find an extra inch or two." At last, Jonathan spun his seat around and looked at his pal. Dressed in a black three-piece suit and a white shirt complemented by a red tie, Brian had a fashion sense that surpassed that of many NISDA officers. A subtle whiff of cologne tickled Jonathan's nostrils. No doubt he took greater care with his appearance than the majority in their profession. "They sent me a list of the equipment they'll ship over." He scoffed. "They ignored my recommendations and went for cheap parts."

"I wish I could be surprised, but..."

"Yeah, yeah, no shit, I know." Jonathan shook his head. "But it's worse than usual. They want us to fill the place with motion detectors. If you're trying to keep out an invisible guy, it makes sense, I guess, but it's experimental technology. Or if you prefer, it doesn't work yet, and they're freaking rare since they're not mass-produced! I tell them it's crazy, but maybe it'll be tolerable if they follow my specs, and it'll cost them a bundle to get so many units on short notice. They're all nodding along. 'Yes, sure, the Melkar's safety is a priority, money isn't a concern.' I figure they lied, 'cause the stuff they're sending us isn't up to snuff. We'll get false positives up the wazoo."

"Is it really that bad?"

"Oh yes."

Brian sighed. "Crap. Jonathan, I understand why you're angry, and I'm worried too, but to be fair"—footsteps resounded as he advanced toward an empty chair waiting beside his companion. The sharp-looking man sat backward with his arms folded around the stiles—"the budget is tight."

"Yeah, sure, but if you can't pay for your insanely expensive dumbass plan, don't buy it!" He groaned. "They even messed up the cameras." Of all the suggested improvements, the thermal cameras proved the only one he agreed with. Level three and below already used them.

They were a reliable technology and a perfect match for the current problem. Unfortunately, the bean counters had convinced those in charge to opt for inferior models and save a few bucks. Not as troublesome as the motion sensors issue, but annoying nonetheless. "Hey, what should I expect from a bunch of idiots who believe in a bird-brained prophet?"

"Whoa, now," Alarmed, Brian rose and shielded his chest with his palms. "Not so loud. You don't want anyone else to hear that kind of talk."

"Why not? Doesn't Nirnivia have religious freedom? I'm allowed to be an atheist."

"In theory, yes, but I wouldn't test it in practice if I were you. There are many zealots out there who might not appreciate your views."

"Don't I know it." After a shrug, Jonathan dismissed his own comment with a wave. "Whatever. My point is, this whole project will be a total fiasco, and they'll blame us."

"That sounds probable, but there's nothing we can do about it. Who knows, it could turn out fine."

Chapter 4

Mashar 30, 2133, on the Nirnivian calendar

The next morning, James woke up early and received breakfast from a nurse. This time, the meal ended up being some kind of gruel accompanied by fruits and proved as tasteless as usual. Not long after James finished and wiped his mouth clean, Dr. Greenberg stepped into the clinic and walked over to the bed. The medic carried a clipboard. He handed it to James and began an overview of the discharge papers.

It was all just a bunch of legal mumbo jumbo. I didn't understand the specifics, but it was obviously to cover their asses. The kind of thing no one really reads. I guessed there were lawyers in this universe too.

—Thoughts of James Hunter, Hocmar 28, 2134, on the Nirnivian calendar

"So, when you're ready, you can sign here and you'll be good to go." Dr. Greenberg tapped the signature line at the bottom of the document. "Don't forget, you have an appointment with a therapist, Dr. Nigel Crane, this afternoon at one thirty. He has an excellent reputation, and I'm sure he'll help you."

Then Greenberg's mouth twisted a tad, and he scowled. "I want to be clear—you're free to go, but you don't have to if you'd rather stay until your appointment. You can even come back after if you—"

"That won't be necessary. He's coming with me," a sultry female voice echoed. Both men stared at the source, which happened to be a beaming Janice Ricdeau. Instead of the uniform most wore in Valardir, she wore a pair of jeans and a strapless red sweetheart shirt, giving her a casual appearance. "We're going to the rec room together right after you sign that thing and get dressed."

"Uh, I don't know, I—"

"No buts." Janice bent over, resting her arms on the bed's footboard. The posture showcased her assets in a most impressive fashion, but James focused on her eyes nonetheless. "It's the Commander's order. Dad thinks you're spending too much time alone, so he gave me the morning off and told me to bring you to the rec room so you could meet people." She waggled a menacing finger. "You're not gonna disobey him, are you, buddy? He's a meanie. I should know, he raised me."

James shrugged. "Yeah, I guess I have to."

"Geez, you sound so thrilled. Wow, I feel really appreciated right about now." She giggled. "Come on, don't be so shy. It'll be fine, I swear. We'll have a ton of fun! First, take care of that." She gestured toward the clipboard. Resisting a sigh, James grabbed it as well as the pen and wrote his name on the designated spot. The instant he finished, Janice straightened. "Okay, great, let's go!"

James stroked his ear. "Uh, I'm still in this hospital gown."

"Oh... what are you waiting for? Get dressed!" Cross-armed, she kept her eyes fixed on him. A few seconds passed with James doing nothing but blushing. "Ooh la la, come on." She laughed. "Nah, I'm messing with you, buddy. Here." With that, she turned around. "Boy, what a convenient mirror! Kidding!"

I would have preferred it if she'd left the room while I dressed, but whatever. I slowly removed my gown and reached for my normal clothes. Let's just say I wasn't in a hurry. My stance on hanging out with the soldiers hadn't changed one bit. At least with Janice, I was pretty sure they wouldn't dare complain or try anything, but I expected some contrived conversations in my future.

—Thoughts of James Hunter, Hocmar 28, 2134, on the Nirnivian calendar

***

A sickness in his stomach assailed James as they entered the recreation room, but mostly for nothing. Two lone soldiers populated the area, the first being a burly man sitting on the sofa and puffing out his cheeks. As for the second, it turned out to be a dark-haired and dark-skinned woman standing in front of an arcade machine, waggling the joystick. She punctuated her effort with encouragement for the character she controlled and even a few curses.

The moment she arrived, Janice waved and said, "Hey, guys!"

The big fellow spun his head and nodded. He then presented his palm, and Janice delivered the requested high five. "Yo, Janice, what's up, girl?" He pointed at the TV. "Can ya believe they haven't fixed that damn thing yet? I'm missing my show, gal."

A chuckle came from Janice. "Yeah, they're taking their sweet time."

"Can you try to pull a few strings with your old man?"

"Like have him put some pressure on the techs?" Janice dismissed the notion with a flick of the hand. "Nah, I won't do that to them. They're busy enough as it is."

"Right, right, the security bullshit." The guy snapped his fingers. "I kinda forgot. Must be why we ain't got no tube."

Through the exchange, James remained silent and fixed his gaze on the floor. He hoped to minimize his presence, but regardless, the man pointed his chin toward him. "A friend o' yours?"

"Yeah, that's my buddy, James." As she uttered the words, Janice subtly pulled James's arm so he'd approach. "He's, uh, the new guy. You've heard of him. He's a bit shy, so I'm forcing him to meet people and have fun!"

The man snickered. "Yeah, sounds like you all right."

Janice ignored the comment and focused on James. "This dude here's Charlie. He's pretty cool, just don't bother him when he's watching TV. Charlie, this is James."

Right on cue, Charlie jumped to his feet. "Yo, man, what's up?" He raised his fist, and after a second of hesitation, James provided the demanded bump.

"Not much…" Though he almost stopped himself, he somehow managed to continue. "Letting Janice boss me around." For her reply, Janice responded with a playful extension of the tongue.

"Ha ha!" Charlie fired a glance at Janice. "That sounds like you too!"

"Whatever, bud."

"Oh yeah, James, I saw you hang out with Her Holiness. That's awesome. I'd like to meet her, but shit, it's intimidating. Can't just go up to a prophet and say hi, right?" He grunted and bobbed his head at Janice. "I asked this one to introduce me, but she ain't gonna do it."

The Melkar's sibling shrugged. "I've been away for months, and she's busy. I'll get around to it."

"Don't believe ya, Ricdeau!" He concentrated again on James. "Hey, pal, how 'bout you introduce me to her one of these days?"

"Yeah, sure, why not?"

The conversation went on from there. It was a bit awkward, but I felt like he was trying to be nice and give me a chance. That was already way better than I expected based on previous experiences. Eventually, he had to leave, though, and Janice had an idea.

—Thoughts of James Hunter, Hocmar 28, 2134, on the Nirnivian calendar

"Hey, James, wanna try a game of Rubarg?"

"I don't know what that is."

She giggled. "You'll be fine! I'll teach you along the way. It's nothing compared to Kuhard." Janice gave him a playful nudge in the ribs. "I bet you're having fun with that!"

James swallowed hard. "Uh, yeah, you could say that, I guess."

"Never managed to learn that one myself, so props for trying."

The duo walked toward a hexagonal table. A thick border guarded its edges, and a reddish rug formed the surface within. Holes graced every point of the contour, while near the middle of the table rested a diamond composed of several numbered balls. Upon the wall was a mounted rack holding a bunch of sticks.

The shape was different, but a little bird told me I had an idea what Rubarg was after all. No, I don't mean Rose, that's silly!

—Thoughts of James Hunter, Hocmar 28, 2134, on the Nirnivian calendar

"By the way"—Janice grabbed a cue and brandished it at the woman enjoying the arcade cabinet—"that's Patricia. Hey, Patricia, I'd like to introduce you to my buddy, James, if you have a minute."

Her gaze remained fixated on the screen. "Hi, James! I've heard about you. I'd shake your hand, but I'm somewhat bu—" A disappointed jingle echoed and Patricia stifled a swear. "Never mind, looks like I'm not that busy." The female soldier spun around and offered James the promised handshake, which he accepted promptly. "Hey, guys, tell you what, I'll challenge the winner, all right?"

Janice shrugged. "Yeah, sure, no probs." Then she wavered. "That's okay with you, James?"

"Oh yeah."

"Great, grab a cue and we'll start. I'll break."

The instant she uttered the sentence, Janice laid a white ball on the table and took aim. She struck it and the orb rolled toward the diamond composed of its colored siblings. After a thud, each then moved in their own direction, but none reached what James assumed to be a coveted hole.

"Guess it's your turn." Smiling, Janice wrapped her arm around James's shoulder and pulled him closer. Her body grazed his, and blood rushed to his cheeks. "It's easy enough. You try to put the right balls in the pockets with the cue. You're number thirteen to twenty-four. Thing is, you can't hit the ball directly, though, you have to do it with the white one." She drew him nearer still, a whiff of her perfume caressing his nostrils, and whispered in his ear. "Wanna cheat? If I were you, I'd go for ball number eighteen, the orange one over there. See, it's almost perfectly aligned."

Tensed beyond what a simple game should cause, James gulped and targeted the sphere. Memories of past pool games entered his mind. All the occasions where he'd missed and Patrick had mocked him with friendly yet still hurtful smack talk. Despite his effort, the projectile ended up ricocheting a few millimeters left of the hole. With a sigh, Janice let him go and patted his back.

"So close... but don't despair, you'll have another chance!" Then she hunched over the table right in front of James. The posture accentuated her hindmost assets, and he reddened even more before averting his gaze. "Hey, James, by the way"—she straightened, forsaking her shot—"thanks for hanging out with Rose. She's too isolated, so it's nice to see you spend time with her."

James scratched the back of his skull. "Um, you said it yourself, I'm isolated too, so it's win-win, really."

"Yeah, I guess. But I appreciate it, and Dad too." She closed her eyes. "I worry about her." She gave a scowl. "She pushes herself too hard for Nirnivia's sake, and prophet or not, she's still only a person. James, I... listen, I get it. The whole Melkar deal, it must be so freaking weird for you, but please don't let that push you away from her. She's not the type who lords her status over others, and you mean a lot to her."

There was something wrong... something strange, a contrast between her words and how I had seen her act before. I wanted to tell her... tell her I was sure she meant a lot to Rose too and she should spend some time with her sister. She'd appreciate it. But I... I couldn't. The words stayed stuck in my throat. I'm such a coward.

—Thoughts of James Hunter, Hocmar 28, 2134, on the Nirnivian calendar

"I... I know. And she means a lot to me too."

"Good." On that note, she refocused on the task at hand and sank a ball, meaning she could replay.

At that moment, the door opened and a tall black-haired man with almond-shaped eyes like Janice's entered. He waved to the trio and said, "Hey, guys! I'll play against the winner, all right?"

Janice chuckled. "Sorry, Dylan, Patricia beat you to it."

"Next round, then!"

I lost the match, but it was fun and the soldiers weren't as mean as I feared. There was some discomfort there, but a genuine effort to welcome the human guy. I was glad Janice forced me into it. After my defeat, Patricia crushed Janice and then Dylan. She had real skills at Rubarg but had to leave, and Janice let me try my luck against Dylan. Let's just say my luck ran out... nah, wait... that implies I had some in the first place.

—Thoughts of James Hunter, Hocmar 28, 2134, on the Nirnivian calendar

The match done, Dylan gave James a thumbs-up. "Nice one, man! You're pretty good for a first-timer! Well, guys, I've got to eat, so I'll see ya later." On that note, he left, and as if agreeing with the statement, Janice's stomach grumbled.

"Hey, he's right, we're like five minutes past lunchtime. Wanna join me, buddy?"

"Yeah, sure!"

Chapter 5

It took us just three or four minutes to get to the cafeteria, but we were still technically late and we paid the price—so to speak. With the length of the line, we'd be there for a while. Ah well, at least it gave me a chance to figure out what I wanted to eat.

—Thoughts of James Hunter, Hocmar 28, 2134, on the Nirnivian calendar

The queue advanced at a slow pace, so James and Janice passed the time with chitchat. Nothing particularly relevant; they exchanged tidbits about their daily lives and discussed rumors circulating around Valardir. Every few minutes, someone completed their order, allowing the rest to step a few paces forward. Little by little, they proceeded this way until they had almost reached the counter. Now able to view the menu fixed on the wall, James studied the available options. He had memorized the whole list several weeks ago, and yet he read it on each visit as if not trusting his memory. Then a feminine voice calling his name, or rather surname, echoed. Surprised, he turned and saw Rose in the distance. Tired but still smiling, she walked toward him. Brucie trailed her and offered a wink, though James suspected it targeted Janice.

"Hunter! Janice!" she said once close enough. "I'm so happy to see you here, guys! I'm sorry, Hunter, I wanted to be there when the clinic discharged you, but it's been a crazy morning."

"Oh, it's fine. I understand. Besides, Janice took care of me, so no worries."

Rose giggled. "Thanks, Janice! I owe you one."

The older sibling dismissed the remark with a wave, though her gaze missed Rose's face by a long shot. "Nah, I meant to drag him to the rec room for a while anyway."

Smirking, Brucie slid beside Janice and wrapped his arm around her shoulder. "Hey, babe!" The stare Janice fired prompted him to withdraw the embrace. James assumed perhaps the threat of being punched in the dick encouraged the strategic retreat. "Ya should bring me along, ya know? Rubarg's my jam!"

A roll of the eyes came from the gigantic woman. "You were busy doing your job, remember? Protecting my sister and all that? Ring a bell?"

"Oh, yeah..." Brucie stifled a chuckle. "Next time?"

"Yeah, sure, whatever."

"Hey, do you guys mind if we join you for lunch?" The alleged prophet joined her fingers in anticipation. "It'd be fun and, Janice, we haven't had the chance to really talk since you've come back."

James almost answered, "Of course," but Janice replied before him. "Um, actually"—a frown appeared on her brow, and she glanced toward the left—"I'm only grabbing a sandwich and I'll eat on the go. I have to make up the hours I spent with James."

She lied. No doubt about it. I mean, it was obvious. It was her idea to have lunch with me. She only split when Rose showed up. And besides, she'd told me her dad had given her time off so she could spend the morning with me. I had a feeling Janice was trying to avoid Rose, and this pretty much confirmed it. What was going on between those two? I wondered if I should tell Rose Janice had lied to her, but I decided not to. I didn't want to start a fight between them, especially since I didn't know why Janice was acting this way. Maybe she had a good reason.

—Thoughts of James Hunter, Hocmar 28, 2134, on the Nirnivian calendar

"Oh, okay." Rose bent her head down and ran her hand through her hair. "Well, maybe tomorrow?"

"Yeah, I'll see what I can do."

***

The trio consisting of Rose, Brucie and James sat at a table situated to the right of the cafeteria. None of them spoke. They each stared at their plate in silence. Even Brucie, the blunt bodyguard, kept his tongue still and avoided his often crude attempts at humor. Remove the sound of utensils scraping the plates and James might have fooled himself into imagining he dined alone. His appetite failed him, and except for the occasional bite, he mostly played with his food. Cutting his meat and tumbling the pieces, things like that. Several minutes of quiet torture passed. James debated attempting a conversation, but in the end, Rose spared him.

"You look well, Hunter," she said, glancing at him before her pupils darted downward again.

"Uh, yeah, I'm feeling all right."

"Good!" An awkward pause followed for a few seconds. "Dad told me you have an appointment with a military psychologist, Nigel Crane."

"Yeah…" James trembled, and he almost dropped his fork. "I'll have to go there right after lunch. I don't even know where it is."

"We'll have someone escort you." The prophet reached for her glass and tried a sip. "Nigel has an excellent reputation. He'll be able to help you through this, I'm sure. Actually, I wish I could consult him too."

I almost asked why she couldn't but stopped midsentence. It wasn't my business, and really, I didn't want to talk about it. I wasn't comfortable with the idea of meeting a shrink in the first place. Never put much stock into therapy.

—Thoughts of James Hunter, Hocmar 28, 2134, on the Nirnivian calendar

"Rose, um"—conflicted, James's lips contorted—"I did something stupid, but I'm fine now. I won't try anything like that again, I swear."

"I believe you, but still... you went through a major change in your life, a traumatic change, even. I can't imagine what it's like. We should've arranged a meeting with Nigel right from the start, and..." She sighed. "You'd rather change the subject, wouldn't you?" Cheeks reddening, James nodded. "I'm sorry, I can't help but worry after what happened, but I'll do my best to put it aside and move on."

Brucie exhaled in relief. "'Bout time, ya know? It's getting all kinda gloomy here." He grunted. "Whole drama is messing with my style."

Annoyed, Rose's jaw tightened as she squinted. "Yes, Brucie, that's what is important right now."

The bodyguard joined his hands behind his head and smirked. "At least ya admit it!"

"I—" She dismissed him with a wave. "Never mind. Hunter, we hardly know anything about you. What kind of life did you live back home?" She blushed and averted her gaze. "Oh, I shouldn't ask about that so soon after. I'm sorry, I don't mean to remind you."

"No, no, it's fine." In an attempt at delaying his response, James chewed a bit of food. "My life was simple. Very boring."

Despite obvious efforts to stifle her laugh, it came through. "Oh, come on, what kind of answer is that?"

"An accurate one." James chuckled and shook his head ever so slightly. "Look, I was just a clerk for a lame convenience store. I sold petty merchandise for a living. A job befitting a loser like me."

A compassionate smile appeared on Rose's face. The red-headed woman leaned forward and patted James's hand. It was such a gentle touch that he barely felt it. Still, the gesture startled him and he almost recoiled. "You're not a loser. You did an honest job. I'd even say an important one. You provided a service and there's nothing wrong with that."

"Yeah, she's right, man." Brucie leaned back, joined his hands behind his head and crossed his legs. "Superior dudes like me need peasant servants, ya know."

"Shut up, Brucie." Rose aimed an icy glare at him, and he hushed as commanded. "Ignore that jerk. He finds himself funny, but he's not. Hunter, you have nothing to be ashamed of. You're not a loser. There are people who steal, lie, and cheat so they can fulfill their selfish desires: those are losers. You survived with honest work. That's a winner in my book."

"Yeah, well, it's not exactly a glamorous job either."

Rose scoffed, rolling her eyes. "Glamour, that's pointless. Nothing but a pleasant distraction that too often steers people toward nothingness. Anyway, Hunter, if you hated your job so much, why not do something else?"

I didn't like the discussion. It reminded me of those talks I'd had with Nadia lately, how she'd slowly realized she de-

served a better man and got ever closer to dumping my sorry ass. I wondered how long it would take before Rose decided I was a waste of time. How long before she forgot I existed? What would happen then? Maybe nothing, or maybe I'd end up in the streets, where I'd die of hunger.

—Thoughts of James Hunter, Hocmar 28, 2134, on the Nirnivian calendar

After a moment of hesitation, James answered. Disappointment tainted his words. "I tried, but I always failed somehow. I wanted to do something important. Like a doctor, an inventor, or a police officer. I was never good in school. I'm not smart or strong. I only managed to get dead-end jobs. My parents... God bless them, they love me, but I can tell they're disappointed. They always thought I was special. Guess they were wrong. I mean, that's logical, right? Every damn parent thinks their child is special. Some of them—ah, hell, most of them have got to be wrong."

"Maybe you fail because you believe you can't succeed."

Unimpressed by the musing, James's body shifted a bit toward the left. "Yeah, right!"

"Okay, I can see this isn't a happy subject. Let's try something else. Did you have friends?"

The tension in James's muscles decreased. "Well, I was never one of the cool kids, but I did have friends. Mostly others who didn't fit in."

"I wish I had been a normal little girl with real friends." The corners of Rose's mouth turned down. A touch of envy stained her voice, and that astonished James. Nobody had ever been jealous of him. Quite the opposite, they'd thanked God they weren't him. "How about your girlfriend? Nadia, Right?"

"Good memory! She's something. Beautiful, smart, kind. She's great, I don't understand why she's with a guy like me. She could do so much better."

In my mind, I added, "And she realizes it more and more." I figured it wouldn't do any good to say that part out loud.

—Thoughts of James Hunter, Hocmar 28, 2134, on the Nirnivian calendar

Rose moved on her seat. "Tell me, Hunter, if you were to show up home tomorrow, how would people react?"

"Um…" He shivered. "I guess they'd be relieved. It's been weeks now?"

"So, your parents, Nadia, your friends, they'd be happy to have you back?"

"That's an understatement." James gave a nervous cackle. "I mean, they must've figured I'm dead. They'd be ecstatic."

Rose beamed. "Then you're more important than you think."

Now that I'm here and confronted with this cruel decision, I wonder: was she right? Did I actually matter? Did I make a difference so far? Who knows, but the choice I make now might change everything. A pointless existence doesn't seem all that bad anymore…

—Thoughts of James Hunter, Hocmar 28, 2134, on the Nirnivian calendar

Chapter 6

Mashar 31, 2133, on the Nirnivian calendar

Pen in hand, Rose scribbled over the mistake until a blue blotch covered it. The deed done, she then wrote the correct spelling next to her previous error. Most people, including her mother, questioned her habit of writing sermons the old-fashioned way. Indeed, a word processor offered many conveniences. One look at the crossed-out words littering her document proved that fact. In a few places, arrows indicated that sentences or even paragraphs should be moved, rendering the text hard to follow. A computer solved that issue, and she often considered modernizing her methods, but when she tried, she tended to stare at the screen for hours without progress. Handwriting set her imagination free. She produced turns of phrase she'd never dreamed of when at a keyboard. Even the sound of the pen scribbling on the paper comforted her. Sure, the result might be confusing, but that was better than a blank page. Besides, Kristina took her draft and typed it before her actual speech.

Thinking of her assistant, Rose paused her work and gazed upward. The blond woman sat at a desk near her and toiled on her minicomp as usual. Across the room, Brucie surveyed the scene with fingers joined behind his head. He and Kristina didn't quite gel. The bodyguard possessed a peculiar sense of humor, and his style failed to amuse Kristina. Rose finally ordered him to keep his distance, mentioning that if Kristina complained or considered quitting, she'd fire him. Though attached to Brucie, her assistant provided greater aid, and she couldn't envision living without her. Thankfully, he obeyed, even if the situation annoyed him. He meant no harm, Rose knew that, but whether he intended to or not, he often pushed jokes too far for his own good. Once Brucie noticed she watched him, he winked at her. Rose ignored him and returned to her revisions.

"Rose," Kristina said less than a minute later, "just a reminder that your meeting with the Kenneth Foundation starts in half an hour."

"What? Oh no!"

"You didn't forget, did you?" Kristina adopted a defensive scowl. "I reminded you this morning, and yesterday."

"Yes, I remember, but I didn't think it was this late." Rose bit her lip. "I have a sermon tomorrow, and it's not even close to finished." Her cheeks blushed. "Kristina, I'm so sorry, I shouldn't ask this as it isn't part of your tasks, but could you finish writing the rest for me?"

"Yes, no problem."

"I know it's inappropriate, and you're overworked, but please. The research is all done, and I have notes." Then Rose realized Kristina was well aware of this, given she had performed said research, and her cheeks reddened further. "It's just putting it all together and cleaning it up."

A rare giggle escaped from Kristina. "I already said yes!"

Rose exhaled in relief. "Thank you! You're a lifesaver!"

"You're welcome!" Not a tinge of sarcasm tainted her voice, and that impressed Rose.

"Oh, and please don't mention this to anyone."

The assistant mimed zipping up her lips, thus assuring her discretion. A wave of tension left Rose. If Madeleine heard that Rose had asked Kristina for such a favor, she'd be furious. Her mother would claim she'd failed in her duties. She pictured the head priestess lecturing her about how, no matter how busy she became, her role as the Melkar took precedence. Also, even though Kristina displayed great competence, she lacked credibility when it came to religious matters. A fair point, yet Rose wasn't worried for a second. As much as she hated admitting her failings in this regard, Kristina had edited her sermons on two or three occasions before, and she excelled at the task. It wasn't that surprising, as Kristina excelled at everything she threw at her, be it by natural talent or relentless labor.

"I better get ready." She smiled at Kristina. "Thanks, I don't deserve you."

***

Rose forced herself to stay immobile as her technician installed the microphone. After years of video conferencing, one might expect she'd learned the process, but the technology baffled her much as it had on the first day. Remove her tech and she'd be lost, a reality she accepted.

On the screen before her, an animated hourglass played above the words "Waiting for the other party to join." The Kenneth Foundation's representatives hadn't showed up yet; not surprising, given she had joined the virtual meeting room early. Punctuality was a virtue she sometimes lacked, but Kristina offset that weakness.

A minute passed and two men replaced the icon. On the right sat Max Kenneth, a Perz sporting a dress shirt and the manager of the Kenneth Foundation, succeeding his father. The headscarf covering his hair failed to conceal his scowl, and between that and his crossed arms, Rose sensed a certain impatience from him. Speaking of the black-and-white headpiece, it contrasted with the professionalism expected of a man in his position, though Rose understood its purpose. A large eye rested on Max's brow, a mutation he had suffered since birth. Max felt no shame about his condition and would've shown it with pride, but alas, the gigantic eyeball proved sensitive to light. When it was exposed to anything but pure darkness, violent headaches assailed Max, explaining the garment.

Meanwhile, the Brig sitting to the right, Leon Serath, radiated with serenity. His face displayed a smile. With his short blond hair, delicate glasses and a sharp black suit, he resonated with style. Perhaps the tentacle serving as his left hand diminished his beauty for some, but it suited his role as the foundation's second-in-command.

Leon offered a respectful bow, then said, "Thank you again, Your Holiness, for meeting us. We know how busy you are and we greatly appreciate it. You've always been beyond generous with the Kenneth Foundation, and we're hoping you'll help us once again."

"With pleasure." Touched, her voice broke a little. "Mutants are the one group still facing major discrimination, and it must change. There are other charities that need my financial support, but I'm sure I can arrange to donate more money. Let me consult my fina—"

"We don't need your money, Your Holiness." The instant Max uttered this sentence, Leon turned his head and glared at him. After a mere second, the reaction passed, and his focus returned to Rose. "We need you."

With a harrumph, Leon lifted his index finger. "Let me explain. From birth, mutants are at a disadvantage. Most mutant families are below the poverty line and have no recourse but to live in a less-than-reputable neighborhood. Because of this, mutant children are assigned to inferior schools and often go to class hungry. If they ever graduate, it doesn't get better." He frowned. "Job interviews are tough enough by default, and in my experience, showing up with one of these"—he brandished his tentacle—"doesn't make a good first impression. I could go on and on, but the short version is that it's hard growing up as a mutant. Our youths are discouraged, so they don't see the point of trying."

Empathic, Rose lowered her head. "I can understand the sentiment."

A snort came from Max. "Yeah, why work your butt off if you get crapped on for it anyway?"

Again, Leon stared at Max, but this time he lingered, as if he didn't mind whether Rose noticed anymore. "I'd rather not put it as crudely as my colleague, but he does paint a vivid picture."

After enduring the glare for a moment, Max shrugged and grunted. "I apologize for my language, Your Holiness. It slipped out." He chuckled. "Leon's supposed to do the talking."

Rose dismissed the notion with a wave. "It's okay, I've heard far worse."

A nod came from Leon. "Yes, I'm quite sure you have." He moistened his lips. "In any event, this poses a major dilemma for our cause. When you are at a disadvantage, you have to try harder for a shot at success. It's unfair, but it's how it is, and if we wait until that changes on its own, it'll be a while." He gave a sigh. "Because our youth is disillusioned, they tend to give up on themselves. And from there, it's a vicious circle. People view mutants negatively, causing them to sink further into poverty, and as a result, the general opinion of mutants worsens. The cycle must be broken. While it would be only fair if the so-called 'normies' broke it, since they're the ones who created it, realistically, I think it will have to be us."

Leon clenched his lone fist. "Mutants need to show their worth, prove we're equal to everyone else. For that to happen, we need to motivate young mutants. What better way than real-life experience? That's why we are searching for spokespersons, people who, despite their mutations, have attained respected positions in society and can speak about how they overcame the odds. Max and I would be honored if you'd be one of them."

Stunned, Rose remained immobile for an instant and then blinked twice in rapid succession before pointing at herself. "Me?"

Max leaned forward and grinned. "Well, yeah, you identify as a mutant, don't you?"

A scowl appeared on Rose's forehead. "Um, yes, I do. Personally, I believe my wings are a mutation and not a divine phenomenon."

Max raised an inquisitive eyebrow. "Then what's the problem?"

"Max, that's enough." Enraged, Leon jumped to his feet, and his cheeks reddened. Once Max relented, his calm demeanor returned and he took his seat. "Please forgive him, he is a brusque man but extremely devoted to the cause." Leon stroked behind his ear with his index finger. "However, he has a point. You are the most respected person in Nirnivia, adored by millions as the Melkar, and you are even the first mutant councillor. You are an inspiration to us all!"

Rose rubbed her brow. "I'm sorry, but I can't accept. It would send the wrong message. The only reason anyone takes me seriously is because they believe I'm a prophet. To have me be a spokesperson is like saying that to be successful, you have to convince people you're not a mutant." A sense of indignation tainted her voice. "Mutants shouldn't have to hide who they are to realize their dreams." She exhaled. "Besides, I never faced the discrimination our kind suffers. It'd be hypocritical to pretend I have."

Leon acquiesced. "Maybe you haven't been through what Max or I endured. But you are a symbol of hope and tolerance. It can work."

Reluctantly, Rose shook her head. "The notion that I may be a mutant is very unpopular. If I parade around the country as a spokesperson for the Kenneth Foundation, claiming I'm a mutant, the Nirnivian public will accuse you of heresy. You'll be reviled and your foundation will crumble. I've supported the Kenneth Foundation and mutant rights all my life, and I don't just mean with money. I've spoken about the subject on multiple occasions in my sermons, defended mutants when they were unfairly treated. I will continue helping you in your fight, but not as one of your own." A few tears graced her eyes. "I wish I could. I'd love to stand with my fellow mutants as one of them. But if I do, I'll hurt them, so I can't accept." Her volume reduced to a whisper. "I'm sorry."

Stunned, Leon finally mumbled, "Your Holiness..."

Max's jaw tightened. "Forget it, Leon. She talks big, but she doesn't care enough to help."

"Don't be so cruel, Max. She raised valid concerns."

"Wait," said Rose, interrupting the potential fight. "I can't in good conscience be a spokesperson, but I know someone who'd be perfect."

Chapter 7

Mashar 33, 2133, on the Nirnivian calendar

James endured another boring day. With no activity in mind and lacking company, he remembered Rose had mentioned during breakfast that the techs had fixed the recreation room's TV. Having nothing better to do, James decided he'd check it out. Besides, television from another universe sounded interesting. Who knew what kind of strange programs he would discover? Perhaps some drama or a sitcom, or a simple news show... even the last one might be entertaining given how little he understood this world.

As James entered, he noticed Rose standing before the monitor, clutching the remote. She stood perfectly immobile and stared at the screen, absorbing every detail. On the couch, he found Brucie the bodyguard crumpled and twiddling his fingers. Due to Rose's intense concentration, James assumed she watched something important and deduced he'd better leave her alone for now. He considered returning to his quarters, but Brucie waved for him to come forward. Once near enough, James remarked the television displayed a meteorological broadcast. Various graphics indicated the coming weather while a droning voice explained what the images already made clear: heavy rain for the next few hours.

"Hey, dude. What's up?" Brucie asked.

"Not much. What about you guys?"

"I dunno. We got 'nother freaking lame-ass meeting, ya know. Rose saw the weather guy go on and on 'bout rain, and she just froze there! We're late and she ain't listening to me."

"I miss the rain," Rose said in a mere whisper.

A frown wrinkled James's brow. "Uh, you miss the rain?" From his own mouth, the words sounded even stranger.

Rose kept ogling the TV. "Yeah, I love the rain. I used to walk around in it, sometimes for hours. We don't get much rain in this underground complex. I miss it."

I certainly didn't share her love for rain. I considered it a necessary evil at best. Nothing I hated more than being surprised by a sudden shower. Besides, walking around in the rain for hours sounds like a bad idea. Maybe she had a pneumonia wish?

—Thoughts of James Hunter, Hocmar 28, 2134, on the Nirnivian calendar

"What's so great about walking around all wet anyway?"

"Nothing, really..." Finally, she turned her head toward James, forced a smile and winked. "Just another one of my mysteries." She then gazed upon Brucie. "We should get going, big man."

"Hey, sure. Ain't me who stopped, ya know."

Mysteries... Nirnivia had plenty of those. They were piling up a bit too much for my liking, but I guess trying to figure them out gave me something to do.

—Thoughts of James Hunter, Hocmar 28, 2134, on the Nirnivian calendar

Chapter 8

Tigal 5, 2133, on the Nirnivian calendar

The lighting ended up being the hardest part for Commander Daniel Ricdeau. Numerous spotlights shone upon him, causing sweat to drip from his brow. He'd performed well on his fair share of press interviews during his career, but he never got used to this aspect.

Several people sat with Daniel at the conference table. On his left, Max Kenneth and Leon Serath from the foundation could be seen. The two mutants beamed with pride. Max even wore a tie for the occasion, a garment he despised. To Daniel's immediate right, Doug Thomson and Jade Carlson offered a show of support from the Council. Though he would've proceeded without their approval, Daniel nonetheless appreciated the gesture. Before them sat a crowd of journalists from various news outlets, many jotting down notes. Flashes blinded his vision as they photographed him, but Daniel continued his speech undeterred.

"You may be wondering why I'm doing this now. We've hidden my mutation for decades, so what's changed? It's simple. I've been thinking about revealing the truth for a while, and when Rose told me the Kenneth Foundation was searching for spokespersons, it seemed like the perfect opportunity." There was a dramatic pause, accompanied by a smile. "I've been hiding long enough. It's time I join my mutant brothers and sisters in the fight for our rights."

Daniel expected a deluge of questions the moment he finished, and the audience didn't disappoint. A reporter named Marisa Clements from MegaNews fired the first one.

"Speaking of the spokespersons, the foundation says they're looking for mutants who attained an important position despite the discrimination against their kind." She scowled. "Doesn't it go against the message that you had to hide your mutation in order to become the Commander?"

While she aimed the query at Daniel, Doug Thomson answered. "Mr. Ricdeau never concealed the truth from his superiors or colleagues. Everyone in NISDA and the Council has been aware of his mutation since he enrolled. Yes, we hid that fact from the public, but Mr. Ricdeau is familiar with the discriminations faced by those like him."

"That's correct." Daniel nodded. "I had my share of setbacks in the military before I got to where I am. Even today, there are some who feel I shouldn't be Commander because of my genes. But they couldn't stop me, and believe me they tried." At this moment, Daniel rubbed his chin, pondering. "Actually, my mutation was an asset. I don't think I'd be at the top without it."

"I don't mean to be insensitive," Marisa said the second he uttered his last sentence, "but I'm curious about what your mutation is. I sure can't see it. Would you mind telling us?"

After a chuckle, Daniel shrugged. "Not at all, it'd be a pleasure. It doesn't affect my appearance. In short, my senses are heightened. I have beyond normal vision and hearing. It gave me an edge on the battlefield as you can imagine, and in other areas too. It's very hard to lie to me, for example. I can spot nervous tics just like that." He snapped his fingers. "This made me quite valuable during interrogations."

A large man Daniel recognized as Joe Baggan from TopNews took a step forward. "It's a fascinating gift, but it brings up another problem concerning your role as a spokesperson. Your mutation is beneficial to you and is one hundred percent invisible. Most mutants don't have that luxury. Many are disfigured at best and suffer from reduced mobility and other ailments at worst. Do you think your experience would have been different if you had been one of them?"

Daniel acquiesced. "Probably, yes, and it has to change. The vast majority of mutations are cosmetic and have no impact on capabilities." In frustration, he clenched his fist. "It's unfair that those mutants are judged on their appearance, especially when it's an aspect they can't control. As for the second group—well, it's a disability like any other. Disabled people contribute to society and have positions of power. No one has a problem with that. Why should it be different for mutants?" Again, he paused for effect.

"I'm proud of who I am. I wouldn't give up being a mutant for all the money in the world. Those with debilitating mutations should be even prouder because the hardships they went through make them stronger. Incredible talent is overlooked, and that could've been my fate if I hadn't been lucky. I'm going to do everything I can so that, in the future, luck isn't a factor."

To everyone's surprise, a lone clapping sound echoed through the room. Everyone turned toward the source: Max Kenneth. "Now that's a wise man, and he speaks the truth. My buddy here, Leon"—he pointed at his colleague beside him—"you think his tentacle means he has less dexterity? Bullshit. He can do things with it that a hand can only dream of!"

A round of applause erupted for Leon. Perhaps embarrassed by the unexpected attention, he blushed, but still waved his uncommon appendage to the crowd. A man Daniel failed to recognize raised his arm when silence returned. Though his face was unfamiliar, Daniel recognized the Corbam Network symbol on the reporter's coat.

"I have a question concerning a controversial subject for Councillor Jade Carlson. Mutants are known to suffer from a disease called brain erosion where their brain cells deteriorate, leading to violence. Was this a concern when Mr. Ricdeau was chosen as NISDA's Commander?"

"Of course not. There hasn't been a case of brain erosion for almost a century. It used to be a major problem, but it's in the past." Jane leaned forward, glaring at the man. "Frankly, I'm offended you dared ask this question. Such blatant ignorance is why we are so far behind on mutants' rights. Mr. Ricdeau deserves your respect, not your slander."

Benevolent laughter came from Daniel. "It's quite all right. He gave us a chance to expose the fear of brain erosion for what it is: outdated and bigoted. We'll have to face those taboos sooner or later to succeed."

Then MegaNews' Marisa returned on the offensive. "Are you afraid there might be resistance from the public now that your secret is out?"

"No, I'm not. Oh, there'll be plenty of critics and letters asking for my resignation, but I dare hope my track record speak for itself and the Council will ignore them."

"You bet," Doug said louder than necessary.

A female voice belonging to Jade Carlson followed, "You are the best Commander we could ask for, and angry bigots can't change that."

"No reason to be scared, then." Daniel winked. "I've dealt with mutant haters before. There'll be more of them, but I can take them on."

***

Rumors spread across Valardir that Daniel would make an announcement on TV. I heard murmurs through the cafeteria in particular. Rose asked if I'd watch it in the rec room with her. Since I had nothing to do, I figured why not? His being a mutant came as a shock, but when he mentioned heightened senses, it explained a lot. When he'd interrogated me, I'd felt like he saw right through me, and I guess he did.

—Thoughts of James Hunter, Hocmar 28, 2134, on the Nirnivian calendar

Inside the recreation area, James sat in the middle of the couch, sandwiched between Rose and a soldier named Charlie. James had met him before, when Janice had taught him Rubarg. Back then, Charlie had asked if James could introduce him to Rose, a favor now fulfilled, though the awestruck Charlie had managed only to mutter a few platitudes.

Brucie stood behind the sofa, leaning on it, resulting in his head popping between Rose and James. While not an expert on the subject, James doubted that his position befitted his role as a bodyguard. Then again, Rose didn't mind, so he supposed that was fine.

Several people filled the room watching their Commander on TV. Janice almost missed the beginning of the broadcast, but she joined the group at the last minute. Unlike her usual social self, she stood silently in the back, her arms crossed. This puzzled James. He realized she tended to steer clear of Rose, but that didn't explain why she avoided everyone else. At least she waved when he greeted her.

Soon after Janice's arrival, the conference started and Daniel made his announcement. The second he finished, the journalists pounced. Their queries were benign until someone referred to brain erosion. James lacked knowledge of the matter, but the mere allusion drew groans and disapproval, especially from Rose, who sighed and shook her head in disappointment. Those reactions distracted James for a minute. By the time he returned his attention to the screen, a reporter asked, "How did the Council respond when you told them you would reveal your mutation?"

Doug Thomson leaned forward in Daniel's stead. "We were thrilled!"

The journalist ignored the answer and stared at the Commander. "You believe him?"

With a smile, Daniel acquiesced. "Absolutely. The Council supported my decision from the start."

As if displeased by his response, the newscaster said, "And yet they made you hide the truth for years."

"Give me a break!" A dark-skinned woman near James frowned in disgust and clenched her fists. After a moment, he recognized Patricia, the dark-skinned woman who had been playing on arcade machines when he'd last visited this place with Janice. "It's like they're trying to start a fight."

"Damn straight!" Charlie forced a derisive laugh. "Drama gets the ratings."

Again, Doug spoke before Daniel. "It was deemed necessary, but that hasn't been the case for a while."

A visible moment of hesitation passed and then Patricia glanced at Rose. "The Council needs him thanks to the uneasy peace, but your dad still put his career on the line for mutants' rights. You must be proud of him."

Rose smiled. "Yes, I am. When I learned that the Kenneth Foundation was looking for spokespersons, I figured he'd be a great choice. I wasn't sure he'd agree, but he accepted without a second thought."

Smirking, Patricia focused her attention on Janice. "What about you over there? You're proud too?"

The muscular woman shrugged. "Yeah, sure..."

"Really? It's hard to see with you back there." She chuckled. "Are you too good for us now?"

"Yep!" She dismissed her own words with a wave. "Nah, I've caught a bug and I don't want to spread it. Dad won't be happy if I infect his whole staff!"

It seemed like complete bullshit to me, and it probably was. Anyway, the interview ended not long after. I wanted to talk to Janice, just say hi or whatever, but she had already left.

—Thoughts of James Hunter, Hocmar 28, 2134, on the Nirnivian calendar

Chapter 9

Tigal 7, 2133, on the Nirnivian calendar

Again, James joined Rose for her workout, though only in a support role. His motivation for training remained near zero, so despite Brucie's encouragements, he declined to partake in the exercises. As usual, the intense session left Rose drenched in perspiration, so she went and took a shower while the two of them waited. James sat on the floor with his arms wrapped around his knees. As for Brucie, he stood leaning against the wall nearby with his hands linked behind his head. The bodyguard prattled on and on about inane nonsense while James ignored him and stared in the other direction. With every word, his grip tightened. While not a master of subtlety, even Brucie figured the one-sided conversation failed to thrill him.

"You mad, bro? Ya ain't talking much, even fo' you."

I wasn't going to bring it up, but since he mentioned it...

—Thoughts of James Hunter, Hocmar 28, 2134, on the Nirnivian calendar

"Uh, yeah, I guess you could say that."

Confused, Brucie scratched the top of his skull and fired a questioning glance at James. Blood rushed to James's cheeks, though not out of embarrassment but rather anger at the brute's obliviousness. He threw his hands in the air.

"Um, I don't know, maybe it's because you yelled 'Hey, Rose, he's checking out your ass' right when she was bending over."

A burst of laughter overcame Brucie, and he slapped his thigh. "That was so freaking funny! Ya shouda seen your face, dude. Why are ya so pissed 'bout it? She didn't care!"

"That's not the point!" Prey to a headache, James rubbed his brow. "It wasn't true and, I don't want her to think I'm the kind of jerk who ogles women at the gym. That's creepy."

Brucie dismissed the notion in a frustrated wave. "Ah, whatever man, she knows I was screwing 'round. You were all avoiding looking at her and shit. Just figured I'd mess with ya, and Rose understands that. Ain't gonna think any less o' you." There was a short silence, after which Brucie shrugged. "What's the big deal, anyway? Dudes like chicks, big whoop. And Rose is hot! Those curves, bro." He motioned his fingers in a way that mimicked Rose's body shape, and James gritted his teeth at the gesture. "Makes me weak in the knees, ya know what I mean? W—"

It's obvious that I'm not the kind of guy who'd normally have the courage to interrupt someone with Brucie's build, but I'd had enough.

—Thoughts of James Hunter, Hocmar 28, 2134, on the Nirnivian calendar

"Please stop, Brucie. Don't talk about her like that."

"What?" Brucie frowned. "Ya don't think she's hot?"

"That has nothing to do with it." He groaned. "It's disrespectful, sexist even. Rose is super nice and she's your boss. Don't talk about her like she's some kind of... she deserves better than that."

Against James's expectations, Brucie lowered his neck. "Dude, I ain't mean it like that."

At that moment, they noticed Rose had finished her shower and stood a few feet away from them in her traditional dress. She glared at the duo with her hands on her hips.

Brucie felt I was pissed, but I had nothing on Rose. I figure he was busted, but she had a surprise in store for me.
—Thoughts of James Hunter, Hocmar 28, 2134, on the Nirnivian calendar

"Thank you, Hunter, but I don't need a white knight. I can take care of myself, especially when it comes to Brucie."

"I.... um... I just..."

She crossed her arms. "Say what you will about Brucie's treatment of women, at least he's not assuming we're so weak we can't defend ourselves." She moaned. "Come, Brucie." On that note, she turned around and walked toward the exist at a brisk pace. The bodyguard followed, but not before he extended his tongue at James in an immature display.

Well, I was in trouble. The worst part is, I wasn't telling Brucie off for her, I was doing it for me. He was making me uncomfortable. I didn't understand why she was so furious, but I soon did.
—Thoughts of James Hunter, Hocmar 28, 2134, on the Nirnivian calendar

***

After the incident at the gym, I returned to my room, lay on the bed and thought about what had happened. That's an understatement. The truth is, I agonized about it, and not because my life was pretty much in Rose's hands. Okay, that was part of the reason, but it was mostly because—well, she was my friend and I hated having done something that bothered her. Turns out, I didn't have to worry. A few hours passed and Rose came for a talk.

—Thoughts of James Hunter, Hocmar 28, 2134, on the Nirnivian calendar

Once James opened the door, he found Rose standing there, blushing. She had a hard time looking him in the eyes. Later, he'd recall this to be amusing, given he'd suffered from a similar shyness when Madeleine had revealed her role as the Melkar. Behind Rose, Brucie waited in the background. Something about the bodyguard's demeanor made it clear he intended to stay in the corridor and let them settle the matter. However, the brute still stuck his tongue out like earlier.

"Hi, Hunter, I wish to apologize about this morning." There was a moment of hesitation. "May I come in?"

"Um, yeah, sure!" James gestured for Rose to proceed. Without delay, she sat on the mattress and patted beside her, indicating he should join her.

"I'm sorry, Hunter, I overreacted."

James scratched behind his ear. "It's fine."

"No, it's not." She gave a sigh. "I want you to understand that I don't condone Brucie's behavior. He's rude, and the way he talks about women can be far less than respectful, maybe to the point of misogyny. I won't defend him, and I certainly wouldn't blame anyone for judging his actions inappropriate. Thing is, it's different for me." Rose's brow furrowed into a frown as she closed her eyes.

"Because I'm considered a prophet, people treat me differently. No man has ever whistled when I walked on the sidewalk or made lewd comments about my appearance. I guess I'm lucky, many women would envy me, but people are strange." The scowl intensified. "There's a dessert I can't stand: trotleberry pie. It's awful, and yet if I were in a group and everyone except me were given a piece, I'd resent being singled out. It's similar with Brucie. That type of behavior is demeaning, and I don't enjoy being treated like that, but... well, unlike most girls, I never lived through that."

Rose opened her eyelids and her pupils darted up as she recalled previous events. "Even boorish men put on a polite facade for me. Everyone plays a role when I'm around." A nostalgic smile formed on her lips. "The day Brucie became my bodyguard, he made a crude remark of the sort he often reserves for women. Once he realized, he was appalled and terrified of how I'd react. He apologized several times. Zargs—um, that's Brucie's race—have pale skin to begin with, but the poor fool was almost as white as snow."

She chuckled and shook her head. "The thing is, I wasn't angry. In fact, it was kind of nice... I mean, being objectified made me feel gross. Yet it was nice to have someone treat me like they would anyone else. Brucie knows this. To him, I am the Melkar, and he doesn't see me as a normal person. Still, he forces himself not to hide his chauvinistic qualities with me. It's difficult for him. When you were telling Brucie off, it seemed like you were trying to take this away." Rose exhaled. "Of course that wasn't the case, but Gorumars sometimes let their feelings get the better of them."

"Yeah, same for humans."

Both glanced at each other as if gauging whether the minor dispute had truly ended. After this quiet moment, Rose rubbed her chin and said, "To be honest, I'm not proud of myself because I'm enabling Brucie. I stop him when he bothers someone else, but still." She giggled. "Ah well, half the councillors are women, so I think gender equity can survive a jerk like Brucie Garland."

Frankly, it's a little hard to relate to Rose in this case. I've never been particularly liked, even less revered. Trust me, no one let me stop them from saying whatever the hell they wanted, and if I didn't approve, they didn't give a rat's ass. And yet, if I twist it around, I could somewhat understand. We both grew up isolated. Me because I wasn't popular, and Rose because she was too popular. I was left alone, she was surrounded by people, but no one ever got all that close to her emotionally. It's similar to a celebrity, which I guess she was.

—Thoughts of James Hunter, Hocmar 28, 2134, on the Nirnivian calendar

Chapter 10

In the evening, Janice came to my room. She finished her shift and wanted to know if I'd play a game of Rubarg with her before she went home. It's not like I had anything better to do, and I rather enjoyed her company, so I said yes.

—Thoughts of James Hunter, Hocmar 28, 2134, on the Nirnivian calendar

Hunched over, Janice aimed at ball eight. Quite frankly, her decision confused James. Number five seemed the obvious choice, being close to a pocket and perfectly aligned. Though not a terrible move, Janice's target demanded greater accuracy and James doubted he'd make the shot. Still, she possessed superior skills compared to his, so perhaps she'd manage. As had happened on previous occasions, her posture accentuated a lower part of her anatomy, and the tight jeans she wore increased the effect. James averted his gaze out of politeness.

"You could just ask, you know?" Janice said, adjusting her cue.

Surprised, James recoiled, his mouth gaping. "Uh, what?"

She giggled. "You're wondering if I'm like Dad and can analyze every little detail about you. Everyone does, but they don't dare bring it up. They tiptoe around the issue like I'm made of glass or something." She moaned. "It's fine, I'm not offended by the question. It's normal to be curious. I get it."

Blushing, James scratched behind his ear. "Um, I hadn't even thought about that."

Actually, it did cross my mind, I guess, but I kind of figured she couldn't; not that it mattered either way.

    —Thoughts of James Hunter, Hocmar 28, 2134, on the Nirnivian calendar

"Not bad, but I don't buy it." A *plock* echoed as the wooden stick struck the cue ball. The white sphere missed the mark by a hairline, and Janice mumbled a curse. "Anyway, yes, I'm a mutant"—she straightened as she turned toward James. Thanks to her impressive height, his vision aligned with the sweetheart neckline her shirt provided. Brucie would no doubt accuse him of stealing a peek, not to mention catch one himself, but again, James remained a gentleman and looked up to Janice's eyes—"but I'm not as good as Dad." She gestured for him to take his turn, and he stepped toward the table. "I can't read people like he does." While she talked, James surveyed the board, attempting to pick a target. "He can spot every small tic just like that." She snapped her fingers. "Not me, and I'm not that great at psychology, so I'm not sure it'd do me any good." Finally making his selection, James bent over. "I do have his balance, though."

Her tone struck him as odd, and James frowned. He paused and glanced at Janice. The soldier stood on top of a chair's back with one foot in the air. A feat especially impressive considering she applied her weight to the chair, forcing it to lean forward so it rested on two legs. Flabbergasted, James shouted, "Jesus Christ!"

Those words said, he withdrew a touch, tripped and tumbled down with a crashing sound. Janice leaped off her perch in a flash and rushed toward him, causing the chair to fly backward and fall on the floor. A loud thud resounded upon contact and James thought he saw one of the legs crack, but soon, the gigantic woman filled his vision as she crouched next to him. James caught a whiff of her druik-inaka-scented perfume.

"You okay, buddy?" Janice asked, red-faced.

"Um, yeah, sure..."

"Sorry about that." She extended her hand and hauled him up. "I thought it'd be cool to give you a demonstration, but maybe I overdid it."

"I didn't expect it, that's all. It's pretty sweet!" He chuckled. "You're pulling off stunts like that and I'm the one falling."

"I have that effect on men!" She winked.

Chapter 11

Tigal 10, 2133, on the Nirnivian calendar

I reached a new stage in the Kuhard lessons. Rose figured there wasn't much more I could learn from listening to her recite the rules. As such, she decided it was time for a mock game. The idea was that she'd explain her every move and correct any tactical mistake I made. While it wasn't for real, I was still a little nervous.

—Thoughts of James Hunter, Hocmar 28, 2134, on the Nirnivian calendar

The wind caressing his skin proved to be such an unfamiliar yet satisfying sensation. To James, it seemed like he hadn't experienced a breeze for years. He realized fans placed in strategic spots in Rose's garden simulated the effect, but between that and the UV lights, it felt like heaven. Maybe it was a sign he should force himself to take a walk outside. Despite how tempting that sounded, he dreaded the prospect.

As much as James wished to enjoy the pleasant room in peace, they hadn't come here for relaxation. Rose finished preparing the board and asked if he was ready to begin. He nodded, and so the pretend match began. Given Rose played the blue pieces and he the red, the first move belonged to her. In less than a second, she dragged her assassin toward James's side without a trace of hesitation. A common opening, based on her teachings.

James remembered she had revealed the best counter in a previous lesson, yet he failed to recall the instructions.

Tapping his finger against his chin, he studied the board. His pupils darted around, observing each piece as if they might reveal their secret if pressed. Though it took several minutes, Rose waited patiently. Eventually, she leaned forward and her lips parted. James assumed she meant to offer a hint, and he presented his raised index finger. Then his hand hovered above his berserker. Before he touched the figurine, he reconsidered and instead positioned his mercenary against the assassin.

"Good!" A large smile spread across Rose's face. "I see you've been paying attention to my rambling. You did great!"

All things considered, he deserved little praise. She had explained this strategy so often that the answer should've popped into his mind immediately. Still, a sense of pride filled him, perhaps due to the genuine enthusiasm behind the compliment. No rest for the student, however. Rose took her second turn without delay, and James had to determine the solution once again. This time, the correct choice eluded him even more. The way she positioned her koporal... she'd never mentioned this tactic until then.

Since the answer wouldn't be spoon-fed, James increased his focus. He recollected his past classes and enumerated the various rules in his head, searching for a possible counterattack. Though he devised a few alternatives, upon further consideration, he discovered fatal flaws in them. Soon, a headache assailed him. James scowled and rubbed his brow. Again, Rose offered help and he declined, but he feared he'd regret his arrogance. He had almost abandoned hope when he saw it. With a slight cackle, James grabbed his berserker and advanced it one space.

Rose adopted a blank expression and said, "Are you sure this is what you want to do, Hunter?"

He had been, but his confidence now vanished and the question fed his doubts. The choice appeared flawless, and yet he scrutinized the board and Rose let him do so to his heart's content. In the end, he presumed she attempted a trick. The move might not be perfect, but it was decent.

"Yes, I'm sure."

She waggled a lecturing index finger. "Really sure?" The grin on her visage widened. "In that case, I can take my mercenary like this and... Kuhard. I win."

James gasped. What a quick victory. She had exploited a glaring flaw he'd introduced in his formation. How could he miss that?

"You've made a very common beginner's mistake." She giggled. "The same thing happened to me on my first game, so don't feel bad about it. Now, then, lucky for you this isn't a real competition." That said, she returned both her mercenary and his berserker to their original locations. "Try again, Hunter. Take your time. This is not a race."

So he did, and he blundered once more. Again, Rose corrected him. She explained his mistake and allowed him to fix it. The match went on like this. Sometimes James did stupid things, to the point where he broke the rules. Rose never objected. Instead, she taught him the subtleties he misinterpreted. Little by little, the flow of the game became clearer to James. By the end of the session, he somewhat understood the rationale behind Rose's tactics, even if several concepts still confused him.

I can't pretend I enjoyed Kuhard at that point, but I saw the possibility that I might one day. That was already a huge improvement. Besides, she loved it so much, how could I have said no?

—Thoughts of James Hunter, Hocmar 28, 2134, on the Nirnivian calendar

Chapter 12

Tigal 11, 2133, on the Nirnivian calendar

Once Rose's workday was over, she showed up at James's room with Brucie. She asked if he had eaten supper yet; despite the late hour, he hadn't, so she invited him to join them. After the meal, both the prophet and the bodyguard stayed in James's quarters for a while.

Rose sat on the mattress and James took the lone chair. Though she insisted on coming in, she lacked energy and talked little. Often, she yawned, and he assumed the day had proved tiring. Brucie, on the other hand, burst with enthusiasm. Declining a seat, the large man remained on his feet and recounted various stories from his youth as exaggerated gestures provided effect. Most of his tales consisted of being drunk and acting like an idiot. Somehow, that fact didn't surprise James all that much.

"So, yeah, man, that dude was so freaking wasted." Laughs peppered his words as he anticipated his own punch line. "Went up to that gal, tried to hit on her, ya know. Made a total ass outta himself. Guess we were kinda jerks for letting him. Anyway, what happe—"

At that moment, a beeping interrupted his yarn. Frustrated, Brucie grunted and crossed his arms. Before he voiced an objection, a female voice echoed. "James, it's Kristina. Is Rose with you?"

"Oh God..." Rose mumbled. "Something bad must've happened if she wants to see me at this hour."

As the assumed Melkar finished her thoughts, James walked to the door and opened it. The blond assistant waited, scolding and holding her precious minicomp with both hands. Again, her beauty, not to mention her resemblance to Nadia, struck James. They had never recovered from their disastrous first encounter. Discomfort filled him just at seeing her. Still, he believed he should be diplomatic and force a smile while adopting a cheerful tone.

"Hi! How are you doing?"

"Fine, but I'd feel better if Rose didn't waste her time when she's supposed to be working."

Something told me it was me she called a waste of time, but I didn't bring it up.

—Thoughts of James Hunter, Hocmar 28, 2134, on the Nirnivian calendar

Kristina looked right past James and focused instead on her employer. "Rose, what are you doing? You have a meeting with Quintus Topton. He's already joined the video conference."

There was a gasp from Rose as she face-palmed. "Dear Ulgorack... I completely forgot it was this evening! I'm so sorry, Kristina. After you agreed to be here so late, too."

"That's all right, but we should hurry. He's a very sick man, and I think he should be in bed by now."

"You're right. I've been so busy, I couldn't fit him in my normal schedule." Rose picked up the small mirror that she brought everywhere and checked her appearance. "I'd be lost without you, Kristina, thank you again for putting up with me." That said, she got on her feet and advance toward the exit. At the last moment, she glanced at James. "Sorry, Hunter, I have to cut my visit short. Come on, Brucie."

And so they left, and I was alone. That was a fairly familiar situation. Everyone was busy, and I admit the loneliness took its toll, but there was nothing I could do except bear it. So I went ahead and grabbed Nadia's photo from my wallet. Then, I started talking to her picture, going over my day. I picked up that habit not long after I was discharged from the clinic. Not sure it was a healthy coping mechanism, but often it was the closest to a conversation I could get.

—Thoughts of James Hunter, Hocmar 28, 2134, on the Nirnivian calendar

***

On the screen, an old man sat in a wheelchair. It had been years since Rose had last seen Quintus Topton, and she barely recognized him. A plastic oxygen mask covered his wrinkled face, allowing the rhythmic rise and fall of his chest. His gaping mouth contorted with every breath, implying pain. The energy still present in his gray eyes when she had first met him in his early hundreds had vanished, replaced by exhaustion. The thick brown hair of his youth, which Rose had witnessed in photos, fared little better; a mere few white strands remained on his bald head. On his right side stood an IV drip, providing Quintus with the nutrients and medication he required.

"Your Holiness," he murmured, "thank you for meeting with me. I know you'd rather not."

Each word sounded ragged and gave the impression they crawled up his throat by force, tearing up his insides. He spoke the truth. In his younger years, Quintus used to be a rich politician, as most are. He served in the Mardaboeuf Delegation and even won one term on the High Council. During his career, he had adopted positions that clashed with Rose's own views. Actually, that would be an understatement: many of his stances had appeared downright cruel to her. Rose admitted a smidge of reticence had gripped her when Quintus's assistant had contacted her for an audience. Then he'd assured her his employer wished to talk not about politics, but rather charity, and that seemed noble enough, so she accepted.

"We have divergent opinions, Mr. Topton, but I don't have anything against you on a personal level."

"Maybe you should"—he coughed—"I wouldn't blame you." He paused for effect. "I'm dying, Your Holiness. I have six months left. A year if I'm lucky—heh, if you want to call it that."

"I'm very sorry to hear that." Though she wasn't surprised; that fact had spread through the media a while ago.

Quintus's left arm trembled as he attempted to dismiss the comment with a wave, but the simple movement demanded too great an effort. "I'm not asking for your pity, Your Holiness. I've lived a long and prosperous life. There are many out there who need it more than I. No, I'm only saying I don't have much time left, and I want to make it count." There was a short silence as he closed his eyelids.

"I am the second-richest man in Nirnivia, but all the money in the world can't help me." He harrumphed. "I want to give away eighty percent of my fortune to charity right now, and the rest once I'm gone."

Rose blinked twice in rapid succession. "I'm touched by your generosity, and proud that you'd trust the Melkar's fund for the needy with such an impressive sum, but I'm not in charge of donations. I'm very sorry that you strained yourself to meet me, but you'll have to see Caleb."

What might have been a chuckle escaped from Quintus's lips. "I'm the one who's sorry. I misled you and I apologize. The money isn't for the MFN." He sighed. "I'm sure you're well aware of my greatest sin."

A few possibilities entered Rose's mind. Quintus Topton had a certain reputation. Rumor had it he had accepted bribes for dubious favors and pushed for controversial legislation that favored the rich to the detriment of the poor, that he'd gained his place on the Council through voter fraud, and so on. Still, she had a feeling she knew what he referred to.

"I think I do." In her head, Rose added, *But I'm not sure we're on the same page.*

"All my career, I've campaigned against mutant rights. I believed mutants should be restrained to restricted areas; be sterilized so their mutations don't spread. I've been accused of hating mutants, but to me, at least, that was wrong. I didn't hate them, not at all. I wanted to protect the population from the danger they posed. Civilization almost collapsed due to increasing mutation rates in the past. Yes, the problem isn't nearly as rampant now, but we have to be careful or it could happen again. While I did empathize with the mutants, they might bring complete annihilation, and so drastic measures were necessary. That's what I told myself, but in my old age, I see... I... I was blinded by fear. I..."

An eruption of coughs overcame Quintus. He twisted in his wheelchair without control. A drop of blood ran down his chin, unless Rose imagined it. Two nurses, one male and the other female, rushed out of the shadows. The first grabbed a syringe and reached for Quintus's wrist, attempting an injection. The second performed CPR. It took five minutes, but the senior returned to normal.

"Mr. Topton, we should take a b—"

"I was afraid, it's as simple as that. Afraid of something possible, but very unlikely. Science stood against my views, but I dismissed it, hiding behind the idea that the danger was so great, we had to be careful despite the evidence. I didn't have much success in my agenda, but I slowed down progress and hurt so many people." Here, he stopped and took a few deep breaths. "I can't undo what I did, but I want to help mutants before I leave. That's why I decided I'd give my fortune to the Kenneth Foundation."

Rose clasped her hand and smiled. "That's a great choice, but I don't see why you wanted to talk to me."

"Max Kenneth won't listen to a word I say. He refused my offer."

"Oh..." Rose touched her cheek. "Well, if you want, I can help you find another organization that fights for mutant rights. There are plenty."

"Yes, but none of them are a match for the Kenneth Foundation. I thank you for the assistance, Your Holiness, but I already found my second choice. Thing is, I'd rather change Kenneth's mind. His foundation can accomplish so much more. I know you spoke to Max Kenneth before. You arranged for your father to be one of their spokespersons, and you are the Melkar. Maybe he'd listen to you." A few tears rolled down the senior's cheeks. "I'm not asking for me. You, Max and Leon can hate me, you can denounce me as a monster for the rest of your life, I don't care. I just want him to take the money and use it to help his community."

Rose closed her eyes, rubbed her brow and exhaled. "I'll see what I can do."

***

Tigal 12, 2133, on the Nirnivian calendar

Rose stared at her blank monitor with wide eyes while Kristina shook her head and said, "That doesn't happen every day."

The instant Rose had mentioned Quintus and the possibility of a large donation, Max Kenneth had hung up on them. He hadn't even uttered a single word or given her a chance to elaborate. Of course, she understood he despised Quintus, and with good reason, but still.

"No, it doesn't. Well, now I know what it's like to be a telemarketer. I thought I'd never see the day."

"It's fine. You should prepare for your sermon, anyway." Kristina rested her minicomp beside her. "If you want, I can try calling them again."

"No, no, I wouldn't do that to you." She giggled. "They're in charge of the foundation, if they won't take Quintus's money, that's their business. I shouldn't be meddling in the first place, but they could do so much for the mutant population if they accepted that I figured I should try for their sake."

"Sure feels like a waste."

"Yeah, it does." Rose sighed. "I guess Quintus will have to settle for his second choice."

Chapter 13

Tigal 13, 2133, on the Nirnivian calendar

I didn't attend all her sermons. Far from it, in fact. I don't know why I went occasionally. This wasn't my religion; I didn't believe the things she said. I mean, it's not like I was going to my own church all that often back home. I guess part of me just wanted to learn more about Nirnivia. I also enjoyed seeing Rose perform. She was good, really good. Watching her was a pleasure, even if her words were nonsense to me. I can only imagine how it felt for her followers.

—Thoughts of James Hunter, Hocmar 28, 2134, on the Nirnivian calendar

Few attended the chapel, so James found an empty pew toward the back. He preferred not being surrounded by strangers when alone. Such had always been the case, and finding himself in a strange new world only increased his disdain for mobs.

Behind the altar, Rose recited her words as charismatically as ever. She managed without notes, reciting complex religious text by memory. From the public's perspective, she made it seem simple, but James understood the truth. While Rose breezed through her speech, most would end up looking like complete fools if put in her position, him included. Why, the mere notion of addressing a crowd left him covered in sweat and shivering.

James watched her without really listening. Though he enjoyed her "performance," the subject remained out of reach. His limited knowledge of the Nirnivian religion reduced his chances of comprehension to nil. The saints' various names alone proved confusing and difficult to remember. The situation changed, however, when Rose began answering questions from her audience. One letter stuck in James's mind, yet he couldn't explain why.

"I received a question about a slightly controversial subject. The writer doesn't understand the theory of reduced reincarnation flow." Rose cleared her throat. "He isn't alone. This particular theory is a popular topic among theologists, but it is rare someone attempts explaining it to the general public. Today, I will try. I hope you'll agree the basics are rather simple." As she gathered her thoughts, she rested her fingers against her chin for a second or two. "When we die, our souls return to Ulgorack and Timagoron for judgment. If the deceased is deemed worthy, they proceed to the afterlife. If they are judged irredeemable, they are banished to nothingness. In most cases, the outcome falls somewhere in between, and we're given a new life through reincarnation so we can keep on learning until we're ready."

Rose then paused and smiled for the camera. "I realize you have heard this on multiple occasions, but this is where the discussion becomes interesting." She took a deep breath. "Before the old war, our population was far greater. We can only speculate, but it is generally estimated that there were five hundred to one thousand times more Gorumars living on this planet. Now, think about it for a minute: fewer people implies fewer pregnancies, which means fewer births. Maybe you are wondering what that has to do with anything. Well, souls are waiting for reincarnation. Since the number of newborns is reduced, those souls have to wait longer for their next life. What are the implications?"

Her pupils darted up for an instant. "This is where it gets controversial. No one knows for sure. There isn't any religious text discussing the issue. As the Melkar, it is said Ulgorack speaks to me. However, I have received no visions concerning the diminishing reincarnation flow, and so I am as clueless as anyone. There are several theories, but none can be proven, and all are widely debated. Theologists agree someday this world will end. The date has been chosen, even if we have no idea what it is. Because there are fewer reincarnations than before, a big question is what will happen to the souls who won't have accessed the afterlife before it's all over? We can't know the right answer—we don't have sufficient information—but many have tried to provide an explanation. Some assume those poor souls will be condemned to nothingness."

She sighed as she squeezed the bridge of her nose. "This is a rather pessimistic outlook, and I hope they are wrong. Others presume that Ulgorack won't condone such an unfair judgment and will use an alternative test. There are even those who insist there are no problems and thus nothing to fear. According to them, a great number of souls attained the afterlife during a short interval thanks to the original Melkar. There weren't enough souls left for the huge population, so the gods orchestrated the old war as a solution. Those possibilities only scratch the surface. Which is correct?"

She shrugged. "I don't know. They might all be wrong. We can't tell. You have to decide for yourself. In my case, I have faith in Ulgorack, and I trust that whatever happens, he will do what is best for all of us."

For some reason, I found myself enthralled by the theory of reduced reincarnation flow. I'm not sure why, since I don't believe in reincarnation. Maybe it's because I never thought about that concept. It's the kind of thing that's completely useless. I mean, even if it's true and there's a problem, we can't do anything about it. This new knowledge didn't help me, and I doubt it ever will. Still, I find it fascinating. In fact, I'd rather discuss this theory than something useful like mathematics or advanced physics. I can't be the only one either. I wonder why that is.

    —Thoughts of James Hunter, Hocmar 28, 2134, on the Nirnivian calendar

Chapter 14

The camera had barely turned off when Kristina dashed toward Rose. The assistant's haste surprised Rose. She almost waved at Hunter in the crowd once she finished speaking, but witnessing the blond woman in such a rush interrupted her. Soon, Kristina arrived breathless.

"Rose, Leon Serath just called. He wants to talk to you about Quintus."

Rose blinked, confused, and then she remembered her earlier failed communication attempt with Max Kenneth and Leon. "He does?" She resisted a sigh. She wished to chat with James before leaving, but that would have to wait.

"Yes, you should call him back as soon as possible. Max isn't there right now, and that means it's the perfect time."

"All right." She nodded. "Go set up the equipment, I'll be right there." Not that she needed to provide instructions for Kristina. The assistant had sprinted toward the exit the instant she'd said, "All right." Gathering her things, she looked at James. "Hey, Hunter, thanks for coming! I have to run, but I'll see you later!"

***

Again, Rose talked to Leon Serath through video conference. Her interlocutor's tentacle twitched around and he fiddled with his glasses, pushing them up his nose at frequent intervals. The demeanor implied a touch of nervousness.

"Your Holiness, we don't have much time." He peeked over his left shoulder before returning his focus on her. "Max will be back soon. If he finds out I'm talking to you about this, he'll be furious."

"I understand why you don't like Quintus." After exhaling, Rose shook her head. "I share the sentiment, believe me, but aren't you two letting your feelings cloud your judgment? With a donation this size, the foundation could do so much!"

"You don't have to sell me on it, Your Holiness. I begged Max to take the money. He won't hear a word of it." Leon groaned. "He's the one in charge. There's nothing I can do, but maybe he'd listen to you. You are the Melkar after all."

Rose shrugged. "He won't even talk to me, so we're out of luck there."

"Well, that's why I called you." Once more, Leon adjusted his spectacles. "You really did us a big favor by finding a great spokesman. Your father is perfect for the job, and to show our gratitude, we won't take your call because of our feud with Quintus." He gave a smirk. "This is kind of rotten of us, isn't it?"

Rose smiled and dismissed the notion with a wave. "Don't be silly, Mr. Serath. I only did what any decent person with my connections would have done and didn't expect anything in return." She giggled. "It wouldn't be charity otherwise."

"I suppose not, but let's say you were offended. I think it'd give me leverage to convince Max to reconsider." Leon winked.

Despite her effort, Rose failed to stifle a laugh. "Hmm... maybe I am a little offended after all."

Chapter 15

The Good Doctor promised we'd have our war meeting, and he kept his word. Only the concerned parties were invited, not the whole cabinet. It was comprised of me, the president, a couple of high-ranking officers and Mr. Roland Cursak, the defense secretary. We discussed our military position and strategy. The Good Doctor complained it was a waste of time; that might have been the case. He was in charge and calling the shots. Cursak agreed with everything he said. As for me and the others, the president politely listened to our opinions, but we rarely changed his mind. For the most part, I figured it wasn't so bad. The Good Doctor had a plan, and while I didn't understand it, he was right about pretty much everything.

—Thoughts of Evelyn Losier, Hocmar 28, 2134, on the Nirnivian calendar

The cup of coffee in Evelyn's hands radiated heat, and with any luck, it would still do so once they started. They had fixed the reunion for 2:00, and the hour drew near. Everyone already assembled around the conference table. Well, everyone except one person, but he'd show up. The president detested waiting when arriving early. He considered every second important, and wasting a mere few in an unproductive manner displeased him. Because of this, he arrived at the last moment, yet according to Evelyn's memory, he'd never indulged in tardiness.

Perhaps due to the serious subject they'd soon discuss, chatter remained low. Most sat in silence, consulting their notes, and that suited Evelyn fine. The lack of conversation allowed her to steel herself for the coming battle. She took her mug to her mouth, and the pleasant aroma of coffee caressed her nostrils as she sampled her beverage. The taste made her lips contort in a grimace. On her doctor's advice, she was attempting to cut her sugar consumption. The effort resulted in her adding one cube instead of two to her coffee. While not bad, she hadn't grown accustomed to the flavor yet. In any case, she believed the time drew near. A glance at her watch confirmed her suspicion. As expected, the door opened and the mechanical man stepped inside. The light glimmered on his metallic body.

They began after a few greetings and courtesies. The discussion started with an overview of the current situation. Nothing really changed. The uneasy peace went undisturbed. Both Ostark and Nirnivia showed no signs of restarting the hostilities. It was a charade; they had failed to resolve the actual conflict and only postponed the fight. Someday, the truce would be broken. Still, for now, the farce held strong and the biggest problem ended up not being NISDA, but rather the terrorist group BBR. Similar to a bloodsucking insect, they posed little threat but brought constant annoyance. Worse, the joint effort with Nirnivia didn't stop them. Fingers joined in a pyramid, General Harold Torn proposed a possibility. Evelyn suppressed a shiver. That warmonger made her skin crawl.

"Mr. President, dear colleagues, I'd like to remind you that back when Laforge was in charge, Ostark invested heavily in genetic experiments. Laforge wanted to create super soldiers, but despite some promising results, the project was shut down." A sadistic glimmer shone in his eyes. "I think we should revive it."

Without hesitation, the cyborg said, "No."

"But, Mr. President—"

The defense secretary, Mr. Cursak, pointed a menacing index finger toward Torn. "I won't hear a word of this nonsense. The ethical ramifications alone are enough to give me nightmares. You know what happened to the test subjects."

Harold crossed his arms and smirked. "I'd say we had two major successes."

"And hundreds of gruesome deaths." Cursak shivered and swallowed hard. "Or worse, in Plague's case. And if you consider Diabo and Stalker successes, that's a low bar. There aren't many soldiers who'd be willing to go through those"—he gestured with finger quotes—"side effects."

A nonchalant shrug came from General Torn. "They enlisted. They're ours to command now."

What a turd of a man. If the president listened to him, he'd lose his incredible record-breaking ninety-two percent approval rating. Not that I was surprised by his ridiculous speech: it was classic Torn. I wondered why the Good Doctor hadn't gotten rid of him. He was a remnant of the Laforge era. I figured the president kept him around for political reasons, though I had no idea what those might be. At least it wasn't like he had any influence. Torn talked big, but it fell on deaf ears. And yet, as much as I hate to admit it, he was partly right about the super soldier program.

—Thoughts of Evelyn Losier, Hocmar 28, 2134, on the Nirnivian calendar

Clearing her throat, Evelyn harrumphed. "While I agree that General Torn's proposition is beyond appalling, I think we should review the data from the experiments we ran back then."

Again, the mechanical man's monotonous voice answered with a single word, "No."

"Please, let me finish." She rubbed her brow. "These experiments created Diabo and Stalker, so maybe if we take a closer look, they'd reveal a weakness we could exploit." She gave a sigh. "Laforge wasted a ton of money on this ridiculous project and destroyed countless lives, but what if it can at least rid us of the horrors it caused?"

The cyborg contemplated her in silence. He remained immobile, but his electronic eye switched from a smiley to a pondering emoticon. "President Laforge forced me to conduct those dreadful experiments on Nirnivian prisoners. I supervised every detail, and I am quite familiar with all the data obtained." There was a brief pause. "It is burned in my memory. I cannot forget no matter how much I wish to. Such an endeavor would be a waste of resource given this fact."

And that was it. Several arguments came to mind, but I knew he'd reject them. There was no point arguing. Every minute that passed, I considered bringing up a subject I meant to discuss. It had been brought up before and ignored, but it was necessary. The thing is, deep down, I agreed with him, but the realities of war... suffice to say, I felt conflicted.

—Thoughts of Evelyn Losier, Hocmar 28, 2134, on the Nirnivian calendar

The president looked at everyone present. "I believe we have gone through everything we needed to review. If you will excuse me, I will take my leave."

"Please wait!" Covered in sweat, Evelyn swallowed hard. "There's one last thing. Mr. President, we should develop IML technology."

A snort came from Harold Torn. "Good luck with that. This administration is too soft to listen to common sense."

Despite his skepticism, an aura of approval filled the room. Several of the officers nodded in agreement. Yet she realized their support granted her little favor. Only the Good Doctor's opinion mattered, and as expected, he dismissed the notion. "That would be most inadvisable."

Evelyn considered debating but deemed the fight futile and so kept her mouth shut. To her surprise, the defense secretary, Roland Cursak, leaned forward. "I'm sure the vice president doesn't mean for us to use them. It's for deterrence purposes." Evelyn was familiar with his favor of IML, but still, his support came as a shock. Cursak toed the Good Doctor's line, even when their view differed. She could count the occasions when he'd opposed the president on a single hand. Roland adjusted his glasses, and Evelyn admired his muscular arms. She'd always had a weakness for the Perz's dark skin tone, and she had to admit Roland possessed an impressive body. "Should Nirnivia build an IML, we'll be caught with our pants down."

The Good Doctor shook his head in disapproval as his smiley turned into a sad face. "Deterrence is overrated. Such was the purpose of our ancestors for building them as well as the dirty weapons they allowed to launch all over the planet. They thought the threat of certain doom would protect them from one another, but it only maximized devastation when madness overtook the world. We are fortunate. The technology that almost destroyed civilization has been lost. If we rebuild it, then it will be used sooner or later, and extinction will be our fate."

Evelyn exhaled and acquiesced. "I understand your concern, Mr. President." A scowl formed on her brow. "I'd rather see IML gone forever myself, but if Nirnivia develops a single launcher, we'll be at their mercy. If we both have one, it's a stalemate."

"There is no reason to believe Nirnivia is attempting to build an IML system. Our spies report no such activity."

Annoyed, Evelyn clenched her fists. "Yes, but we can't be sure."

The president dismissed her objection with a wave. "I submit that we can. Nirnivia lost the Chestnut War. Their country is on the verge of collapse, and NISDA is a shadow of its former self. Even if they were to pursue IML technology, it is years away from their grasp. Daniel Ricdeau is well aware that if we catch them playing such a reckless game, it would doom the uneasy peace and Nirnivia with it. The Commander is many things, but suicidal he is not."

Her fists tightened further. "What about Rose? You've been saying for years we need to capture her to reach true peace between our nations. With IML technology, we could force her to surrender to us."

"Nirnivia would rather die than surrender their precious Melkar. To capture her by force would bring Nirnivia's destruction, and bringing forth such a tragedy would be both morally unacceptable and illogical. Whether you like it or not, they are people. Irrational hatred nearly wiped out intelligent life before. They represent roughly thirty-five percent of the species. Should we wipe them out, we would be thirty-five percent closer to extinction."

I understand his perspective, I really do. I'm not insane, I don't want extinction, but if thirty-five percent of our species had to be destroyed, I'd prefer it if it wasn't from my half.

—Thoughts of Evelyn Losier, Hocmar 28, 2134, on the Nirnivian calendar

A shrug came from the cyborg. "Besides, it is unnecessary. Now that I have my deus ex machina, the one you call the human from Earth, she will be our prisoner soon enough."

"How?" The defense secretary tilted his neck sideways. "You plan on kidnapping the human and using him as a bargaining chip?"

"That might work. My sources say Rose is quite fond of him, perhaps unnaturally so. Should the possibility arise, I will exploit it. However, I doubt we will get the chance. So far, he is as isolated in Valardir as she is." He rose from his seat and turned his back on them with his head bowed and his arms crossed. "Reaching Rose is too complex and dangerous, so I will have her come to us, and Mr. James Hunter will play a key part."

"How so?"

An annoyed clicking sound came from the president's speaker. "I realize it is difficult for you to be kept in the dark, but the plan in question is in constant flux. There are countless possibilities, some simple, some delightfully complex. At the moment, it is impossible to gauge which is our best bet. I must proceed carefully reevaluating my options after every move. For now, be aware this visitor is a weakness for Rose. Our source tells us she already left Valardir once because of him. If only we had been informed of this fact before she had returned. But I digress. Mr. Hunter is one of the many elements that can be used to manipulate Rose, and I intend to do just that."

It was maddening. You could never get a straight answer from him. In his mind, he was always ten steps—no, make that a hundred steps ahead of everyone. He mapped different potential outcomes to positions in a tangled graph and predicted which branch the future would take. The whole thing was so complicated that I guess he couldn't have explained his plan even if he'd tried, but it was frustrating. Still, we'd all learned it was best to trust him and follow his lead no matter how ludicrous it seemed. Fate tended to prove him right. I only had one last question.

—Thoughts of Evelyn Losier, Hocmar 28, 2134, on the Nirnivian calendar

A sneer formed on Evelyn's visage. "What happens if it doesn't work?"

The Good Doctor stared at her in silence for a second. His expression didn't change, couldn't change, yet she sensed an immense sadness in him. Such raw emotion, even though he forgot to convey it through his smiley. Distressed by his reaction, Evelyn almost apologized, but he stopped her.

"Failure is a possibility one must account for. Should I fail, then I shall have to consider the possibility that this conflict cannot be resolved without bloodshed."

Chapter 16

Tigal 14, 2133, on the Nirnivian calendar

"Thank you for finally meeting me, Mr. Kenneth." On the screen, Max barely reacted to Rose's greeting. He remained in his chair, his arms crossed. A few feet behind him stood Leon, fidgeting and keeping his distance. There was no need for a detective to deduce that the two had had an argument. Rose expected the cause to be this very call.

"Yeah, no problem. Sorry 'bout hanging up on you before." The grumpy voice sounded anything but sincere. Still, the forced apology drew a smile from Leon. "That wasn't the polite thing to do, and I wanted to apologize. But I've got to say, I don't see you changing my mind."

"That's fine, I don't have a stake in this." Rose's mouth contorted in disdain. "I'm not a fan of Quintus Topton either. My only concern here is the well-being of the mutant population. The Topton fortune could do so much for your cause."

"She's right, Max!" Nodding, Leon stepped forward. "Topton is a monster, but his money is worth just as much as anyone's." For added effect, he slapped his tentacle against his palm. The resulting squishing noise proved quite different from the usual clapping, and Rose stifled a giggle. "It'd fund our lobbying budget for a decade, and we'd still have plenty left over. Think of all the hungry mutant children we could feed. The school's programs we could finance. It's a game changer, Max!"

Unimpressed, the bandana-sporting mutant groaned. "Yeah, yeah, but you're not looking at the big picture. Quintus Topton is the biggest enemy of mutant rights in recent history. Just take reproductive rights." Though it seemed impossible to Rose, his self-embrace tightened further, causing slight tremors in his muscles. "We're free to freaking have kids with anyone now, but that's only been for like thirty years. A while back, mutants weren't allowed to have children."

He paused for effect, and after a polite delay, Rose harrumphed. "In fairness, that was enacted before Quintus's time."

A shrug came from Max. "Sure, ain't gonna pretend he was responsible for that, but he supported the idea. In his time, as you call it, some mutants could have children, but there were restrictions. Stuff like, two highly mutated people couldn't have a baby together to protect the gene pool. My parents..." He gritted his teeth for a moment as he uncrossed his arms. "They had to live in fear and hide me from the authorities." Blood flushed his cheeks. "Same for Leon. We were raised in secret until we were twelve. That's when they finally changed their goddamn law. If we had been found, we wouldn't be here today." Enraged, Max lifted his fist and slammed it on his desk, which trembled as a bang echoed. Rose gasped, shocked by the sudden motion, but she regained her composure almost immediately. As for Leon, he averted his gaze and shook his head in disappointment, though not surprise. No doubt he had witnessed his partner's temper before. "That's what Topton stood for."

Rose swallowed hard. "Mr. Kenneth, this is a complex subject." She swept a few drops of sweat from her brow. "In every other case I can think of, discrimination has no logical reason to exist. Long ago, before the old war, racial prejudices were rampant even though they weren't backed by science. In fact, science taught us they were false. Same with women's rights. There used to be a time when women were prohibited from owning a business, or becoming a successful politician or, if we go back far enough... driving." She rolled her eyes at the ridiculous idea.

"Nirnivian women prove these stereotypes wrong every day. It sickens me to say it"—and indeed, she suspected she grew paler simply considering the notion—"but when it comes to mutants, the situation is a little different. It's easy to forget now, but back then, mutations almost brought about our extinction. You're well aware of the Rockter scale, I'm sure. Mutations are rated from one to six—the higher the number, the worse the effects. William Adamant, the most mutated person in Nirnivia, is so deformed that someone unaware of his condition might not realize he's a Gorumar like you or me. He was born paralyzed and suffers constant pain."

An annoyed grunt came from Max. "Who do you think you're talking to?" He threw his hands in the air. "I know who freaking William Adamant is!" He scowled. "What's the point of bringing him up, anyway?"

"My point is, Mr. Adamant is level three on the Rockter scale. Back when Nirnivia was formed, level sixes were common, and their numbers increased daily. Can you imagine what it must have been like?" A shiver ran down Rose's spine. "A life of nothing but constant agony. Scientists were clear: unless mutation rates decreased dramatically, we'd be extinct within the century. The only way they found to save us was to limit mutants' rights to reproduce, and for better or worse, it worked. The data proves it beyond a doubt."

Max's frown intensified as he leaned forward. "Are you saying the end justifies the means?"

"No, I'm saying our ancestors were faced with a choice where all options were terrible. No matter what they did, there'd be blood on their hands. These were extreme circumstances. So extreme they defied morality." Her lips quivered at the implications of her own words. "I don't know if they were right or wrong. I doubt it was possible to be right. It's easy for us to judge sitting in our comfy chairs, but they were living it. I for one am glad I'll never have to make such a cruel decision." Rose stopped for a moment and then added, "I couldn't take it."

Against her hope, Max slumped back in his chair and returned to his former cross-armed position. "Hmm... yeah, all right, it was tough. I ain't agreeing with what they did, but I understand why they did it." He shrugged. "Doesn't change a damn thing for Quintus. By the time he was around, scientists everywhere shouted from the rooftops that the restrictions weren't necessary anymore. We were past the danger, and he still persecuted us."

Rose acquiesced. "There's a simple but unreasonable explanation for his actions: Quintus was afraid. Afraid of a repeat of what happened back then, despite the assurances of scientists. Fear knows no logic. That doesn't excuse him, of course, but he realizes now, far too late, that he acted like a fool."

"A coward who blamed the victims. Do you really want the foundation to associate itself with that kind of man?"

A second of silence passed while Rose stroked behind her ear with her index finger. "That's a valid concern, and I agree, Quintus Topton treated mutants like trash and I certainly won't defend him." She averted her gaze. "There is another way to look at it, though. He committed atrocities, but now he sees how wrong he was. He's devastated by the horrors he brought and wants to make amends. Nothing he can do will ever repair the damage he caused, but at the very least, he hopes his donation can help the people he persecuted. It won't be nearly enough to repay his debt, but it's the best he can do in his condition." Without realizing, Rose wrapped her fingers around the arms of her chair and applied pressure. "Thanks to the Kenneth Foundation, the biggest bigot alive admitted he was wrong. That's quite a headline right there and would be proof of all you've accomplished."

His jaws tightening, Max squinted at Rose. "That geezer doesn't care about us! He knows he sinned and he's scared for his soul! He's trying to buy his way into the afterlife using the same mutants he oppressed!" Again, he hit the table, this time with his open hand, though Rose had expected it given his previous blow and didn't react. "Me, I say let him rot in nothingness."

Rose exhaled and bent her neck. "You don't need to be concerned about that." Then she straightened and looked Max in the eyes. "I don't know what Quintus's true motive is. I admit I share your suspicions. It doesn't matter, because if that's his plan, well, it won't work." There was a slight smirk. "The gods aren't fools, and they don't only judge our actions. Intentions matter, and we can't hide those from them. If Quintus is making his donation for selfish reasons, he'll only buy himself a ticket to nothingness. It goes further..."

About to utter what might be a bombshell, she leaned forward. "You can refuse his money, but if he is sincere, then it will count as if you accepted it. From a religious perspective, your decision here has no impact on Quintus's fate. After all, his soul will be judged for his actions, not yours."

After a painful moan, Max began massaging his temples. "You're giving me a headache! Why do you care so much if I take the old geezer's cash or not?"

Rose allowed herself a brief chuckle and then dismissed the notion with a wave. "I don't, but I want you to decide based on what matters most to you and not hatred. There is no right or wrong here, Mr. Kenneth. Religiously speaking, both options can be valid. If you accepted Topton's money out of greed even though you believe it would actually hurt the foundation, it would steer you toward nothingness. Refusing out of spite and thus hurting the mutant population for your own ego's sake would produce the same result."

A sad smile grew on her face. "Even the Melkar can't see what's in your heart, so I can't offer guidance except for this. Think of what matters most to you—think of your values. Mr. Kenneth, you've fought for mutant rights all your life and have often said it's the most important thing to you. Is it? What matters most? Fighting for fellow mutants, or making sure Quintus doesn't buy his redemption in the eyes of the people? Both are fine and defensible positions, but whatever you choose, please do so for the right reasons and not out of anger."

Chapter 17

A meeting with senior officers waited for Daniel Ricdeau as he headed for what they called the war room. Said chamber consisted of the heart of operation for Valardir. There, you could monitor the complex at a micro level. It contained a multitude of high-tech equipment, making it the perfect place for military presentations. To his side walked his good friend and colleague, Ron. The Koporal advanced at a brisk pace, sporting a frown that suggested a sour mood. After years of friendship, Daniel understood nothing could be further from the truth. Ron Tigh always looked pissed off no matter the circumstances.

The reunion in question concerned BBR. In an effort to keep what they called the uneasy peace going, Nirnivia had agreed to help Ostark stop the terrorists. Diabo and his cohorts proved to be a thorn in the Ostarkirans' side despite posing little threat. Ostark's desire to rid themselves of their nuisance had grown until they'd granted Nirnivia permission to enter the neutral zone when it came to hunting them. Restrictions applied, of course. Both countries had to warn the other and seek their consent before such an excursion, and obtaining it required hard evidence of BBR's presence in the targeted area. Size limits for sent troops also meant no hope of a small army attacking BBR.

Regardless of Nirnivia and Ostark's collaboration, the assaults against BBR brought rare successes. Most often, their soldiers arrived too late and discovered the remnants of an abandoned cell. A recent mission of that nature had failed recently, explaining the meeting in question. They planned to review what had gone wrong, determine why their intelligence had ended up flawed, and find solutions. The Commander and his Koporal had already started discussing the issue as they marched.

"It's freaking shameful," Ron Tigh said in an irritated tone while he clenched his fist. "Tell you what, these young'uns aren't up to snuff. No way we would've screwed up so bad back in our day." He grunted. "We took pride in our duties."

A shrug came from Daniel. "You're too hard on them. It's not easy. There's so much red tape before we can enter the neutral zone, by the time it's done, it's too late."

Shocked by the defense, Ron threw his hands in the air and glared at his pal. "What the freak?" Even with his lower rank, he waggled a lecturing index finger. "Dan, there was nothing there! Not a trace of BBR!"

"I know, we had pretty bad intel on this one."

"That's putting it mildly." He gave a groan and a couple of inaudible mumbles. "Have you heard from our bud, Doctor Death, about our latest cluster freak?" When he finished uttering the words, they arrived at a closed door. Daniel picked up his key card.

"Well, he complained as usual, but it's empty threats." He inserted the plastic slab into the reader. "He's not willing to start the war again, not without a good reason." Obediently, the door slid open. Daniel passed through and Ron tailed him. "Besides, Ostark doesn't have any more luck th—"

Then the door closed with a bang, separating the two on each side. After a sigh, Daniel scanned his card again, allowing a fuming Ron to join him. "That's pure bullcrap!" the Koporal yelled. "I keep forgetting about it. What a pain in the ass. Those damn techs."

Daniel chuckled. "They're following our guidelines, remember?" High Command had feared Stalker might slip through a door as someone crossed. For this reason, they'd instructed the techs to install motion sensors that determined when a person passed through and closed the door. Should tricksters attempt cheating the system by traversing side by side, an alarm would blare a warning, indicating the presence of a suspicious individual. "They told us it'd be trouble."

With a wave, Ron dismissed the notion. "Nah, they said annoying. I can deal with annoying. This is a whole new level of idiocy." He groaned. "Anyway, yeah, it's by design, fine, but they still messed up. These motion detectors we asked them to install, they keep giving false positives. They're supposed to use the cameras to figure out if the detectors made a mistake, but it ain't working for shit. Freak, Nicky was just complaining about it. She got trapped twice today already."

Perhaps to reinforce his point, a sudden sound echoed. Both seniors covered their ears and recoiled in pain. A robotic voice warned, "Incoherent motion detected. This section will be locked down until proper inspection."

Ron glared at Daniel. "See, I'm not making it up! We're gonna be so freaking late."

Daniel chuckled. "It's fine, they won't start without the bosses." He gave his friend an affectionate tap on the shoulder. "Relax, they'll work the kinks out."

"Whatever... once the meeting is done, I'm giving those goddamn techs a piece of my mind."

***

A series of clicking noises echoed as Jonathan pounded on his keyboard. Next to him, his friend and colleague, Brian, stretched, then massaged his neck. They remained in a sitting position for hours, and it took its toll. With a sigh, Brian eyed the screen and said, "Everything seems in order."

"Yep," Jonathan replied under his breath. While Brian's remark sounded reassuring, it represented bad news. The motion detectors they had installed often triggered without reason, a fact Jonathan had predicted since they used experimental technology. It remained to identify the source of the problem, the most likely explanation being their own programming. The system was intended to detect an invisible man like Stalker, but it'd be fruitless if it raised an alarm whenever a person budged. To prevent this outcome, they wrote custom codes so that the sensors communicated with the cameras and verified whether a visible object caused the movement. Despite the effort, the result suffered from false positives, and they hoped the fault lay in their software. Fixing their own error would be simple enough, but the alternative ended up far less palatable.

For a few days now, Jonathan and Brian had scanned every line they had written and run the program through various debugging sessions. They tried any test they could imagine, both automated and manual. So far, they'd failed to locate any mistake in their logic.

Brian rubbed his chin. "Should we just admit it's a hardware problem at this point?"

A shrug came from Jonathan. "Probably. It's unreliable tech. I said from the start it'd be a pain in the ass."

"Question is, how do we fix it?"

"Psssh"—Jonathan threw his hands in the air in defeat—"freak if I know! The experts who built them couldn't do it right, and they had years. And a large budget. Ours is a shoestring. Literally."

Brian opened his mouth, but before he uttered a word, the door behind them slid open with a swoosh. Shocked, Jonathan rotated his swiveling chair and then sprang to his feet. Only someone with a high clearance level could've entered his office without his permission, and indeed, a short balding old man stepped inside. Jonathan recognized him as the Koporal. Whatever his purpose might be, his tightened jaw and clenched fists implied a bad mood.

"Koporal Tigh, to what do we owe the honor?"

"Don't try kissing my ass, it won't help you. This isn't an honor, it's a freaking disgrace. Valardir isn't a playground for you to toy around with your gadgets."

Jonathan frowned. "Sir, with all due respect, I don't understand."

"Oh, sure you don't, you whippersnapper!" The Koporal kept marching on until he stood too close for Jonathan's comfort. Enraged, Ron waggled a lecturing finger that scraped his nose. "What kind of shit job are you doing, you freaking idiots? Doors are closing in my face!" For effect, he slammed his fist into his opened palm. "This morning, your stupid motion detectors locked me and Dan out for fifteen minutes! We were late to our meeting. If it had been an emergency, people could have died!" Perhaps surprisingly, the worst part of the tirade ended up not being the message, but Tigh's breath. The officer must've lacked time for proper oral hygiene. The odor almost caused Jonathan to recoil, but he forced himself to remain in place. He refused to show any sign of weakness to this man. "We're NISDA, not a puppet theater! We don't pay you to screw around!"

Despite the tirade, Jonathan stayed calm. He glared at the Koporal in silence, adjusted his glasses with his index finger and then said, "Clause thirteen, paragraph six."

Puzzled, Tigh's mouth contorted. "What the freak does that mean?"

Jonathan crossed his arms. "Look at our work contract. You can scream and insult your soldiers all you want, but technicians like us aren't actually part of the military. Any communication with us is supposed to be polite, courteous and nonthreatening. Your rank doesn't apply. You're giving me no choice. I'll have to file a formal complaint."

Every muscle in Tigh's body tightened. The glare he fired at Jonathan might drive a lesser man to crumble and apologize, but Jonathan stayed firm and met the Koporal's stare, unflinching. "Now, about your own complaints. The Commander himself wanted the doors to work this way. We warned him it'd be annoying, but he didn't care. And the detectors, I said it was a bad idea right when that Perz woman told us about them. I also wrote a detailed report explaining that they were experimental technology and that installing them in a place like Valardir was downright dangerous. When I was ignored, I gave High Command recommended specs so it at least wouldn't be a complete disaster. They weren't followed. We're not the problem, Mr. Tigh"—he accentuated the word mister so the geezer would remember that no rule obliged him to use his formal title—"but if you want to find it, part of it is standing before me."

The senior's lips quivered as if he considered retorting, but he resisted the temptation. His formerly red cheeks intensified in color until they almost reached purple. Then Ron spun around and started to leave, muttering, "You goddamn lazy imbeciles."

"What was that?" A smirk spread on Jonathan's face and he leaned forward while arranging his fingers like a cone circling his ear. "Can you repeat that? I want to make sure you didn't say something I should add to my formal complaint."

Tigh denied him even a glance as he mumbled, "I didn't say anything."

Once the Koporal left, Brian exhaled in relief. He took a few deep respirations and turned toward his friend. The goose bumps on his wrists proved evident, and he trembled. "You think that was a good idea? He's super pissed."

Jonathan nodded. "It was. I had to put him in his place. You can't give an inch to guys like that. If you don't defend your rights, they'll trample all over you."

Chapter 18

Tigal 18, 2133, on the Nirnivian calendar

It felt like déjà vu. A bunch of soldiers gathered in the rec room. Rose, Brucie and me were there sitting on the couch. This time, though, Janice didn't bother to show up.

—Thoughts of James Hunter, Hocmar 28, 2134, on the Nirnivian calendar

The crowd size failed to equal that when Daniel had revealed his mutation, but it still ended up impressive. Around twenty people watched the ceremony on television. James didn't quite understand what was happening. Some kind of huge donation to the same mutant rights organization as before. Whatever the case may be, the event seemed important based on the enthusiasm filling the chamber.

An elder citizen who was slumped in a wheelchair spoke at a podium: "...great honor to be here with Mr. Kenneth and Mr. Serath." His words sounded slurred and weak, as if uttering a few sentences demanded incredible strength from his ravaged body, and that might've been so. "I don't deserve their company." He paused. "To be blunt, I've been a fool, and while I can't rectify my past mistakes completely, I can at least acknowledge...

On each side of the orator stood two persons James recognized from Daniel's TV appearance. One wore a bandana that contrasted with his black suit. He stared at the senior with a forced smirk on his face. The other sported a tentacle in place of his left arm and fixated on the floor as he stroked his nose with his normal index finger. His octopus appendage wrapped around his torso and quivered.

Charlie, a soldier James had introduced to Rose a while back upon his request, turned toward her. "I never thought I'd ever see Max Kenneth and Quintus Topton in the same room without 'em strangling each other." This was by far the longest sentence he had uttered to the Melkar. When they'd first met, he had held his tongue, still overwhelmed by the alleged prophet's presence. Now that he had overcome his shyness, without quite realizing it, he blinked twice and shivered.

Rose looked at him and smiled. "It almost didn't happen. If I've learned one thing about Mr. Kenneth, it's that he doesn't change his mind easily."

Surprised by her acknowledgment, Charlie stepped back. He hesitated for a moment, fidgeting in place, but soon he recovered. "Doesn't seem like he wanna be there at any rate."

An unknown woman said, "Neither of them do!"

Rose giggled. "Leon is probably worried Max might make a scene. I'm pretty sure he has it in him."

On the monitor, an aide passed a giant check to Quintus, who then handed it to a man James assumed to be Max. The mutant took the gift, though his somber expression remained. Quintus offered a handshake, which Max accepted despite evident disdain. After that, Quintus spun his chair toward Leon, turning his back to the camera. A fraction of a second later, he let out a chilling scream. Two guards charged Leon and jumped on him. He didn't resist, and they grabbed him. The same aide as before rushed for the wheelchair and moved it. Red stained Quintus's shirt, no doubt from the knife stuck in his chest.

The rec room became very quiet as we processed what just happened. Then, utter chaos. Everyone talked at the same time, trying to figure out what was going on. We were all shocked, especially Rose.

 —Thoughts of James Hunter, Hocmar 28, 2134, on the Nirnivian calendar

Pale as if struck by sudden sickness, Rose got on her feet. She slowly advanced toward the television, eyes and mouth wide open and palms resting on her cheeks. She dropped to her knees, breathing heavily, almost to the point of hyperventilation, and lowered her eyes to the floor. Then she gazed at the screen again and said, "He... he used me."

Chapter 19

Tigal 20, 2133, on the Nirnivian calendar

Leon would face her, and not by video conference. Gritting her teeth, Rose paced around the small chamber with her arms crossed. The murder had come as a shock, but once she'd recovered, her resolve had grown to an immeasurable proportion: Leon would explain himself in person. As expected, her father and Ron Tigh balked at the idea. No way would they allow a murderer in the same room as the precious Melkar. Besides, they wouldn't have granted Leon access to level five of Valardir even if he hadn't killed Quintus. Rose stood firm and countered that there'd be no danger. Leon would be restrained and guarded. As for Valardir's security, her quarters were isolated from the military. Why, they let James live there. Since she refused to relent, they reached a compromise: the meeting would occur on level two.

For five minutes at least, perhaps ten, she waited. In her state, time hardly mattered. Eventually, the door slid open and Leon Serath stepped inside, shackled and encircled by six guards. The mutant advanced with his head bowed down, not daring to look at her. Rose stared at the prisoner with her hands on her hips.

"I wish I could say I'm glad to see you, Mr. Serath." His eyes darted toward her for a fraction of a second, and then he averted his gaze again. His lips quivered, but no reply came. "Look at me." He ignored the request. "I said look at me!" One of the guards grabbed Leon's head and forced it upward. Out of reflex, Leon struggled, but he lacked strength compared to the soldier, and soon he gave up. "I made you come here for a simple reason—to ask why. Why did you murder Quintus? Why did you use me to set him up? Don't tell me it's because he lobbied against mutant rights. A ton of mutants hated Quintus for that, including Max, and they didn't kill him. He was a dying man... why ruin your life when he would be gone in a year at most?"

Leon frowned and said in a mere whisper, "What's done is done. My reasons don't matter."

Enraged, Rose brandished a menacing index finger. "It does to me! You manipulated me and planned everything to reach Quintus. Don't deny it!"

"You're right." A few tears ran down Leon's cheeks. "I'm sorry..." Guilt-ridden, he whimpered, "I didn't want to get you mixed up in this, Your Holiness, I swear. I didn't have a choice."

"Really? You didn't have a choice about stabbing a senior citizen?"

"No... well, yes, but at a terrible price." He took a deep breath. "My parents suffered a lot because of Quintus Topton. Like Max said, they had to hide me until I was twelve because, according to the laws of the time, they weren't allowed to have children. If the authorities had found me, I'd have been"—he performed a finger quote—"purged for the good of society."

Sorrow gripped Rose and she exhaled. "Such an awful law."

A few nods came from Leon. "Yeah... back then, the Kenneth Foundation and other groups fought to repeal the law as the relic it was. That bastard Quintus Topton financed a smear campaign and stalled the efforts for another twelve years. What Max didn't mention is that I wasn't an only child. I had a brother." He sobbed. "He fell sick and we couldn't take him to a hospital or he'd be executed. My parents tried taking care of him, but it was serious, and without a doctor, he had no chance. On the night we lost him, my father took an Elolian oath that he would murder Quintus with his own hands. Then he made me take one too. If he died before he succeeded, I would kill Quintus in his place."

Upon hearing the words, Rose recoiled, her mouth gaping. Eyes opened wide, she shook her head in disbelief. How she wished her ears deceived her, but somehow, she knew he spoke the truth.

"No...," she whimpered. "How could a father do such a thing to his own child?"

Leon shrugged. "It was in the heat of the moment. He regretted it right after, but as you are well aware, you can't take back an Elolian oath."

Assailed by a headache, Rose closed her eyelids and rubbed her brow. "Yes... what a nightmare..."

"Dad failed to fulfill the oath, and I thought I'd suffer the same fate. Quintus Topton is a powerful man protected by the best bodyguards in the business. I'd never reach the old buffoon. Then, not that long ago, he contacted us to talk about a large donation. It was a shock, as you can imagine." Leon exhaled. "In his condition, Quintus doesn't get out of the house much, but I figured if he gave his fortune to the foundation, there'd be a ceremony. Maybe he'd show up for that, and if so, I'd have my chance. Except Max refused. There was only one person who might be able to change his mind—the Melkar herself. I suggested to Quintus he asked you for help. You know the rest from there."

With a sickening sensation filling her stomach, Rose said, "Elolian oath or not, if I had known what you planned to do, I wouldn't have helped convince Max. You made me an unwilling accomplice, Leon."

"I..." He gulped. "I'm truly sorry, Your Holiness. I'm sure you must despise me, but I hope you at least understand my actions."

"I'm not proud of you, Mr. Serath. In fact, I'm downright disappointed." The tone of her voice lightened a touch. "But despise is a strong word. Your father put you in an impossible situation."

***

On his mattress, Rose sat hunched and dispirited, twiddling her fingers. As for James, he chose a chair and faced her. Her hair lay in disarray, and based on her swollen eyes, he assumed she had been crying before she showed up. When Rose had arrived, they'd exchanged greetings and she'd asked if he minded some company. Other than that, they'd barely uttered a word.

She didn't say how her meeting with Leon went, but it wasn't hard to tell it hadn't gone too well.

—Thoughts of James Hunter, Hocmar 28, 2134, on the Nirnivian calendar

Several minutes of silence passed. An emotional heaviness weighed in the air more and more with every passing second. No doubt Rose had come to talk, probably about what had happened with Leon, yet she remained tongue-tied, perhaps too drained to find the words. James decided he should try making the first step.

Filled with hesitation, he scratched the back of his skull and said, "So, uh, did Leon, um, tell you why he murdered Quintus?"

Rose looked at James. "Yes, I've found my answer." She sighed. "His father made him take an Elolian oath," She mumbled the words as if they were self-explanatory but caught her mistake once she saw James tilting his head and lifting his nose. "Oh, right... sorry. An Elolian oath is an atrocity that shouldn't exist. If you swear such an oath and fail to fulfill it in your lifetime, your soul is instantly banished into nothingness. They're actually illegal now because they were often forced on people through coercion, like what happened to Leon. His father had put Leon in a horrible predicament. If he didn't kill Quintus, he was doomed. If he did, then he'd stain his soul and get closer to the edge and might tip over. Then again, should the gods show mercy, he'd have another chance during his next life to redeem himself." Her mouth contorted. "It's a big if, but it was his only hope, so he murdered Quintus."

The scowl on James's brow intensified. "So, his parents made him swear he'd kill Quintus?" A nod from Rose confirmed the notion. "What the hell? It's messed up. How can someone be so cruel to their kid?"

"I've been wondering that myself. I also wonder whether Leon will be spared nothingness. I doubt it. You know, our religion, Ulgoronisoism, isn't a united front. Several branches split from the original one." Rose enumerated them on her fingers. "You have the orthodox, the progressive, and the centrist. The orthodox are rigid and strict." A movement resembling a blow though far gentler accompanied the sentence. "There's a single true answer, that's it. Your actions are either right or wrong." She exhaled and squinted. "With the progressives, it's more flexible. Sacred texts point to the truth, but they aren't literal. And, yes, actions matter, but intentions are more important." As she thought of an example, Rose rubbed her chin. "For instance, theft is sinful. Yet if you save your family from starvation by stealing food, it might be seen as a good deed by the gods nevertheless. Centrists are somewhere in between, like their name suggests."

That speech about the branches wasn't expected. To be frank, the whole thing seemed irrelevant to the conversation, but I figured talking helped her avoid thinking about Leon. A kind of coping mechanism or something similar. Besides, I found it sort of interesting anyway, so I didn't mind listening, especially not if it made her feel better.

—Thoughts of James Hunter, Hocmar 28, 2134, on the Nirnivian calendar

"Though each of them has such different views, when it comes to an Elolian oath, they all agree Leon is finished." Her pupils darted up. "For the orthodox, it's because—well, murder is among the biggest sins, no matter the circumstances. For the progressives, even if the oath forced Leon's hand, his intentions were to save himself. Taking a life for your own benefit is a cruel, selfish act." Rose gave a defeated shrug. "There's little hope for Leon. He sealed his fate the instant he took that goddamned oath."

After that, neither of us had anything to say, and it became awkward. Thank God it didn't take me too long before I thought of a question that might break the tension.

—Thoughts of James Hunter, Hocmar 28, 2134, on the Nirnivian calendar

James leaned forward and smiled. "So, which one are you?"

Confused, Rose blinked twice and slanted her neck sideways. "What?"

"The branches. Based on your sermons, you're a progressive, right?" He stroked his ear. "Um, I mean, you don't sound like an orthodox."

A laugh echoed from Rose. "Hunter, I'm not allowed to answer that." She waggled a lecturing finger. "Since even the Melkar can be mistaken, whichever branch I believe in might not be the correct one. If I endorsed a branch, people would follow my example, and I could be steering them wrong. They have to choose on their own. For this reason, it was decided that I wouldn't belong to any specific branch regardless of my beliefs."

"Oh..." James pondered for a moment, tapping his chin. "Um, you still don't seem like an orthodox to me. Maybe a centrist?"

"Stop trying to get me in trouble, Hunter!" Though she pointed a menacing index finger, she giggled. "Thank you for listening—I needed it." She grimaced. "I shouldn't take it so hard. Quintus was near the end, and he managed to give his fortune to the Kenneth Foundation as he wished. Leon will spend the rest of his life in prison, but it was his choice." Rose's cheeks flushed as a touch of rage returned. Her voice intensified. "He used me as a tool!" The anger left as soon as it had appeared, and she moaned. "I played a part in this madness, but even the most devoted orthodox would agree I'm not responsible given that Leon tricked me." She lifted her fingers and gazed at them. "Still, I feel like I have blood on my hands."

Revolted by the notion, James threw his arms up in the air. "You don't! Rose, it wasn't your fault. You were trying to help the mutants. You couldn't know what Leon was planning."

"You're right, Hunter, but somehow that doesn't make it any easier."

That was just like her. I would soon find out Rose often blamed herself even when she didn't do anything wrong. I guess part of it was the fact that she was seen as a prophet. Whatever she did, she influenced people in unintended ways, and so being the Melkar weighed on her.

—Thoughts of James Hunter, Hocmar 28, 2134, on the Nirnivian calendar

***

The door slid open and Rose entered her room. She glanced at the bed. Tiredness overcame her, yet she knew sleep would elude her. She'd spent the night twisting and turning while reliving Quintus's murder in her mind. No matter what James said to comfort her, she had played a role and she couldn't deny it.

Instead of heading for her mattress, Rose walked toward her desk, sat in the chair and studied the reflection in the mounted mirror. The stress from recent events showed. Her skin had become a touch paler. Dark circles surrounded her eyes. A disarrayed lock of hair encumbered her vision, so she moved it. Doing so, she noted red stains on her hand. She wiggled her fingers, twisted her wrist and said, "At least this time it's not my fault..."

***

Now that you've finished reading, please consider leaving a review, or at least rating the book. This helps a lot and would be a great show of support.

Do you want a free short story that serves as a prequel to The Cyborg's Crusade? Then, join the cyborg's fan club on my website,

https://thecyborgscrusade.com/fanclub.html

Note that you can buy books, and follow me on social media with this link:

https://thecyborgscrusade.com/hub.html

Thank you for reading, I hope with all my heart you enjoyed The Cyborg's Crusade.

ABOUT THE AUTHOR

My name is Benoit Lanteigne and I'm a French Canadian (outside of Quebec) who's trying to write in English. That can be tricky. I'm a computer programmer and I enjoy it. I see many inspiring writers who hate their day jobs and hope to quit someday, but that's not my case. Mostly, I've worked on websites and web applications.

Back in school, I enjoyed writing and according to my teachers and classmates; I had a talent for it. Well, not so much for grammar and spelling, but they liked my stories. Once I went to university, I dropped writing as a hobby. There were other things I wanted to focus on, such as my career. Then, in the early 2000s, around 2006 I'd say, I had a flash of inspiration. At first, it was a single character: a winged woman with red hair. I didn't even know who she was, but the image stuck with me. From there, I began figuring out details about her origins and her world, but I only started writing for real in 2009. After over ten years of hard work, books of The Cyborg's Crusade are finally ready for release.